When Gods Bleed

By

Njedeh Anthony

Dedicated to my daughter Obi, to let you know I was thinking of you before you were born and I will be thinking of you after I am gone.

ALSO BY NJEDEH ANTHONY

The Seventh King

The Devil's Switch

Adulterer

Last Call from the Devil's Lane

The Dragon's Covenant

Mind Crawlers

Queens of the Revolution

Symphony of Extinction

After the Fairytale

Prologue

Barb Horses stomped in through the gates, he got off his beast and slowly walked to the palace. Men, women and children all had their heads bowed. The men wore the hides of cattle. The women wrapped the skins of cheetahs, zebras and gazelles around their waists and upper bodies.

He took paces through the surrounding limestone buildings, which under the sun's rays reflected hues of green and yellow. The roofs and ceilings were made of split date-palm trunks arranged diagonally over the corners, forming a square center that was covered by split-palm beams. Twenty-nine foot high mud walls surrounded the palace, and individual enclosures gave the surrounding edifices their independency within the mud walls. There was a taller tower by the gates, which gave a wider view into the kingdom. The houses around the palace were rectangular, unlike those of the poor, which were round mud-plastered houses with conically thatched roofs.

A woman stood by him. She didn't bow. She tried to speak but the words were too heavy, and her eyes told him everything he needed to know. In a mark of pride, she walked off without any expression.

Though he entered the palace every day, this day was different—death was singing its love song. His hand shook. He held it firm, stood straight and used his fingers to check if any tears ran out of their cage. One final time he walked under the ornate arches that supported the palace's acacia wood and mud roof.

The King smiled at the two men escorting him and said something they could not understand. Soon after, death arrested him. A scream resonated from within the walls of the palace. The marketplace blasted with the wails of people of the kingdom. While some predicted the birth of disaster, others expected life to flourish with the wings of a new beginning.

BOOK
1

Chapter 1

King Nwosa appeared, covered with the skin of a lion, the head of the beast hanging on his shoulder. When he walked in, everyone in the conference room bowed. He looked around at the uninvited guests, namely the elders and the Ogun priest who was the Headman to the Oracle as well as the King's personal bodyguard.

After the King sat on his throne, all the men sat down. The elders broke kola nuts and distributed pieces in order of respect and then age, as is customary in such gatherings. The expression on their faces bothered the King and he knew they would not assemble at this time of the night for good news.

Probably the Wazike kingdom has declared war on us —the King thought to himself— but why would they break the peace treaty when my first wife is the daughter of their king?

To his immediate right sat the bony, big-eyed Headman to the Oracle, who wore the hides of a panther, and at his waist dangled the skull of a monkey. The Headman to the Oracle is a position that could only be ascended to by a Tikpapa, someone who has dedicated his life from youth to the study of supernatural powers, for curative and lethal applications. Around his neck hung the teeth of men and animals with whom he had done battle—a sign of a fearless chief, which he would need to be for the task ahead.

1

"To be the Headman to the Oracle, you have to not only be a warlock but you have to play politics with your King. Ogun Priest, you better have a good reason for waking me at this time when the sun fears to give out its light or you would soon be an ordinary Tikpapa of the Ogun God," King Nwosa said, with an attempt at composure.

"Sire, the lion does not kill a cub that is not his because it's wicked, but to prevent the growth of another generation that will grow to be his enemy. Winds—"

"Please," the King interrupted, "I hope you did not wake me up to lecture me on lions."

"No, Your Majesty. How long since your queen gave birth to an heir?"

"Eight full moons ago," the King responded through clenched teeth.

"Have you seen the child in the eight days?" The Ogun priest asked, knowing the answer.

"Ogun Priest, are you trying to spice my anger? You and I both know that I have not seen this child because," Nwosa arched his brow, "custom demands that the heir has to cry before being brought to the presence of the King."

"Sire, a normal child cries immediately after it leaves its mother's belly and nobody except your wife's servants have seen this child," one of the elders joined in.

"All right, you men have proved a point; my son is not your normal child. Or are you trying to tell me that the child did not come out safely?" The King pounded his right hand in his palm.

"The child was delivered safely, but the child hasn't cried for eight days," another Elder replied.

"I hope you have something else to tell me or else heads will roll for this disturbance."

"Yesterday I went to the oracle to inquire about the abnormality of the child's birth and the reply is what has brought all of us here," the Ogun priest said solemnly.

"Speak man!" the King shouted, leaning forward.

"The oracle says the south wind has touched the earth at a point where the blood of life has lost its sweetness. Destiny has created dispute between man and gods. Wisdom carries a weight that is unbearable to man with a poisonous form of reality. The birth of joy has brought a change in the color of the wind and the transformation of a legacy."

"Talk to me in a language I can understand."

"The child your wife gave birth to will end a chain that was bound by our etiquette."

"What exactly are you saying'?" the King stammered.

Looking down, the Ogun priest responded. "The prince has to be sacrificed to the gods or there will be damage in the dynasty."

"I have heard you all, now I would like to speak to my Tikpapa alone."

Immediately, everyone except the Ogun priest left the room.

"How dare you go to those old men before coming to me with this information?"

"I was positive you would not want to give the life of the child to me if it was a secret," the Tikpapa said in an apologetic tone and still avoiding eye contact.

"So what if I did not want my only son dead?"

"You do not know the extent of danger this child your wife bore carries. The gods are hungry for his life."

"'Ogun Priest, you and I both know how difficult it is for people in our family lineage to produce men. I was the only male child of fifty-six children and even now I have eight and all are girls."

"If it be the will of the gods that you bear no more sons, then so shall it be. But as King, it is your solemn duty to produce this child for sacrifice to earn the respect you deserve from both your ancestors and this generation. My King, understand that this offering is unavoidable. When you met with me," the Ogun priest chose his words carefully, "about the assassination of your father, the late King Burobee, I was with you all the way."

"Would you stop deceiving yourself with all that patriotic rubbish? Before we poisoned the man, were you not just an ordinary Tikpapa? And see how long it took you to overcome the Awnu priest. Sometimes I begin to wonder if the Awnu god is greater than the Ogun," the King retorted.

"The delay in overcoming of the Awnu god was my fault, but there is no comparison between my god and the dead man's god. Sire, this is not about your fatherly stand, but the sacrifice of a child whose destiny we cannot understand."

"Then take the child if it will make all of you sleep better at night, but the first man who comes to me disturbing me about an heir, I will personally slash his throat."

The Ogun priest lay flat on the floor as a mark of maximum respect as he spoke. "Every man who walks in this kingdom will walk with pride that they have a great King."

"I said take the child now before I change my mind," the King shouted.

As the Ogun priest left, the King sat down and felt how transient life really was.

*

Queen Aneaton paced to and from the walls of her room in anticipation of receiving her elder sister, who arrived in the still of the night. Queens dwelt in their own palace; only their female servants, female relatives, female guards and the King were allowed inside.

The Queen's palace was guarded by female Omees, trained warriors who have dedicated their lives to either the government or an institution. There were two types of female warriors—the Ikuvamee and the Wovamee.

An Ikuvamee was a girl who was given to the government at age eight by parents who believed she was not pretty enough to attract a husband. The parents received a settlement from the government instead of waiting for a dowry from a husband that might never come. After all their training procedures, they were assigned to a particular queen or the wife of a chief. They were women of high regard and extremely dangerous.

The Wovamee did not belong to the government; they operated under private ownership. In most cases, they were extremely beautiful and extremely dangerous. These female warriors infiltrated fortresses and got their tasks done by any means necessary— using sex, dressing and behaving like a man, or even killing men, women and children. They came to join the organization out of their own free will, and most were married and poor. The kingdom did not recognize the Wovamees; people in the top hierarchy denied their existence; their identities were secret. Even the Wovamees didn't know who their leader was; they hardly cared, as long as they got paid. Before these women were accepted, they underwent a training and test period under supervision of Ikazas. An Ikaza was either a publicly dismissed chief or general. Only the Ikazas had access to the person or people who owned the organization and they took the secret to their graves.

Queen Aneaton wondered why her sibling, who had just given birth, would come to see her at this time of night. They had never been close, and her jealousy of Nneka went back to their childhood. She did not understand why, because she was prettier, smarter, and was even their mother's favorite child. Notwithstanding the envy, she knew she would never let harm come to her sister, the woman who should have been queen.

Everyone but Nneka knew the King had come to take her to be his bride—until he saw Aneaton. At the time, Aneaton had no regrets, but she later began to covet the happiness her sister found in a simpler life. Nneka got married to an Ikaza who made her his only wife. She had fewer possessions than the Queen, but more of the things that mattered. However, the Queen never forgot they were sisters. When the King tried repeatedly to arrest her sister's husband because he believed all Ikazas were involved in Wovamee contracts, the Queen each time made sure the case went away.

As soon as she saw her sister, she wanted to run and hug her, but the Queen is expected to disengage herself from physical contact with anybody in the midst of observers. Nneka came toward her with a child in her arms and bowed. The Queen responded by nodding and waving to the Ikuvamees and her servants to leave the room.

"Nneka."

"Your Highness, I came immediately after I heard."

"Would you stop fooling yourself? Since when did you start addressing me as your highness when we are alone?"

"The hyenas continue to eat the cubs of lions until they become full grown lions, then they fear them."

"Nonsense, my dear sister, the blood that flowed in my veins before I became queen is still the same. Now let me see my little nephew. How old is he?"

"He is ten days old. Sorry about the way he is crying. Since the day I gave birth to him, the child has been crying continuously." Nneka's tone was soft.

"The tortoise looks up into the sky and wonders why he cannot fly like a bird, whilst the bird wonders how it feels to roam the earth on its feet. Your child cries and it brings you grief, while my child refuses to shed a tear."

"It happens at times. When I gave birth to Odagwe, he did not cry for close to a day."

"A day? Do you come here to poison my heart?" The Queen angrily turned her back to her sister.

"Aneaton, I do not understand the language you speak. I came here with the softest heart to see the man who will be king, whose mother is my sister. If not that I, too, was giving birth to my own son, I would have been here sooner." Nneka spoke softly, the teardrops

8

falling from her eyes. "If you want me to leave your palace then I suggest you tell me now."

"I am sorry Nneka, but things are not going the way they are supposed to be and I am losing my sanity," the Queen said, now facing her sister.

"I came with my son in the dead of the night to meet you. Believe me when I tell you that I am here for you."

"Nneka, since I gave birth to the child, he has not shed a tear. Even the King has not seen his son. At first I thought it was normal, but now even a dunce would recognize the abnormality of the situation. Very soon they would take my baby away from me. Maybe the child was born to be a thorn on the gods so they might have to take its life."

"You do not have to lose control, Your Majesty."

"Stop calling me that! I can accept it from a farmer who walks on the road, chiefs who come to my presence, traders who offer me the finest linen, northerners who offer us their horses, but I refuse to accept it from you."

"Okay, Aneaton, nobody can hurt your child," Nneka said confidently. "He is the heir to the throne."

"Someone heard under the mango tree that elders are coming for my son. My heart wishes that the words you speak were strong enough to hold water."

"Now let's replace this darkness in our mood with some sunlight. So where is my nephew, the son of the soil, the firmness of the earth, and the greatest king our kingdom will ever produce?"

Queen Aneaton clapped her hands. Her servants approached. She made a sign to them and they brought the prince to his aunt.

As Nneka held the child, she felt a bond. His eyes seemed to open doors into her heart.

"What's his name?"

"How can I name a child that has not shed a tear and may never?"

"Stop talking this way, Aneaton. I do not like it."

"Forget my son. What is the name of yours?"

"His father calls him Obi, but I prefer calling him Obiani."

"Obiani. You named the child, the heart of the land," the Queen said with smile.

An Omee with an axe in hand entered the room and bowed. "My Queen, sorry for disturbing you, but the Ogun priest requires your presence at the gates."

"What does he want at this time of the night?" the Queen asked, not really wanting to know.

"He refused to say. He said it required your personal attention."

"Tell him I am on my way."

As the Omee left, Queen Aneaton looked at her sister and said, "Look after my son."

Nneka wanted to say something, but the words could not find their way out of her lips. She watched her sister walk away and wished he came for anything but the child.

As Queen Aneaton walked toward the bamboo gates, she saw the Ogun priest outside with two-dozen Omees, all carrying burning torches and armed with ivory-handled bronze swords. The seriousness in the Ogun priest's face made her realize that blood could define the end of the day. She saw the readiness of the Ikuvamees and her confidence level rose.

"I wonder, what brings the Ogun priest to my home at this time of the night?" the Queen asked him.

"Accept my apologies for coming at this time, but your son is required for sacrifice," the Ogun priest said in a direct manner.

"Let me understand this situation. You wake me up to tell me I should produce my son for sacrifice—my only son. A vulture waits for its prey to die before it devours it, so let's cut the long story short. I will never, I mean never, give my son to you."

Immediately after Queen Aneaton spoke the word "never," her warriors drew their swords, spears, axes, knives, bows and arrows while the men around the Ogun priest raised their weapons for battle.

"Aneaton, I can understand your maternal instinct over my orders to you to bring the child, but I have directives from the King, your husband, to take the child, so please leave this unnecessary boldness behind and give me the child."

"Orders? You are a knowledgeable man, and I expect you to know when a Queen says no, she means it." As Queen Aneaton spoke, she could feel the tension burning on both sides of the gates. Her heart pounded harder than festival drums. Her words were the only things that didn't shake.

"I don't think you understand the situation. I will pretend you did not disobey the laws of our King, our custom and this kingdom. People will die for your stubbornness and I guarantee you I will have that child before the cock crows. For the last time, woman, give me the child."

"Over…my…dead…body!" Queen Aneaton screamed.

"Then so it shall be."

The Ogun priest spread his arms, a horde of men broke down the gates, and the collision began.

Arrows and spears flew in the air, swords clashed and warriors cried in pain. During the battle, Queen Aneaton knew that she could never win. Notwithstanding the fact that her warriors outnumbered the priest's Omees, she was aware that nature made men physically stronger than women and even if her warriors won the war now, it would mean total annihilation later. So she chose to get her satisfaction by another means. She sighted the Ogun priest walking majestically around the battle zone killing any female warrior that came his way. Then she took a bow and arrow, aimed, and fired from behind him. The arrow traveled like a hawk seeking its prey. When it was about a hand's length from his back, the Ogun priest made a swift turn and caught the arrow in the air. He looked at Queen Aneaton, grinned and made a gesture with his fingers.

At that point she knew it was over. She ran up to see her child for the last time. As she got to the top of the platform leading to the palace, right in front of her the Ogun priest appeared. He gripped her firmly around the neck, clamping hard enough to make her breathless.

"Aneaton, save me the trouble of looking for the child and I will give a very quick death. Where is the child?"

Queen Aneaton tried to speak, but the words weren't coming out clearly.

"I can't hear you. Sorry, forgive me. I am holding your neck too tightly," The Ogun priest said, releasing his grip. "You may talk now."

"Over my dead body," Queen Aneaton gasped.

"That will not be a problem."

The Ogun priest took his dagger out of the scabbard and was about to strike when Nneka shouted, "No! I am with the child, take him."

As she spoke, she gave him the crying baby.

Queen Aneaton was still gasping when she saw the child. She tried to shout, but the words came out very soft. "No, Nneka, no."

"Is this life not funny? All the child had to do was cry about two days ago and he would have been the prince. Now the oracle requires his life," the Ogun priest said with an ugly grin.

"Now you have the child. Please let my sister go," Nneka pleaded.

"Queen Aneaton has committed a crime against the King, the customs and our kingdom and that is punishable by death." Without a thought, the Ogun priest plunged the knife deeply into her chest and took the child away.

Nneka ran to her sister's side as she was dying. Her sister wanted to say lots of things, but the only words that came from her mouth before she died were, "Thank you."

Chapter 2

Nneka returned home to her husband, Ifeanyi, and older son immediately after her sister was buried. News of the Queen's defiance and the battle at her palace had spread around the kingdom with the aid of the market women and tradesmen. They looked for means to console Nneka but concluded the best way was to give her time to herself.

That night in the depth of her sleep, she heard her baby cry. She went to the child, picked him up, and started laughing.

With a frown Ifeanyi said, "I also wondered whether the child was okay. Since you came back he refused to cry."

The smile on her face vanished and she turned toward Ifeanyi. "This child is not Obiani, it's Aneaton's child."

Ifeanyi's face tightened. "I noticed. I am not that stupid that I can't differentiate my child from another. Where is my son?"

"They took him thinking he was…" she said, her voice fading and tears rolling down her cheeks.

"Speak louder woman, I cannot hear you."

"They took him thinking that he was Queen Aneaton's child."

"Don't lie to me woman. The reason I did not question you about the child was because you were in mourning. Why would they think my son was the King's son?"

Nneka realized the truth would destroy her family, so she lied. "Aneaton gave them my child claiming that it was hers after the Ogun priest tortured her. I screamed to let him know it was the wrong child but they ignored me."

"But the Ogun priest should know the difference between a prince and a peasant."

"No man has seen the child."

"The King took my son for sacrifice." Ifeanyi spoke covering his face with his palms, as a tear slid down his cheek.

"I tried my best, Ifeanyi. I really did try to let them know they had the wrong child."

"They took my boy."

"The King took your boy, but you have his prince. Our child would have grown to a limited existence, now we have a child with the power to change everything we care about."

"Does anybody know about this?" Ifeanyi for the first time spoke firmly to his wife.

"I don't think so," Nneka responded, sounding confused.

"I don't want you to think. I want you to know. Does anybody know about this?" There was an intense seriousness in his voice.

Nneka raised her head to look the towering bearded man in the eye and spoke with firmness.

"No one."

"Good. Now that my son, Obi, has gone to bed, I insist that you come back to bed."

She did as he requested, immediately her eyes closed, she fought to hold back the tears. She had sacrificed her child for the Queen, not for her sister. The ugly truth was she felt her child was worth less than the future king of the kingdom. She loved her son but her duty to the kingdom she lived in came first.

*

Time passed and the baby who once could not talk, stand or walk was now ten years old. Obi was in the forest with his father and big brother Odagwe. [As they squatted in the bushes, they watched the lion and the lioness mating slowly, as though the world would last forever.] The two boys laughed while leaving the forest with a dead deer on Obi's shoulder.

When they got home, they met their mother preparing supper with her servants. "Odagwe, pound the yam. Obiani take these cowries and get me some salt from the market. Make sure you hurry so the night will not catch up with you. Where is your father?"

"He saw some grasscutters on our way, so he decided to set some more traps," Odagwe replied.

Obi ran because that was the only way he could make it to the market and back in time, before his brother grabbed every decent looking meat on the table. Their home was far from where the other inhabitants of the kingdom lived, due to his father's

Ikaza nature. Ifeanyi used to be the general in the Didasu capital, until his predecessor ordered him to destroy the Gwanji tribe. He confronted the Gwanji warriors in battle; their men were few and lacked experience. After obtaining a victory, as the general, he ordered the death of every man in their village, but he left the women and children. This aggravated the chief, which led to the general receiving fifty lashes publicly and banishment from the province.

When Obi got to the market, he met an angry mob chasing after a man who had stolen a bag of salt. "Ole, Ole, Ole," they screamed. They all kept shouting as they chased the man. They eventually caught the thief, but before the Omees came to pick up the looter, he was beaten and burnt to ashes. Everyone was transfixed by the event. After the corpse was taken away, the rumors kept flowing in the air.

By the time Obi got the salt—then among the most prized possessions on earth—the sun had gone to bed. He started to run, not because he was scared of walking in the dark between deciduous trees, but because his mother would block his ears with insults if he were late. On his way home, three boys blocked him. He looked at the boys, all about the same age as his elder brother and also about the same size.

"Is it not a little late for someone like you to be out without your mother?" asked the one with the broken tooth as he played with his nails.

Obi looked at him and walked past him as though he did not exist.

The shortest amongst them held up his hand saying, "Do we look like people of your age group?"

Obi continued walking away. This time the two boys grabbed him and brought him toward the biggest member in the group.

"I like your spirit young man, but we did not follow you from the market just to harass you like a gang of jobless criminals," the biggest boy said. "Odagwe owes me and it seems he does not have any intentions of paying back. If I had my way, I would have killed your brother personally. But since I have been installed an Omee, I can't kill anyone except by orders from my general or the chief."

"The youngest Omee ever to be initiated!" the boy with the broken tooth yelled.

"And the greatest Omee this kingdom will ever provide," the shortest boy among them added. They started hailing the young Omee, who had a grandiloquent smile on his face.

Disgusted by this scene portrayed by the bunch of delinquents, Obi nodded and started walking home. What irritated the bullies was that he could not give them their dignity by running away; instead, he chose to walk—majestically.

"Bring him here."

They could feel the anger in their leader's voice. This time it was not easy to hold the child. There was an intense struggle and Obi broke free.

"Stop," the young Omee screamed and everyone paused. He walked toward the boy. "Your brother, Odagwe, refuses to pay the debt he owes me. Each time I look for him, he is nowhere to be found. I could decide to beat you up, but the pain is not yours, so I'll take what they sent you to buy as a reminder to your brother that he owes me and I will continue seizing anything you are sent to buy until I find him or he pays back with interest."

The two boys released their grip. Obi took the salt, dropped it on the ground and drew a circle around it. It was a challenge to wrestle.

In all the provinces men of equal respect who desired similar goals that could not be settled amicably, normally preferred not meeting with a chief, which put them at the mercy of the law. But a wrestling contest needed nobody's consent. This contest did not have to be public; the only people required were the witnesses from both parties. Whatever the common desire, a circle was drawn around it. It could be a dispute between family members for land, the uncertainty of parents about to whom they want to give their daughter's hand in marriage, or an item to buy. To win you had to make the opponent's back touch the ground, and if a speck of dust was noted on your back, you lost the contest.

The two smaller boys started laughing. They realized Obi was tenacious enough to prevent them from overpowering him, but they knew that the young Omee had the strength of an elephant.

The process of becoming an Omee normally took about ten to twelve years. The training did not only teach about how to use strength and weapons, it also taught the Omees about honor, respect, patience, diligence and self-control. To enter the training program, an Omee, or someone of greater respect, had to vouch for the person; few people in the program were accepted. It took this boy only seven years to become an Omee, which made him the youngest Omee ever in the kingdom.

"Amazing the time we live in, a time where a bag of salt is more expensive than the life of a man." Smiling, "Okay, you have won. Take your salt and go," the young Omee said with admiration.

Obi spoke as though the young Omee did not say anything. "The terms of the wager are: If I win, my brother owes you nothing anymore; if I lose, you take what is in the circle and my brother still owes you."

The young Omee laughed. "Do you think I would wrestle with you over a pinch of salt? First, we are not in the same age group; secondly, we are not of equal respect; and thirdly, I prefer dealing with your brother personally to make an example to others. Let's leave this frustrated baby to his delirium."

"I am still talking to you. Don't turn your back on me," Obi shouted, and all three boys turned toward him, astonished. "Am I to believe that the Omee is scared to go on a bout with someone greater than him? Then I was right all along. I knew I smelled the womb of a woman in front of me."

With restrained anger the young Omee looked deep into the boy's eyes. "Do you know who I am?"

"You are Gbangba, son of Ikechukwu the general of the Ozuoba. Now that I know who you are, can we create some action instead of standing here like market women?"

Obi took some sand and poured it on the young Omee's body. This was a form of provocation to an individual challenged to a bout. If the individual did not heed the challenge, then the witnesses had the right to spread the word that the person was a coward.

"All right, if this is what you want, but the terms of the wager will change. If I win you will be my slave."

"Gbangba, don't you think you're over doing it? Imagine what people will say, that you fought with a child to make him your slave. You would kill the respect you have created for yourself," the shortest amongst the trio whispered in his ear.

"He is man enough to call me a market woman, pour dirt on me when I gave him a chance to walk away and still look me in the eye. Or has the young man realized that he is a baby where men stand?"

"Definitely not. I accept your wager. Please, can we start? My mother is expecting me to deliver the salt."

"The only thing you will be delivering will be to my hut."

Both boys walked in circles, their eyes fixed on each other, watching for the slightest flaw in positioning so they could attack. Obi ran and attacked his opponent. Gbangba gripped him by the crotch, lifted him in the air as though he was a feather, and dropped him, but he landed on his feet. Gbangba nodded to show he was impressed.

They took their stances again, crouching with their hands spread out like claws. This time Gbangba attacked. He caught Obi by the waist and started to squeeze him in a bear hug. Obi used the back of his head to hit him continuously until he started to bleed from his eyebrows. Gbangba staggered back a little and Obi then used the back of his leg to hit him on the chest.

As Gbangba was about to land on his back, with the agility of a monkey he turned in the air and landed on his hands and feet. He rushed at Obi like a wild bull. He tried to grab the boy, but the child kept swerving through every little gap between them.

Obi attempted to trip him from behind, but his opponent was by far stronger. Gbangba threw him like a stone against a tree. Obi hit the tree forcefully with his back and then landed on his hands and knees.

Gbangba walked to him. "Are you still ready to play this game?"

Obi again threw sand on his body. His opponent kicked him in the jaw. The force of the kick made him land on his stomach. The older of the opponents tried to turn him over, but Obi refused. He coiled himself to prevent from being overpowered. Gbangba put an arm around his neck and squeezed. He gestured for the boy to give up, but Obi shook his head. When Gbangba saw the look of declining pride in both his friends' eyes, he loosened his hold on Obi and started walking away.

Obi staggered to his feet, picked dirt from the ground and threw it on Gbangba again.

Gbangba turned to the boy's direction thinking, If I walk away, everyone will say I could not defeat this needle in a man's heart. An experienced hand trained this boy. He should be able to take an experienced punishment.

Gbangba charged at his opponent like a bull, while his victim stood in the same position like a dead animal. As he was about to pounce on the boy, Obi sidestepped him, gripped Gbangba at the back of his neck, and used his momentum to throw him on the floor on his back.

Everyone was astonished, including the victor. Gbangba went to Obi and gave him a slight bow as a mark of respect. Obi answered the bow and started home.

"Don't forget your salt." Gbangba threw the salt to Obi.

"Thank you, Omee."

"Call me Gbangba. To you I owe the respect."

The victor walked toward home, unable to run, without looking back.

Obi got home with the rays of the moonlight as his only source of light. He reached his home to meet his mother waiting for him.

"What happened to you?" she asked, carrying the boy inside.

"I was attacked by a hyena."

"You were fighting again," Odagwe said.

"This is not the time for you to be asking those kinds of questions. And by the way, woman, why would you send him at this time of the night?" the father asked.

"It wasn't that late when I sent him," she replied while applying herbs to the injury.

"Father, I have something to tell you." Odagwe's tone was soft.

"Then talk, I am listening."

"It's something I would like to talk with you about privately."

"It's okay. Obi and I will finish up in the other room," his mother said.

"Nonsense. If you have something to say, you can say it in your mother and brother's presence. If your sisters were here, I would ask them to be present. So what do you have to say?"

"It could be something that requires only your ears," his mother said in a soothing manner.

"I have spoken. This family is built firm by the things we share together. Now Odagwe, what is the problem?"

The boy looked up in the air then faced his father and spoke harshly. "I have been offered a space in Omee training."

"So why are you telling me?"

"The general has vouched for me."

"Is there anything they teach Omees that I have not taught you? The constitution of anything good has been debased by their lust of power."

"With all due respect, Father, I want to be an Omee with a future to look forward to. I would rather be a ruthless warrior than live in this isolated place you call home."

"Odagwe!" Nneka shouted.

"You are now a man to choose your destiny, but I expect you not to hide under the skin of your prey. Why don't you say what hangs by your tongue, 'Your father was weak. That's why he did not finish what they sent him to do.'"

"I did not mean to say that."

"I did not raise a liar and a coward. That's exactly what you had in mind, so be bold enough to say what you mean." Ifeanyi was burning with rage.

"If you are interested in my opinion, I know you are weak and the fact that you cannot handle the niche you are in, doesn't mean you would bring us down to your level."

"Ifeanyi," his wife said shakily, "forgive Odagwe, I think he drank too much of that old man's palm wine."

"Mother, stop defending me. I am no longer a child. I have watched the world turn around without me in it. I am over here wasting my life as a diminutive trader while my mates like Gbangba are now Omees. I am not drunk. My eyes are as wide as an owl."

"I respect your decision my son. You know the way out and don't bother coming back."

"Ifeanyi, you are not serious."

"Yes, Mother, he is serious and I, too, am serious about my decision."

Odagwe bent to the height of his brother. "Come with me. They even take children of only seven years. The way we are, we would make it through their training in a year. Forget what is in your heart; think with your head. In every way, you are a man and it's time to let the world know. There is no future here for us here."

"Odagwe, you are stupid. You want to take my son away."

Nneka was silenced by a signal from her husband's fingers; nevertheless she grabbed her son close to her.

27

"My brother, follow me. Let us create a pathway for our destination. Tears come and go, but the experience is something we can't buy, even if we possessed everything we touched. I know you are younger than I am, but there is nobody I trust to be at my back more than you, and nothing in this world or out of it will ever touch you as long as I live. Come with me. The general also vouched for you."

Obi left his mother's arms and went to his brother. His mother's mouth was open in astonishment; his father's face was indifferent. He shook his brother with two hands, telling him goodbye.

"Don't make me beg, Obi. I will never forgive you if you don't follow me."

"I can't come with you, Odagwe." Obi stepped back toward Ifeanyi.

"Please come with me," Odagwe said, his gaze intent on his brother.

Obi said nothing but remained still by his mother. Odagwe grinned and walked away, his mother chasing after him to change his mind, but it was to no avail.

Chapter 3

With time, the kingdom of Didasu's idealism was transformed imperceptibly to something nobody could comprehend.

It started with the encroachment of the lighter-skinned Nomads, who felt their cattle were best raised within that region. These Arabians provided an excellent breed of horses, their women's faces were covered and they were relentless about introducing their philosophy of life and religion to everyone. Then came the white men with their straight hair and narrow noses. When they first arrived, everyone in the kingdom thought the gods sent them direct from heaven. But after they sweated, bled, ate and had sex like the black man, the people's impression changed.

They kept coming with gifts that meant nothing to them compared to what they received in exchange. They were not all from the same land. Their religion was not the same, but they claimed to have the same god. They did not speak the same language and they had intense hatred for each other. They brought horses, copper and some luxury items like salt to trade for gold, cloth, ivory, beads, bronze carvings and even slaves.

People sold their land, slaves and heritage for salt. They used the salt to heal their wounds, wash their clothes, preserve and cook their food, and dry animal skins used as clothes and footwear. The only problem was the kingdom of Didasu did not allow the trading of slaves to men outside the kingdom.

The white men often attacked small villages in the outskirts of kingdoms and exported the people as slaves. They preferred the extremely strong nature of the Negroes in Didasu Kingdom, so they paid criminals large amounts to capture anyone they found. Some chiefs had private dealings with them.

*

Obi was twenty years old when his mother died, not long after her husband's funeral. Ifeanyi died from snakebite when he was in the bushes. His son tried to suck out the poison, but it spread too quickly into his body. It took them about two weeks before his spirit was let out of his body. In this time, every man who was a friend or a relation to the deceased pays their respect. Very few men were present for the interment of the Ikaza because their presence would have been unforgivable to their superior. Most men came out of gratitude for services Ifeanyi had done for them. He was recognized for making the antidotes for any kind of poison, which happened to be his major means of taking care of his family and increasing his land. For this reason, most people were surprised he died from snakebite. Everybody expected Odagwe, the general of Ozuoba, to be present, but he did not come. The chief of Alloida, Gbangba, came out for every man to see that he was present for the funeral of his friend's father.

Gbangba was a feared man for his heartless missions. When he was the general, his predecessor, Chief Hejieto, tried many times to assassinate him but to no avail. His predecessor died with a spear in his heart on a sunny day. The general headed the investigation of the mysterious death of their chief. Everyone knew Gbangba did it, but no one ever uttered a word except the dead man's wives, who were screaming all over the market place that the general had killed their husband. People pretended they didn't hear anything. A few elders challenged the general; they seemed to die of old age afterward. Only one Omee, named Vacoura, vehemently challenged Gbangba's investigation and he was made general when Gbangba became chief.

As chief, Gbangba lived under constant threat from the outsiders, his Omees, his wives, and even his children. Attempts on his life were routine; his enemies were more than the men in his province. He was a true Omee to the core. His people feared him, yet they respected him because he expanded their province by encroaching into other chiefs' lands and annihilating the tribes. They had reported the matter to the King many times, but Gbangba had a way of expanding his taxes as he expanded his land. The King allowed Chief Nonso of Iyatu to go to war with him because the man was insistent. The battle ended in a flawless victory—Iyatu's province no longer existed and the land was used to form a greater Alloida.

Gbangba's servants always picked the coquettes he slept with, to quench his insatiable sexual appetite after his wives and concubines. His servant had been telling him of a girl whose skin was smooth as the fur of a lion, whose smile opened up the heavens and whose beauty was unmatched.

During a feast celebrating the birth of his son a few months before the funeral of Obi's father, Gbangba ordered his servants to bring the girl to his presence. When she arrived, he was positive she was a goddess. The closer she got to his private chambers the faster his heart beat. She bowed with flawless humility. He studied the female and noticed a combined asset of lust and purity.

"Please rise. It is I who should respect your presence." He snapped his fingers and everyone in the room left, closing the door behind them. "Why have I not been aware of your existence till now?"

"Your Grace, my existence is not worth a space in the midst of your knowledge."

"Nonsense. My servants underestimated your beauty. What is your name and who is your father?" As he spoke, he tried to keep his distance, but the voluptuous animal had a power over him that made him reach for her bosoms.

The coquette pushed him away in a highly seductive manner and started walking around the room asking, "What is your desire?"

"My desire is you in my bed."

"Patience, Gbangba, or am I too little to call you that?"

"I am whatever you want me to be. Now come to me."

"No rush," she said, smiling and playing with the palm wine keg on the table resting on the ivory tusk. "You realize it will be highly indecent for me to spread my legs for you to enter me this soon."

"What you want I will provide. Even if you want to belong to me, then I am yours. Any dowry settlement I will pay, but now I want both of us to join as one."

She poured palm wine from the chief's table into a calabash and knelt in front of him.

"I hope I am worthy to offer my Chief palm wine to drink."

"If I want to be served palm wine, I would snap my fingers and have over twenty servants waiting to serve me. Now I want to enter inside you."

"A tortoise knows it will take him a long time to get to his destination, but it still moves. Now please drink the wine I offer you and soften my heart."

Gbangba got up and paced around the room. "Women! You are all the same. You prefer to be acted on with intensity."

"How do you expect me to let you enter me when you refuse to drink the wine I offer you from your calabash?"

"Why don't you drink and offer me the rest?"

"Are you trying to imply that I poisoned the wine?"

"Definitely not, but our people have a saying that the woman spices the path of a man, so please help yourself."

"If that is your desire, so shall it be." She took the calabash in one hand and her other hand delved into her braids, where she took out some sharp pins from her hair and threw them at the chief.

Gbangba succeeded in deflecting the first set of pins, but she kept throwing more at him until one finally entered his eye. As he pulled the pin from his eye, there was blood everywhere and he found it hard to see. The Wovamee dipped her hand into her miniature wrapper around her waist and brought out a jagged edged knife. She jumped on the table and dived at the chief. Gbangba could not see; the blood had covered his second eye. As she landed on him, she drove the knife into his shoulder with a powerful thrust. She missed her aim for his heart because the chief swayed. He wanted to scream, but what example would he give to his men, allowing them think the great Gbangba could not take care of a Wovamee.

She pulled the knife from his shoulder like a tigress. With a greater force, she aimed for his heart with no intention to miss this time. He used his hands as a blockade. The knife passed through his hands, but did not get to his heart. He held her wrist with the knife still inside his hand. She punched him hard continuously with her other hand, but he did not let go. As he rose to his feet, he got hold of her other hand.

She kicked him, but it seemed to have no effect on him. She started giving him head-butts until he released the grip and staggered back.

The Wovamee broke out one of the tusks from the legs of the table and ran toward Gbangba. The chief could now see the figure in a blurred manner, approaching him forcefully, but he instinctively dodged her, grabbed her by the neck and twisted it. He continued squeezing her neck until he was positive she was dead, then he opened the door to his chambers and fainted.

His servants, on seeing him, went to inform the Omees. These men then sent the message to the general who sent for the chief's Tikpapa. The general got to the chief's home about the same time as the Tikpapa. They saw Obi, the Ikaza's son and friend of Gbangba, dressing the chief's wounds.

"The pins she threw at his eyes were poisoned as well as the knife. I suspect we can still treat it before—" Obi began explaining before being interrupted.

"If I want your opinion I'll ask for it," the Tikpapa said as he surveyed the invalid's wounds. "He is right. He has been poisoned, but the antidote cannot be found in these parts."

"You are speaking rubbish, man. All Wovamees use ugra poison that can be cured by using aniye leaves," Obi said angrily while applying pressure to his friend's shoulder.

"Listen, you might be the son of an Ikaza but it does not put you in a position to interfere with things higher than your level."

The Tikpapa removed Obi's hands and started applying a mixture from the bark of a tree on the shoulder.

"Everyone in this room should leave except the Tikpapa," Vacoura, the general, ordered. "Whatever you have to say with the chief lying here, you say in front of me," Obi said. "Whatever you have to do with the chief here, you do it in front of me, because I am not going anywhere."

"Look here young man, we are not prepared for contests, so for the last time as general of this province I am ordering you to—"

"You are ordering me to what?" Obi interrupted. "We are wasting time. Let us send someone to get these leaves or else he will not make it—unless that is what you want."

"How dare you accuse us of such a crime," the Tikpapa said.

"If the Tikpapa said there is no cure, then there is no cure," the general said.

Obi ran to where Gbangba lay, used his elbow to push the Tikpapa away, and hefted the chief onto his shoulder. Before the general could reach him, he used his back to push the door open. On the other side of the door the chief's wives were wailing and crying, while the Omees and the elders were talking amongst

36

themselves. When they saw Obi with the chief on his shoulder, the Tikpapa on the floor, and the general trying to catch him, silence filled the room.

"Great people of Alloida," Obi dropped the chief on the floor gently as he spoke, "Chief Gbangba was stabbed in his shoulder and in the hand with a poisonous knife. The pin that entered his eye was also poisoned. The Tikpapa said the antidote is aniye leaves and it should be given to him before morning. Your general said I should drop the chief in the midst of his people so that everyone can witness his recovery while I go and get the leaves."

When he finished talking, he faced the general and Tikpapa along with every other spectator in the room.

The General raised his head high and without looking at anyone and said, "Now that you have told them what I told you to tell them, go and get the leaves before the day is over."

Obi got the antidote for the poison and gave it to the chief. His convalescence took a short period but eventually Gbangba was himself again, though with only one eye—the other one was damaged beyond healing. The servant who introduced the Wovamee to the chief died mysteriously. Gbangba looked for a million excuses to kill the general, but he was good at covering his tracks and was loved by both his Omees and the elders. The Tikpapa was not so fortunate; he was killed by the general for treason. The general claimed to have killed him immediately after he told him about assassinating his beloved chief. Gbangba knew that the Tikpapa was killed to cover all the loopholes, but he really did not mind the loss. Now he had only the general to take care of.

The burial of Obi's father was not too ceremonial; a few commoners came and danced around his grave and some poured palm wine on it. His wife was kept in seclusion from everybody for a week, except her daughters who provided her food and anything she desired.

Obi looked at everyone dancing and rejoicing at his father's burial. His father told all of his children he wanted them to be happy when he died because he lived a good life and he expected them to dance vigorously. Ifeanyi raised him as an Omee, taught him about the art of physical combat, the different poisons and their antidotes, to understand the deception of man, and gave him systematic information on the laws and politics of the land.

On more than one occasion, Nneka told Obi about his real mother, but he would always say that she was his only mother. She died immediately after she came out of seclusion at the end of the funeral. Nobody could detect what she died of, but everyone knew she went in search of her husband's soul. Nneka's funeral was not crowded because she was a woman of lower respect. Top delegates from her province of Utagba were present. The people who came were of a younger age than she was because it was forbidden to go to the funeral of someone younger.

The people from his mother's province were known for their loyalty to anyone who was still accepted by them. The men from Utagba gave Obi a chain made out of the teeth of lions, letting him know that he had a home at Utagba at anytime. The whole funeral was organized by Obi; he was the only son in the house and the first daughter did the cooking for everyone in the funeral, as was custom.

His two sisters were both married and he cared deeply for them. He was positive when they left he would drown in an intense form of loneliness. Obi wished the funeral would last forever so he could feel the presence of his parents within him. When the ceremony was over and everyone had gone, his sisters stayed with him for a while.

After they had gone back to their former lives, Obi started working on the family land. Day after day, he tilled the soil. In the evenings, he sold the antidotes for different kinds of poisons. He never left his land for anything pleasurable. Traders came to his farm because his harvest grew in a very healthy fashion. Alone at night Obi wondered about who his father was planning to arrange for him to marry; all he knew was that she was the daughter of another Ikaza named Ikpong.

On one of those provocative sunny days a man came to his home with a haughty aura. His horses were a fine breed and he was escorted by more servants than was required. The man definitely dwelt in the realm of luxury and he was not an Omee; he did not have the beads on his hands to show his position in society. He walked through the land with a certain determination that made its owner come into view.

"May I help you?" Obi asked politely.

"Depends. Who owns this land?" the man said as he continued walking around the farm.

"If you are talking to me, I suggest you stand and look me in the eye whilst you speak, or else you leave my property."

"I take it you are the son of the Ikaza who owns the land."

Obi did not say a word, but kept his eyes locked on the man.

"I am Okonjo. Some say I am the greatest merchant who has seen this earth, but I just let them know I am an ordinary man. I have lots of things to do. I came to inspect this land they say flourishes with great crops, and I am impressed. I would like to purchase it from you."

"You are not the first to ask for this land, and what I told the people before you is what I am telling you now—the land is family land and it will remain that way for generations to come."

"You look devilishly familiar," Okonjo said, looking intently at Obi. "By the way, I am ready to offer you more than you can imagine."

"Okonjo, goodbye."

"You have a sharp tongue for the son of an Ikaza. Listen young man, I can get this land in two ways— either we make a peaceful bargain, or you learn the price of being the son of an Ikaza."

"You see this land, my father and his father before him sweated and bled on this land. Before you can take it, you will have to wash this land with my blood."

After Obi spoke, Okonjo looked at him as though he missed something.

"Do you really know who I am?"

"I have never set eyes on you before, but your name I know. You are the nephew of the King-Mother."

"If that is your final decision, then I will have to get what I want by other means." Okonjo turned to leave, but looked back and said, "Has anyone told you that you look and talk in an identical manner to the King?"

Obi turned around, leaving the man still standing on the same spot, wondering how such a person could come close to resembling his distinct looking cousin.

As Okonjo left on a carriage pulled by servants, he thought more about the King and Obi.

The King has only one son alive who cannot stand on his feet. He has no resemblance to the King and is weak with words. A so-called prince that cannot stand where the wind blows. The men in power all long for the King to die. I don't blame them; even I wish the bastard would choke in his greed, but the man was born with an immortal spirit. His poor excuse for a son is the opening of power for anyone who can get access to him. Apart from him being young in the head, he also is young in the heart of a man.

Okonjo frowned at the thought of the sardonic Obi coming out publicly in the capital.

All the elders would claim him the lost prince. How ironic this life is—the elders pushed the King to kill the only heir at that time and now they would rather give the throne to a demon than the only son the King has. There is no way that arrogant Obi can be the son of the King, unless he is the son of Aneaton, who was positively killed by the Ogun priest. Unless, the Ogun priest did not kill the child. That can't be possible; he suggested the death of the child. What is going through my head? Obi is the son of Nneka and she is also the sister to Aneaton. She was supposed to be the King's wife, but he chose her sister and continued sleeping with Nneka during her marriage to the Ikaza. It is outstandingly obvious that he looks like the King. How come no one has ever spoken of it?

Okonjo's servants had gotten to the town and were heading to his home. Their master kept looking at the people in the capital, how they crowded together talking of anything they could think of. He smiled knowing that the walls of status prevented him from having anything to talk about with these commoners, but at the same time being the subject their gossip.

Disgusting sets of beings, he thought, they talk so much about me and most of them do not know what I look like. He scratched his head for a while, then his smile was rekindled. That is it. Most men have not stood in the presence of the King and looked him in the eye; that is why they can't detect the resemblance between Obi and the King. His friend Gbangba never noticed the resemblance because they grew up together.

Now, he grinned and rubbed his chin, how can this information benefit me?

When he arrived at his home, his servants and slaves along with his family were all waiting outside. He ignored all three wives and nine children, who were trying to get his attention, and ran into his house like a mad man. He grabbed a servant, who followed him at the same pace.

"Where is she?"

"In her room, sir," the servant answered submissively.

Okonjo went to the room to see his most prized possession. If someone did not recognize his arrival, he took it as an insult. The woman he was looking for knew that and purposely did not come out, letting everyone in his home see her power over him. Only she, Weruche, had the fullness of the earth he craved. He had begged her a thousand times to let him dispose of the thorns of his flesh, but she preferred to remain the fourth wife than the only wife. Everyone believed she put him under a spell, but he did not seem to care, and those who voiced their view were no longer under the blanket of his generosity.

*

The loneliness started eating into Obi's spine. On a few occasions he went to visit his only friend, Gbangba, but these visits were rare because of the intensity of his friend's position. One sunny morning Obi's oldest relative, who was from his mother's lineage, came to his home with his sisters and their husbands. He welcomed them in, and his youngest sister offered kola nuts and palm wine to everyone in order of age. After the oldest relative had blessed what was being offered, eaten the kola nut, and drank the wine, they began what they came for.

"Obiani," his oldest relative spoke while everyone sat down and listened attentively. "Your sisters came all the way to Utagba to tell me that you are still living alone without a wife. Listen young man, if you take one broomstick, it can break with ease, but when it forms a broom it does not break."

The old man coughed and then continued.

"A man cannot stand alone without women or at least a woman. Do you intend cooking for yourself forever, or sweeping the ground by yourself? As much as the chicken spreads its feathers and rises above the ground, it can't fly like an eagle. May the gods forbid such a destiny for you, my son?"

"Papa, I really do not understand why they have to put you through all this trouble because they want to choose a bride for me."

"It is not they, it is we, who have chosen your bride. The girl is the daughter of an Ikaza with lost honor. Your parents before they died introduced you to her father. We have checked their background and noticed nothing of concern, except the fact that the father is an Ikaza like your father, but his case was a little different—he was embezzling the chief's dues. Anyway, we tried other women and their dowries were too high because you are the son of an Ikaza and we all know you are not that wealthy."

"How am I sure that I will like this woman?"

"Believe me, my brother, she glides with the wind and she is his first daughter," the younger sister interjected.

"Beauty is but a spice; the inner desire is the main dish, my dear sister," Obi said.

"Why don't you meet her first?" suggested his younger sister's husband.

The oldest relative continued as though he was never interrupted.

"The dowry is five healthy looking cows, one bull, two he-goats, thirteen kegs of palm wine, a basin of kola nut and garden eggs, twelve fowls, and enough lace material for their whole family."

"I have to admit the dowry requires quite some funds but it is relatively cheap. Why don't you people tell me the truth? Ikpong's daughter is as ugly as a monkey."

"Even if she cannot capture your fancy, the major thing is that you have a woman to look after your house and bear your children," said his oldest sister. "Maybe you do not realize it, but you are the only accepted son of our father. We intend to let his legacy flow forever."

"The introduction is in four days, so look for the sweetest palm wine you can find today. By tomorrow morning we shall all leave."

*

In three days they got to Ikpong's home in the Ozuoba province. As any Ikaza, his house was secluded from the main town, but he seemed to keep a level of affluence. His home was built to a man's exceptional taste. Although he bore the title of Ikaza, all his sons were Omees in the same province and he had constant dealings with Chief Atani, who treated him like a doormat.

Immediately they arrived, they directed them to Ikpong who was surrounded by slaves. They all bowed as a mark of respect except for Obi's oldest relative, who was the oldest person in the room.

"Great Ikpong, in your days no man could look into your eyes in battle and live," the oldest relative said.

"I understand the procedures that this introduction requires, but could we leave the flattering behind and move on." Ikpong replied.

"I, too, always liked to kill the fowl by cutting its neck instead of playing with it," the oldest man grunted. "We have come for the hand of your daughter in marriage. We intend to build a dynasty of sons from her."

The oldest relative glanced at Obi giving him a signal to proceed. Obi's head was still low, and he stretched out his hands with the keg of palm wine and calabash of kola nut.

"Good friend of my father, I come to your glorious presence to humbly ask for your daughter in wedlock."

"Your father was a good friend to me and he had a spirit I will respect till my grave. Please sit," Ikpong replied, taking the gifts as if they were dirt.

Everyone sat on the raffia mats. Hanging on the walls were elephant tusks and feline skins.

"Did your father tell you people what the price of the dowry was?"

"Yes, he did," the oldest relative replied confidently.

"Well, the price has doubled."

"Why?" Obi's youngest sister screamed.

"Has anyone not told you that when men talk women listen?" Ikpong said.

"Forgive her," the oldest relative said, "the youth in her blood overcomes her. I think the women can wait for us outside while we conclude."

The women hesitated and then left angrily.

"Let's face it, the only reason I wanted my daughter to marry into your family was because of Ifeanyi. In spite of the fact that he was an Ikaza, he still commanded respect. But now he is dead and you are not even an Omee. I watched you grow and I was proud of what I saw, but you will end up putting our name in a deeper hole than it already is. You are the son of an Ikaza and it haunts you wherever you go. If my daughter married a man with respect, no one will ever remember that her father was an Ikaza."

"If it is double the dowry you want, then I will provide it for you," Obi replied, not wanting to leave with a wounded pride.

"I don't think he means what he is saying," the oldest relative interrupted.

"I mean exactly what I say."

"So that is settled," Ikpong said before turning and clapping his hands. "Tell Amina to come here."

Facing them again he said, "I wish I could bring Amina's mother here, but I do not want to disgrace your humble presence by calling my concubine to your view."

"Are you trying to tell me that your first daughter, is the daughter of a concubine?" the oldest relative yelled.

"Of course not. The general of our province came for her hand two sunsets ago, and who am I to resist such a man of prestige." Ikpong said proudly.

"But you had already agreed to give the girl to Obi. Why would you choose to give her to his own brother?" the older sister's husband snarled.

"That is the stupidest question any man has ever asked me. Odagwe is general now and very soon he will be chief. Apart from that, he possesses two qualities that I like—he is rich and he has power."

They all stood looking at Ikpong, the words trapped in their mouths.

"I really do not see what the problem is here. Before I accepted the dowry from your brother, I told him you had already asked for her hand in marriage and he said that had nothing to do with him."

"You men should forget about my first daughter. See the beauty in Amina. Her mother was given to me by an Arabian who sought my help in the possession of slaves. At first I chose to refuse him because she was his concubine, but then sight of the woman was irresistible. If you get to know her, you will forget she is not one of us."

"Am I to understand that you want Obi to marry these people? Maybe you are not aware that strength of the people of Utagba lies in our darkened roots," the oldest relative fumed, looking at the half-Arabian girl. "The annoying thing is, you brought this poor excuse for a woman to our presence because you have put us all on the same level. In fact, how dare you bring the daughter of a concubine to be our bride? It's been awhile, but I smell blood."

"The dowry of any commoner's daughter is less than a quarter of your dowry," Obi's in-law blurted.

"I admit you are slick negotiators. We will use the former dowry we agreed on."

"You openly insult us. You bring this child of a concubine and you expect us to pay a dowry for her," the oldest relative said, shaking with anger.

Amina stood without making a sound, her head down and tears falling from her cheeks as she listened to her devaluation as a human being.

When the tears touched the floor, it was as though they awakened Obi's spirit. He looked at the beauty she held and refused to give her away.

"Wise old man, you are quick to lose your temper. How can I even imagine giving such a wench to a son of Utagba? Actually, I wanted her to prepare the road for my other daughter, the first daughter from her mother. She is truly a rare human being and her dowry will remain the same with what I agreed with Obi's father."

"That is generous of you, Ikpong, but we are no longer interested. We shall take our leave," Obi said.

All four men got up and started leaving. Ikpong followed the men and tried begging, but he did not know the words to use. As the men stepped outside and started arranging their departure, Obi looked back into the house and saw Amina standing in the same place. As though his glance touched her, she raised her head and looked back into his eyes. That was all it took. In a month's time, the marriage ceremony between Obi and Amina had begun.

The marriage was a day of bliss, but nothing too flamboyant. Most of the crowd came to dance, eat, and say goodbye to the girl they once knew because she belonged to another man. Obi's sisters, brothers-in-law, relatives and representatives of Utagba were present, but they all objected to him getting married to the daughter of a concubine.

Although the elders never showed themselves in the burial of an Ikaza, it didn't prevent them from being present at an Ikaza's daughter's marriage. Also, her suitor paid an outrageously high dowry for her hand, which made everyone curious to see the Arabian's daughter. Obi could have paid a lesser dowry, but he chose to pay double the amount to let the world know she was worth the fortunes of a man's land.

The ceremony involved throwing alcohol on the ground by the elders and blessing the ground where the union was taking place. Then the father of the bride stated, in the presence of everyone, the way he required the groom to take care of his daughter. Afterward, the groom was blindfolded and a stream of coquettes led by his mother-in-law came in claiming to be his bride, but he rejected their advances with a smile. If Obi had accepted any of their advances, then he would have lost his bride even though her father had already taken the dowry. At the end of the occasion, Amina followed her husband and waved goodbye to her mother. As much as the mother was sad that her daughter was leaving, she was happy for her, too. Amina had never seenher mother smile and walk with so much pride. The day was the best in her life because it helped her mother realize she was special.

Chapter 4

King Nwosa's palace was crowded with men of all kinds, of different races and places, waiting to see him. As the King's mother passed everyone, with Okonjo and her servant behind her, all of them bowed. All the foreigners had quickly learned the customs, a necessary knowledge for those seeking certain possessions. Also, it was no secret that Gbangba cut the head off a white man who approached him with disrespect. Since then, everybody was positive the whites could live and die like anyone else.

As the mother got to the chambers of the King, the Omees tried to stop her from passing through the doors, begging her to let them announce her presence, but she ignored everyone around her until she got to her son.

He was talking with the envoy of the Didasu Kingdom and the Ishu priest, who succeeded the Ogun priest, who died of old age. He saw his mother and totally ignored her entry and discharged the Didasu envoy. The envoy bowed to the King and then the King-Mother before leaving. The King stared at the Omees who let his mother pass through as they lay flat on the ground, begging for mercy for being lax in their duties. He waved his hands, and they thanked him and went out the door.

The King's chamber had cushioned seats from animal skins. Tree trunks elevated his throne and the stairway leading up the throne was made of skeletons.

Crafts hung on the walls and the entire floor had the softness of animal fur.   His mother began to sit but he told her, while staring lustfully at her servant, "I did not offer you a seat."

She got up, snapped her fingers, and pointed to the ground. Her servant went down on her hands and knees and she sat on her.

"Mother, I really do not think where you are sitting is comfortable. You may now take a seat," the King growled.

"I am comfortable where I am," the King-Mother replied.

"I was actually referring to the welfare of that sweet little girl you are sitting on. If you crave to sit on someone's back, let me get an Omee that you can torture."

"Save your manly needs for another day, we have come here on a matter of great importance."

The King-Mother directed Okonjo to sit as she spoke, but he knew better and claimed satisfaction in his standing posture.

"You better have something worth talking about or else—"

"Or else what? I carried you for nine months in my belly and till today you have not brought pride to my weak heart. What I have to say to you is for your ears only."

"Mother, save the melodramatic statements. You are aware that the Ishu priest is the Headman to the Oracle and he is the High Chief."

"I know he is a High Chief. I know there are only three men in the kingdom that can be High Chief. I know they are the Head-Of-Government, Okpalaukwu and the Headman to the Oracle. But as I said before, what I have to say is for your ears only."

At that point the King wondered where was the Okpalaukwu, the oldest chief in the kingdom. "I trust his loyalty over that of your spoiled sister's child, Okonjo," the King retorted pointing at her nephew.

"Okonjo is the reason I am here. The servant with me is deaf and dumb, so you can forget about her. It has come to my knowledge that you were supposed to marry Aneaton's sister."

"Yes, so please do not tell me that is why you came."

"Were you sleeping with her?"

"Mother, maybe you are not aware of the seriousness of the position I carry."

"Were you sleeping with her?"

"No, no, no. I was supposed to marry her then I saw her sister. Since I married Aneaton, I have not laid eyes on her. Why are you asking me these questions?"

As Okonjo stood there during the mother's interrogation, he feared he was going to lose his head at the hands of his King for spreading unfounded information.

"Okonjo showed me her sister's child. He looks, walks, and talks like you," the King-Mother said.

"Are you sure of what you are saying, mother?"

"When Okonjo told me, I wanted to personally castrate him, but I decided to see this man myself. So we dressed like commoners and went to his wedding at Ozuoba. From afar I saw this young man and I had to admit he looked like you from the distance. Then when I stood right in front of him and he asked me, 'Are you a relative of the bride?' I could swear he was you when you were younger and I fainted. My blood is in his veins."

"Okonjo, thank you for your observation. We will get in contact with you." The King's hand drummed on his lap. Okonjo bowed and left.

"It is not possible," the King said. "The Ogun priest did the ritual personally."

"The young man was born at the same period as Aneaton's son. His head is oval like yours, he has the same birthmark underneath his chin like you and his eyes are deep like yours," the King-Mother added.

"When the Ogun priest took the child, where was the sister?" the Ishu priest asked.

"She was with her sister," the King replied, rubbing his chin. "He can't possibly be my child. Or are you trying to tell me the women exchanged their children?"

"That can be the only reason for the gods not telling us anything about the future. They did not get their sacrifice," the Ishu priest said.

"What are you saying?" The King screamed for his messenger. When he came, the King asked, "Where is Arubi? I told you when the day was younger, to tell him to come."

"The Head-of-Government is on his way, Your Majesty."

"Who exactly is this boy?"

"His supposed father was an Ikaza with a good reputation and his supposed mother was your former wife's sister," his mother answered.

"You keep referring to his parents with the term supposed. I find that uncomfortable and I have never heard of an Ikaza with a good reputation."

Just then, his round-faced, dark-skinned Head-of-Government entered the room, bowing as he got near the King.

"My superlative King, forgive me for making you wait for a man as unworthy as I, but the day was in the hands of evildoers."

"Forget all that, Arubi. The King-Mother said she saw a young man who walks, talks, and looks exactly like me."

"So what? It could be coincidental or just a game the gods chose to play."

"My mother and the Ishu priest are under the impression that the young man is my son. They think he was Aneaton's sister's child and he was born in the same period as the child the Ogun priest killed."

"If Aneaton's sister was in her palace on the same day her sister was killed and the children were supposed to be of the same age, then something is wrong. No woman who has just given birth to a child would leave the child behind," the Head-of-Government said.

"Precisely. She did not leave the child behind—they switched both of them. That is why the Ogun priest did not notice," the Ishu priest surmised.

"Okay, let us imagine he was my son...so..."

"Sire, I don't think you understand the gravity of the situation. With all due respect, the heir is weak and that gives you peace of mind. If the people know this newcomer is your son, a new heir will emerge and that makes him immune to any crime—including assassinating you," the Head-of-Government said, leaning back in his lion-skinned chair. "The boy could be aware that he is your son, which I doubt, or else the whole kingdom would have known by now. If this information leaks, all your enemies will want to make contact with him and form an alliance with him. Not to mention the defiance that will come from your chiefs and elders. Take it from me, they will be fighting from a solid foundation because the people will back him. They want a King who can walk, talk and look like a King."

"So what are you suggesting?" the King asked.

"Depends on the town he lives in. How come nobody ever noticed he looked like the King?"

"Well, Arubi," the King-Mother said, calling him by his name to provoke him, "the boy has lived most of his life away from towns because his supposed father was an Ikaza. Since the death of the man, he has been taking care of the land and expanding it. The people he comes across don't notice the similarity because they only see the King from a distance. Although they say he is a very good friend of Gbangba, the reason his friend might never have noticed could probably be their growing up together, so he never noticed any similarities."

"Sire, I feel we should first eliminate any means of this information getting out publicly and then kill the boy in the most accidental manner possible," the Head-of-Government suggested.

The King looked at the Ishu priest. "What do you think?"

"I agree. The commoners are ready to make anybody who can walk and talk the next King. Your son lacks the power to invigorate the men of the King's court to stay together."

"Mother, what do you think?"

"You have to realize that you killed this young man's mother."

"I did not tell the Ogun priest to kill her."

"But he did. If the boy is aware of what happened, his adulation for her will be deep and he will have to avenge her death. The boy grew up without a single

59

pinch of emotion for you; someday he will not hesitate to take your life."

"Don't you people think you are exaggerating? This boy might not even know, and even if he does, do you think he can even get close to me, not to mention killing me?"

"We can't take chances, Your Majesty," the Head-of-Government replied.

"Sire, if your mother died the way his mother died, would you not avenge her?" the Ishu priest asked.

"Arubi, do what you have to do, but nobody should know except the people in this room."

"What about the girl your mother is sitting on?" the Head-of-Government asked.

"You don't have to bother about her—she is deaf and dumb—but you might have to dispose of Okonjo because he is aware of everything."

"May the gods forbid,'' his mother said. "Why do you want to touch my sister's son? That boy has been more of a son to me than you have ever attempted to be."

"I send my sympathy. He has to die. This regards the security of the King...your son." There was bitterness in the Head-of-Government's response.

"I understand, but if you feel he has to die, then you also have to consider me a means of insecurity and I should be dealt with in the same order as Okonjo."

"That won't be a problem. We would lay the two of you side by side after your execution," the Head-of-Government said indifferently.

"Mother, you were strong on emphasizing your grandson should die, even though the boy doesn't know a thing about me. But Okonjo, who is not trustworthy…you are ready to die for him to live."

"So you want to replace his good deed of giving you this information with punishment."

"If he ever whispers anything concerning this issue to anyone—"

The King was cut off by the Head-of-Government. "But Sire."

"I am still talking," the King snapped. "I will wipe out his generation. You all know what you have to do. Now leave me, I want to see my art."

He left them and told the messengers to inform the men waiting for him to come the next day. He entered the Art Room and admired the crafts of men of talent. He ran his hands across the bronze lion that was staring him in the face. Then he went to the area of the room with sculptures of the heads of kings and stopped at his grandfather's head…King Anawanti. Then he saw his father's sculpture, King Burobee, and his past haunted him.

All to remain in power, I killed my father and now I am going to let them kill my son again. It would have been nice to have a strong fit son to teach the way of a King, but that I can't risk at the expense of a knife at my back. They all rejoice at my handicapped heir. They want someone they can tell what to do. I have to admit it feels good to sleep at night without thinking of my son planning to kill me like I did to my father. If these men succeed in getting rid of this boy, the kingdom would definitely be divided at my death. That would be a pity.

*

Obi and his wife had been in their home for three weeks and happiness was within. He lived everyday not wanting it to pass. He never wanted her to follow him to the farm, but she had a stubborn spirit and chose to help him any way she could. The emptiness that used to consume him disappeared; the pain of life had found its way into a distant world. He started singing folk songs with her and acting in plays like a child with her. Every time he held her, his grasp was tight because he did not want to lose her. He never ever wanted to lose her. On the few occasions they went to town, he was cautious of any man who made contact with his wife.

One night while he was sleeping with his wife, he opened his eyes and saw leaves whirling around. He got up and the leaves seemed to be leading him to the bushes. He followed, curious yet cautious of everything. The leaves stopped in front of a blind man who was sitting with his legs crossed.

"Who are you?" Obi inquired.

The skinny blind man with a long stick rose and bowed.

"Your Majesty, forgive me for obstructing your dreams, but what I have to say is urgent."

"Are you a madman? Why are you referring to me by that title? Or has your blindness taken you in the wrong direction? The King's palace is at Didasu."

"My two eyes might be blind, but I see better with my third eye over here," he said, pointing to forehead.

"I am impressed you have a third eye and you can do a little magic. I'd like to continue this conversation, but I have to go back to bed," Obi said, then started walking back home.

"Are you not Aneaton's son?"

Obi stopped. "My mother was Nneka and my father was Ifeanyi the Ikaza."

"You can lie to me, but to yourself is simply unforgivable."

"What is that supposed to mean?"

"Did I not tell you I see better with my third eye? Do not try to pretend ignorance with me. Your lies are sieving through every word you say. Both the Ikaza and his wife told you who your mother was."

"How would I put this to you, blind man? I really do not care if my father is a god. I cared for the mother and father that watched and taught me how to grow and I have a deep affection for the life I am living now, so leave me alone."

"I understand and I see how your heart has brightened since you had your bride, but I would like to let you understand a picture. Yes, the Ikaza's wife had pure feelings for you, but your mother's feelings were also genuine. The only reason you are alive and she is dead is because she sacrificed her life for you."

"I have heard this story before," he said with his back still to the blind man. "She let me live so I could grow up a man and not a King."

"It is no longer about what you want; it is now about her honor. She was buried like a criminal. Even under torture she never let you go and the man who let this happen is living in the bosom of indifference," said the blind man, putting his hand on Obi's shoulder.

"How long have you known I was the son of the King?"

"From the first day I saw you."

"How can you see me? You are blind."

"I was not always blind. I chose this destiny the day I saw you during your mother's funeral. I used to be the protégé to the former Ifa priest."

"So!" Obi exclaimed.

"I succeeded him."

"That is not possible. The worshippers of the Ifa god would not let you be their highest priest. You are too young."

"That is why I had to offer my eyes to the shrine to prove I was worthy. There are some other things I had to do, but I am sure you don't want to hear them."

64

"Why are you here?" Obi asked.

"The King is aware that you are alive. They are coming for you, so you and your wife should go and hide somewhere."

"How do you know this?"

"I have been following you everywhere you step since I became the Ifa priest. During your wedding, a woman fainted when she confronted you. She was the King-Mother. I followed her back to her home and it took awhile before she confronted her son. Probably she wanted to make sure she was in her right senses."

"Wait. Am I to understand that you followed us all of this time and we did not notice the presence of a blind man behind us?"

"I was not in the form of a man when I followed you. When I followed the King-Mother, I did not want to attempt to transfigure and enter the palace because I knew the Ishu priest would detect my presence in any form I took. Luckily for me they let the King-Mother's servant enter with her, so I used her because she was deaf and dumb and got to listen to what they said."

"You are saying that you changed into some form of a creature or an animal and followed me all over the place and then you entered the body of a deaf and dumb girl and listened to everything they said in the palace."

"Yes."

"I am not going to ask how that was possible but I want to know, why are you helping me?"

"Because it is your birthright and, like any other human, I am moved to do what is right."

"Your lies are sieving through every word you say."

The Ifa priest smiled.

"The height of every Tikpapa's ladder ends at him becoming the Headman to the Oracle. To become the Ifa priest I had to give away my source of vision to everything around me and now I see only through darkness. I killed everyone in my family line, then I begin to wonder what I have to give up again to reach the top of the ladder. Did I not mention that I am also too young? You have to be old with your hair totally white before you are deemed worthy."

"What are you trying to say?" Obi asked in a soft tone.

"I would like to serve as your High Chief, the Headman to the Oracle, if you would let me," the Ifa priest said, now flat on the ground to give maximum respect.

Obi chuckled.

"Honestly, this King thing is not for me, but if I ever make it there alive, I will not have anyone else by my side as my Tikpapa. But are you sure you can match with a man like the Ishu priest?"

"Till then, Sire. As of now, I suggest you head toward the river. When you cross to the other side, go straight. I will join you at Utagba when I can. Make sure you don't take horses, or they will trace you," the Ifa priest said before he vanished into the darkness.

"Obiani, Obiani," Amina shouted as she entered the bushes.

"I am over here."

"What are you doing here at this time of night?"

"Pack some food and a few things for yourself, we are leaving here now."

She never argued with him when he was serious so she ran back to the house to do as she was told. Obi gathered his sword, knife, bow and arrow. When she came out, he took the bag from her and gave her a knife, but she refused it. She raised her wrapper to show him her own scabbard tied at her waist. He smiled and knew that if anything touched her skin, death would be the only redemption.

"Are we not taking the horses?" she asked.

"No." He released the horses and smacked them, making them run in the opposite direction. "We are walking."

*

The Head-of-Government watched his general come toward him with his head very low and he knew something was wrong.

"I sent you on a mission over three days ago, why are you coming now?" the Head-of-Government said in a very harsh tone.

"There was nobody in his home."

"Did they travel on a leisure trip?"

67

"I doubt it. They left everything behind except the horses. We traced the horse path on a fruitless adventure. Their horses were purposely released to mislead us."

Arubi got up and left his home with the general behind him. He sent two messengers on errands, the first to the King to announce his arrival and the other to the King's envoy. By the time he got to the palace, his presence was already announced, so it did not take him long to appear face to face with the King.

"Talk to me," the King said, clearly agitated.

The Head-of-Government signaled to the general to speak.

"We did not meet them in their home. They seemed to have fled—"

The King's servant interrupted the general in announcing the arrival of the King's envoy.

"You may leave and get the best pathfinder around," Arubi told the general. "He will probably be heading toward his mother's people in Utagba."

Arubi then asked the King's envoy to explain the status of the relationship between the King and the provinces.

"We are all aware that we have only nine provinces because the Utagba people have still refused to merge with our kingdom and they are growing stronger under total allegiance to their Okpala. They still don't have a chief," the envoy responded.

"Okpala? Who is an Okpala?"

"An Okpala is the oldest retired chief in a province, My King."

"I know what an Okpala is you fool." The King sighed and put his left hand on his waist. "Forget about them. We will talk about them another time. Continue."

"We have Ihua of Ahoda. As long as you can give him the power to do what he wants, he is for us. The Ezeonisha of Abogima is indifferent to the King, but he is strict with the customs of the land. Atani of Ozuoba has an unshakeable loyalty to you. Okon of Ndemili still despises you since Arubi became the Head-of-Government. He still feels the position was taken from him. Akuna of Ogwashi is loyal to you because he has not gotten a better offer. We can't say what Gbangba of Alloida is capable of doing. Ike of Ogbe will give you his honor till his death. Otiotio of Suyema is a man that you can rely on, but I don't know if his allegiance to you is till his death. Last of all is the Head-of-Government, who is by your side."

"Thank you, Envoy, for your explicit dialogue. That will be all for now."

The Head-of-Government discharged the King's envoy, who was disappointed that they did not let him share the other information he had to give.

"Somebody told them," the Head-of-Government continued. "They were aware when we were coming. The leak came from this room."

"Talk me to in a straight manner," the King said.

"Okonjo's loyalty is questionable."

"Be logical, he won't be stupid enough to warn them because he has nothing to gain."

"Then someone dangerous to us is protecting the young man. We are not sure how long we can keep the information from reaching the commoners. The boy will definitely have chiefs who will embrace him when he gets to them, not to mention that he happens to be a good friend of Gbangba."

"How do you know?"

"It's my job to know, Your Majesty. He grew up to have a brother who happens to be the general of Ozuoba, but it seems they are now grave enemies, all the better for us."

King Nwosa shouted for his servant and told him to get the Ishu priest and the Okpalaukwu. Then turning to the Head-of-Government he said, "Give me an open view of where we stand."

"Sire, we are not sure, so let's look at it from the worst perspective. He is definitely supported by a man or men of some degree of power, so we call a meeting inviting all the chiefs to the Conference Room. Anyone who does not make himself available has violated his allegiance to his King with death as the only punishment. But if they should all be present, then we take advantage and eliminate any chief capable of dishonor."

"Supposing he really is my son?"

"That has nothing to do with the situation at hand, Your Majesty."

"I was under the impression it has everything to do with the situation at hand. I have this painful intuition that he is my son and the people seem unsatisfied with my successor...I was thinking about accepting him publicly as my son because the thought of shedding a drop of blood from my own son...burns me somewhere inside."

The Head-of-Government smiled and nodded.

"That is an alternative. But I doubt if your other son will give up the chance to be King. Even though he is crippled and weak, there will still be chiefs who will be ready to back him and I have not mentioned how delicious your death will become. Sire, once there is room for another successor as strong as you are...everyone will seek your death, especially your chiefs, so they can take advantage of the months the princes are battling."

"Whatever chaos this creates, I ought to have separated my spirit from this body."

"You seem to forget one more thing—his mother died for him to survive. That is one sacrifice no man can ever forget, especially if the order is linked to the man whom he should call father."

"I did not order her death."

"But you let it happen."

The King closed his eyes and then opened them with a look of concern. "What do we do now?"

Before the King got an answer, the Ishu priest and the Okpalaukwu walked in. The Ishu walked around the room with his fingers twisting in the air.

"What are you doing?" the Head-of-Government asked.

"I am trying to think."

"What is going on?" the Okpalaukwu asked impatiently.

"Aneaton's son is alive," the King said.

"With all due respect, Sire, that is impossible. I witnessed the ritual death of that child by the Ogun priest," the old man replied.

"Then you saw the death of another."

"The Ogun priest would never have betrayed you by sacrificing the wrong child."

"We never said he did, but somewhere along the line, the child was switched."

"What makes you so sure the Ikaza's son is not just someone taking advantage of the similar physical traits that the two of you share and then claiming to be your son?" the old man asked.

"How did you know he was the Ikaza's son?" the Head-of-Government asked.

"Everyone knows about the young man who claims to be your son. Even the market women have gotten access to the information and they seem to be playing with it in whispers."

The three younger men in the room seemed dumbfounded and then the Head-of-Government asked, "Who told you about this?"

"The elders just told me about the situation before I was brought here. From the way they addressed me it seemed like the rumor is fresh as a baby's buttocks. Or is it not a rumor?"

King Nwosa adjusted himself and began.

"Our people say a child that cries can still see with his two eyes. Before I became King the oracle said, and I quote, 'Fear will come within the laughter of men. The pain that is hidden will find its way through. Time will not stand in the way, but it will try to cover the dark colors and the mountain that holds the grains of our integration will collapse, leaving behind a naked ridge.' That was what the Anwu priest told my father."

"So what does the parable mean?" the Ishu priest asked.

"If I knew what it meant, I wouldn't have shared it with all of you. In fact are you not supposed to be the Headman to the Oracle, or am I to understand that you cannot use your tongue to count your teeth?"

"Sire, whoever gets the oracle understands what it means and I am positive the Anwu priest told your father what it meant. The oracle no longer responds to us, but I think it's talking about a mishap that will come and we will not be able to prevent."

"The oracle no longer responds to you!" the King yelled. "It seems the god you worship is impotent. I wonder how you became the Headman to the Oracle."

"Your Majesty, forgive my incompetence, but I am sure your father was aware of the translation."

"Maybe I forgot to add, my father did not share the information with me." With irritation, he faced the Head-of-Government. "So what is your plan?"

"I have to communicate as soon as possible with all the chiefs to understand the magnitude of our situation."

"What do you mean by 'our situation?'" The King seemed confused.

"We are at war."

Chapter 5

The clouds were changing form and darkness was encroaching into the day. The people of Alloida went about with their normal trade, ignoring the threat of the imminent storms. They were known for being insatiable, this was the result of a curse put on them by a virgin girl they burnt on a stake, claiming she was a witch. The real reason for her death was either her blatant refusal to marry Chief Hejieto or the acceptance of the religion of a group of missionaries.

As much as the people tried to deny it, from that day, the respect for the missionary's God grew to extreme heights. They watched these white missionaries kneel and beg for the life of this girl while the other Portuguese tradesmen laughed at them. After the girl's death, the missionaries migrated from the province. Gbangba's beheading of a Portuguese trader made the other white men in the province flee.

Gbangba sat on his throne-like seat, which had arms made of elephant tusk and the hides of bulls, awaiting his guest. His visitor, the highest priest of the Ifa god, emerged looking fifteen years older than he was. He also did not have the characteristics of the highest priest. Firstly, highest priests were typically old and wrinkled, but this man was middle aged. Secondly, he seemed to have verve in his bones. Lastly, he did not seem like the kind of man who would bend over to publicize his god. The fact that he was blind was no surprise. In the past, the highest priests of each god always had a form of defect because of old age. Some could not see; they were normally unable to speak aloud, or they were partially deaf. As the blind man approached, the general and the chief's envoy were surprised by the unconformable features of the highest priest of the Ifa god.

The Ifa priest ignored the presence of the men in the room. He walked directly in front of the chief. "I would like to talk to you alone."

Gbangba waited a while, looking at the blind man, then he signaled the men in the room to wait for him in another chamber. As they left, the blind man sat down.

"I was under the impression that the custom of our society made a man like you require my permission before you sit," the chief told the Ifa priest.

"I could tell you a thousand apologies, but none of them would weigh as much as a feather."

"Now I see why they always choose an older man with eyes to be the highest priest of a god."

"I would love to engage in this petty encounter with you but my time is limited."

"I am so sorry, great one," Gbangba said with great theatrics. "If only I realized how totally useless my time is and how valuable yours was, I would have treated you as the King you are."

"Save your sarcasm, your friend's life is in danger."

"Which friend?"

"Obi."

The anger in his face radiated and he rose as he spoke.

"Who is the dead man that wants to touch a hair of his skin?"

"The King."

"The King." His voice faded as he sat back down. "Why?"

"Did you ever hear of Queen Aneaton?"

"The queen who refused to sacrifice her son when asked to by the King."

"Well, that son is your friend."

"That's impossible. The Ogun priest sacrificed the child."

"Yes, there was a sacrifice, but there was a switch."

"It still does not make sense. I grew up with him and he does not look like the King. He is slim, whilst the King is as big as I am. Not to mention the King is lighter than he is."

"Your friend's life is in danger and he needs your help."

"How long has he known?"

"A long time now. He always kept it to himself, but as of now he does not know that his secret is now with his father, the King."

"How did you know?"

"I have my ways and I have a limited time to inform him before they get to him."

"What makes you think you will get to him before they do?"

"As I said, I have my ways."

"I am to believe that you have Obi's infinite trust?" Gbangba's voice rose.

"Honestly, I have never been acquainted with him, but by the end of the day, I will be serving him."

"Does King Nwosa think I am stupid? Do I look like a fool? Do you not have any pride? I thought you were supposed to be a highest priest of the Ifa god, or are you people now so easily corruptible?"

The Ifa priest got up and started walking away and the chief followed him, now shouting.

"Is this how the King intends to test me? Have I broken any of the laws or not paid his taxes? Let him know that when it comes to my duties, the law comes before any woman, child, and especially friend of mine."

By the time he finished, the Ifa priest had left the room. The Omees wanted to reprimand the Ifa priest, but the chief waved his hands, allowing him to go without stress. He walked around the room moving in circles. He laughed at the thought of his friend becoming King.

The Ifa priest could be working with the King and high chiefs, but what does he have to gain? Probably because the Ishu priest will never let him become the Headman to the Oracle, even at his death. If I was the King and I wanted to get rid of a man like me, how would I do it? I probably would start my destruction from within. Vacoura. Why would he want to destroy me now? Greed or insecurity? This still does not account for the Ifa priest. Why would he go all this way for Obi? To become the Headman to the Oracle? That's not possible. There is no King alive who would make a man so young his high chief...unless he owes you a favor. He really is Queen Aneaton's son.

The chief laughed insanely. His Omees came to check if he was okay. He told them to get his general and envoy.

As the two men entered the room, he sat down on his throne-like seat and told everyone near the parameter to go away. Both men knew a big event was about to take place and they hoped it was not a tragic one, involving them becoming deceased. Gbangba still sat, not uttering a sound.

Vacoura was about to explode with defensive rage, accompanied by fear. His mind was trying to guess what the Ifa priest told the chief. Gbangba has finally found an excuse to kill me. As our people say, when you have trapped your turkey, it has no choice but to fight back. It is a pity. Just when my son started walking, this dilemma chooses to surface. That stupid brother of mine will now marry my sweet wife. No way. If I had known this was the time for me to die, I would have kept a scar on my son's arm so he would remember his father. If only I could just hold him one last time, I will...

"Vacoura, Envoy, the King has declared war with us because he was told that we have accepted his son from the late Queen Aneaton to be our King."

Vacoura could not say anything. He was still catching his breath after the prelude to his supposed death. Anything he wanted to do now was all right, as long as it didn't concern him.

"Everyone knows her son is dead," the envoy said.

"That's where we were wrong. He lives."

"Who is he, and why are we helping him?" Vacoura asked.

"He is Obi, supposed son of the Ikaza, Ifeanyi."

"I guess that answers why we are helping him," Vacoura said. "With all due respect, as envoy of this province, we are not going to be able to match the whole Didasu Kingdom. I understand your ties with him, but I don't think his life is worth making a multitude of women widows, children fatherless, and freemen slaves."

Gbangba rose in fury. "Are you telling me that you and my people are not ready to die for your King?"

"We are not sure if he really is the son and as of now, he is still a prince," the envoy replied.

"He is the King I now serve and I would like to know if we serve the same King,"

"Who am I to go against my chief?" Vacoura immediately replied.

The chief watched his envoy, waiting for his reply.

"Since I became your envoy, I have never had thoughts of being disloyal. Even now, the thought does not cross my mind. Your king is my king but my duty is to tell you the pure truth."

"Good. Now the kingdom is not aware of this, making it easier for the King to get access to Obi and kill him privately, so we have to let the kingdom know of the new King without the provinces acknowledging where the information came from. Envoy, you will get your most trusted messengers and send them to all the provinces to spread the news to anyone who walks, talks and crawls. Firstly, the people of Utagba should know everything in detail and as quickly as possible. Give the messengers my fastest horses. Vacoura, from today we will be checking the entry of people into the province. You prepare and station the Omees for anything. All the elders who are corruptible should be persuaded to fight for our cause amongst the other elders. Whatever price they ask, give it to them. This job I expect you to do personally, Envoy. All the market women and any gossiper should be given the story in whispers to speed its travel. As for the war against the kingdom, we have no intentions of going to battle now and, as of this time, our loyalty is still with the kingdom, the persuasion of other allies from the other provinces I will take care of personally. You may leave us, Envoy."

The envoy bowed. As he was about to leave, the chief said, "Thank you." He pretended not to hear, but those were the things that made him loyal to Gbangba.

"What else do you require me to do?" the general asked with enthusiasm.

"Stop deceiving yourself. I do not trust you, Vacoura, and I am positive at the first opportunity you have, you will stab me in the back."

"Never."

"Face it, Vacoura, you can't be chief as long as I am alive. I know how much you crave this seat. By the time I leave, nobody will let you succeed me."

"Chief, why would you punish me with such ill thoughts?"

"If we succeed in this battle, then I shall take over as the Head-of-Government of the kingdom and Alloida will be yours."

A grin finally came to the general's face and he said, "You are too kind."

"There is this tiny problem that is still bothering me," the chief continued with a deadly look on his face. "The province can still belong to you if you betray me to King Nwosa, so I decided to keep your son as my personal guest till King Obi is crowned ."

"You can't do that. He is my only son," the general begged.

"Don't worry, everything is going to be all right. You of all people have no intentions of betraying me."

"I beg of you. I swear total allegiance with any god you mention. Please take any other member of my family, but not my boy."

"Look at it like I am showing him around his new home that his father will soon inhabit. Enough." The Chief clapped his hands and his Omees appeared. "Escort him to his home so he can hand his son over to you."

With hatred in his eyes Vacoura said, "This is all about power to you."

"No Vacoura, it is all about my friend." Gbangba turned his back to them while they left. Yes, Vacoura, it's all about my friend, my only friend.

Chapter 6

Obi and his wife had passed through the river. Though they saw no one behind them, they maintained their pace. The areas after the river were muddy; they stopped to eat on a few dry patches. As they traveled, Amina stopped once to vomit. He was positive she was pregnant, but being the proud woman she was, she refused to let him carry her. It was not until she sprained her knee that he forcefully put her on his back and continued the journey.

The farther he went, the more he felt guilty for dragging his greatest asset into such a quest. He wondered why he left everything he had and started this journey with this priceless human being. His thoughts raced, looking for a reason why the Ifa priest would lie to him, but there was none. As he kept moving, there were only two things he was sure of: the first was that the direction he was traveling in led to his mother's province; and secondly, he was not interested in being King, prince or anything that was offered. He just wanted to go back to his way of life.

Dawn approached and he wondered if the people of Utagba would accept him during this crisis. He had nowhere else to go. There was also the possibility that they were not aware of what was happening. The thoughts were getting too heavy for his mind to carry, but he was consoled by their nearness to the boundary between Utagba and Abogima. He found a shelter underneath a pile of boulders and they spent the night there.

As he slept he heard his wife scream his name, "Obiana." He opened his eyes to see his wife dash out of their shelter. He quickly got up and followed her to see what was wrong. He saw the hyena running with their food bag. The scene was funny to him, but his wife had a different view of the scenario so he started chasing the animal. The hyena swerved around the trees as it ran. Just when Obi was about to grip the animal, his legs seemed to become glued to the muddy waters. The more he tried to struggle, the faster he sank. Amina had trailed her husband and looked horrified when she saw that his predicament scared him. She walked in circles like a mad woman, seriously confused.

"Amina, relax," Obi said, and it seemed to make her a little more composed. "Look for a thick and long branch and stretch it to me."

She scanned the area and found a branch. She stretched it to her husband, but it was not long enough. She removed her wrapper and threw it to him, but it, too, was not long enough.

"Cover yourself," Obi said, sinking slowly.

"There should be something we can do. Please help me think!" Amina cried.

"There is something I always wanted to tell you, but I was too proud."

"I don't want to hear anything you want to tell me of that sort now. You can tell me tonight, tomorrow, or even the day after that, but I don't want to hear anything of that sort now."

Her voice was now firm, but when she looked at her husband covered up in mud to his chest she started screaming and crying to the wilderness.

"Please, somebody help me! Is there anybody out there? Please help me!"

When she realized it was to no avail, she started entering the quicksand to join her husband.

"What are you doing?" he shouted, only his head sticking out of the loose wet sand.

She ignored him and continued moving toward him.

"Listen to me for once in your life. I beg you with my soul, please do not join me in this my tragedy."

She ignored him and was still approaching him when a man with pale white skin ran over to where they were and stretched a branch to Obi, pulling the husband and his wife out.

After they settled on dry land, Obi shook Amina violently by the shoulder screaming, "Do not ever do that again! Why do you think I was happy to live? It was because of you. You are my life and if you live, then my life was worth something."

"Without you I also have no life worth living," she replied with no remorse.

He was about to slap her when the white man cut in. "Please, such violence is unnecessary." The man spoke their language fluently.

Then Obi finally acknowledged the presence of the third party. "Kind sir, how can I repay you for your kindness?"

"Please forget about it. My reward comes from my God," the man replied.

"Which god might that be?" Obi inquired.

"The one God up in heaven."

"I take it that you are a missionary," Obi inferred.

"Yes I am, but we will talk on that topic later. There is a stream in front of us; you and your wife can wash up there. I live just across it and I insist you be our guests tonight."

"No sir, your kindness is more than enough. We do not want to encroach into your home."

"Nonsense. Let us go."

The missionary led them to the stream and then into his home. They lived in a small hut with an attached house made up of rafia branches. The attached house was built for a congregation, and opposite the entrance was two sticks crossed together. As Obi and Amina studied these structures, the white man and a woman of his complexion, apparently his wife, approached them.

"It's church," the wife said with a very unclear dialect.

Both man and wife gave a bow to show respect for their guests. They led them into their home and offered them something to eat, but Obi and Amina politely refused. It was very dangerous eating in a man's home when you did not know his background. The white woman insisted on pressuring them, but their refusal was adamant.

The woman seemed to be hurt that they rejected her meal.

"You'll have to forgive my wife," the husband said. "We are not used to people coming to our homes to visit, except on the seventh day when some people sneak here from the province."

"Come to think of it, I don't think we have eaten today, or have we Obi?" Amina said.

He smiled. "We have not."

They offered them rice and stew, which they ate and were grateful. When the meal was finished, the women took the dishes away and left the men alone.

"There must be a way I can repay you for your kindness."

"As I said, my reward will be given to me by God in heaven."

"You must have deep respect for your God."

"Do you say that because I saved your life and require nothing for it?"

"And also welcoming us into your home."

"What is your name?"

"Obi, and yours?"

"Michael."

"Mekell."

The missionary laughed at the pronunciation of a name he felt was easy to pronounce. "No, Michael," he tried to correct Obi.

"What does it mean?"

"I am not sure. All I know is that I was named after an angel of God. What does your name mean?"

"Obi means heart. My mother called me Obiani, which means the heart of the land."

"Your mother, where is she?"

"She died along with my father."

"I am sorry."

"Don't be sorry for me. She lived a good life and died well." Obi tried to cover his emotions, but it was obvious the memory touched him.

"I hardly have guests in my home. What kind of host would I be if I prevent my only guest from opening his mind?"

When Obi was about to ask his question, the women came in and he stopped, which Michael noticed.

"You can ask me anything, we are all family."

"What are you and your wife doing in this secluded area and why leave your home to come to this world where the people are different from you?"

"In my country since I was born, I have always dedicated my life to my God. That is why I became a missionary," Michael quickly replied. "When I first came over here with the merchants, I was forced to by the cardinal and I found this place greatly to my disdain. I stayed here for a year and quickly went home the first chance I could, but when I returned, I realized there was no room for me in that world. The only good I did was getting engaged to Mary, but she did not want to come to Africa with me, so I left her. After three years I went back to report to the church in my world to ask why they stopped sending amenities. They told me that they had cancelled the project in these parts and reassigned me back home, but over there was no longer my home. This was my home. So I decided to come back. Due to a force greater than I was, I went to see Mary, expecting her to already be married, but she was engaged."

He held tight to Mary's hands and, though he was in tears, he continued.

"She was still engaged to me after all those years. This time she did not hesitate when I asked her to follow me. We got married and came over here. We were spreading the word about our God in small villages, but we heard they started to kill people who joined our religion. We decided to come here, near the boundary between Ozuoba and Utagba, so the people who come here are not really noticed because of its seclusion from the populated areas."

When he finished, nobody had anything to say. The hosts noticed how tired their guests were and led them to where they would spend the night.

As Obi slept, he dreamed of coconut trees all around him. Then one of the fruits landed on his forehead and cracked a little. He picked up the fruit and opened it. The Ifa priest's face came out of the coconut and he screamed, "Leave now."

Obi woke up immediately and told his wife to hurry up so they could leave. She got up and started getting ready quickly. He knew he was not worthy to have this woman as his bride and wondered why throughout the journey she never asked him the reason they were running or where they were going. When she was getting prepared, he took out his knife and took out his back tooth. As Michael slept, Obi walked to where he was. If he had his way, he would not have woken him, but it was against their society's etiquette to leave your host's house without thanking him. Such things led to the birth of enemies. In a soft voice he called to him, so his wife would not wake, "Michael, Michael."

"Yes?"

"I am sorry to wake you, but I have to go now. People are after me."

"Stay here, we can hide you."

"No. Our people say, 'The day a snail leaves its shell to find another one, it can never go back to the former.' When these men come here, deny me, or else they will hurt you."

"Don't worry about us. There is something about the white men here that always make them not touch us."

"Please take this." He placed his gift in the missionary's hand.

Michael opened his hands and saw Obi's tooth and he was puzzled.

"It means I owe you and when I repay your goodness I will ask for it back."

Michael was still puzzled by the gesture, he wanted to say something but both man and wife were on their way.

*

They were walking very fast and when Amina's foot started to hurt, he carried her on his back. They had been traveling from the night into the day. When darkness was finding its way again, he saw the boundary to Utagba about a thousand paces across a river from him, but then they heard the horses' hoofs. He could see Utagba, but he knew they could not make it there before the horsemen caught up with them. He found a space within a group of hard rocks, so he squeezed his wife through it. There was no room for two, so he climbed up a tree away from where his wife was.

There were nine men, eight were armed fully on horseback. They rode up to the area with fires on sticks for better illumination, then one of them shouted, "Halt." He was not dressed like an Omee and he was not armed. As they stopped, he picked the sand and rubbed it. Obi now knew he was a pathfinder and hoped he was a bad one. The man kept his ear to the ground and slowly started walking toward Amina's hiding place. Obi tried to hold him back with his eyes, but the man kept getting closer and closer to where she was. He was still touching the ground and seemed to be tracing where Amina was through something on the ground. Then he reached the rock where she was hiding. All he had to do was walk around the rock and his victim would be found.

Obi jumped down with a loud landing. Immediately all the attention was on him; he started running in the rain. Six of the Omees chased him, the other two stayed behind in case of any surprises. Obi was always as fast as a man could ever be, but horses were faster. During the chase, the general who followed the Omees stopped his horse and fired an arrow. The flight of the arrow echoed in his ears as he got to the mouth leading to the river, so he dodged, using his hand to block the destination of the arrow into his heart and he dived into the river. The Omees got to the mouth of the river and started firing arrows at him underwater until he disappeared. The Omees tied their horses to trees and swam across to the other side of the river.

As Obi got to the other side of the river, he saw Utagba in front of him, but he deviated into a house. He had no intention of entering Utagba while his wife was curled up between rocks. Before he approached the house, he pulled the arrow from his hand; the blood gushed from it profusely. He tore a piece of cloth from what he was wearing and tied a bandage around it to prevent himself from losing excess blood. He looked behind him to see a trail of blood, but he hoped for the rain to wash his trail away. He searched the house for a weapon, but there was nothing he could use to defend himself. He had dropped all his weapons during the chase; the only thing left on him was his knife.

Before he knew what was going on, they had reached the house. He climbed to the roof, clamping roof stripes with his hands and feet, with his knife in his mouth, trying hard to hold firm with the pain from the pressure between his grip and his injury. Below, he saw a child looking up at him. He did not know whether to beg or threaten the boy to be quiet.

A man, probably the owner of the house, came out and answered the Omees. The boy looked away from Obi's direction as though he wasn't there. He watched them search the house and even question the boy. Strangely, the boy seemed to be protecting Obi. When the Omee was talking, blood soaked in the wet cloth around his hand fell on the floor. He tried to cover up his wound properly with the other hand. It was getting pointless staying where he was because he was going to be caught.

By the time he noticed what was going on below him, the small boy had the Omee's knife with blood on it and was laughing. It seemed he had been doing some cutting. Next thing he saw, the Omees evacuated the house because of the incident, assuming the spirits of an angry god possessed the boy.

Obi waited till the parameter was clear. He overheard the general saying that he had not yet entered Utagba, so they should spread out and keep searching. When Obi came down, he went to his hero. He heard the house owner call him Otuturex. He met the young boy lying on his mat, he said nothing but in their silence, they made a pact and Obi entered back into the rain.

As he left the house, he knew that he would never forget the favor the child did for him. He would have pulled his tooth and given it to him, but you never give someone younger your tooth. He surveyed the area around his location and saw that the Omees were well spaced out. He did not bother looking toward Utagba because he was going back to get Amina. The area back to the river was neglected except for one Omee. He watched the Omee surveying the area carefully. Obi crept near him and pulled back a branch of a tree. He held the branch firmly, waiting till the Omee got into target. As the Omee walked into the target spot Obi released the branch and with a great force it hit the warrior's neck. The Omee was motionless on the ground.

All that drilling and training can finally be used for something after all, Obi thought. He did not have time to waste. As he quietly crossed the river, he hoped the Omee was not dead. He had never killed a man before.

The two Omees and the pathfinder had been waiting by the river and they were getting impatient. They all shared the premonition that their comrades might be in trouble of some sort, probably a wild animal attacked them or their target had entered Utagba. None of the Omees knew why they were chasing this man, but their orders were clear. They did not want to see the man alive. If they were ordinary men in the kingdom, they would have asked why, but they were Omees. They never ask why, they just follow the orders their superior give them.

Amina still remained curled up between the rocks. Her body seemed to crumple, but she stayed where she was because the dread still lived. She heard them chasing Obi, but from the conversation between the Omees closer to her, she knew he had escaped. She hoped he got to Utagba. She knew that was where he was going from the Omees' conversations. She never wondered why. Such information did not seem necessary to her because her husband was such a positive force in her life. Even being squeezed between rocks with danger around her, she knew she was happy and these past months were the best days of her life.

While trying to get comfortable she heard a hiss. She looked behind her and saw a rattlesnake. She slowly started crawling out of the rock, but the snake was not ready to let her leave its home without a bite. The snake struck, aiming for her neck. She grabbed the snake's head before it got to her and threw it away.

She breathed a sigh of relief as she landed on the floor, but when she looked up her eyes met the three men. She got up and started running and they chased her, laughing. She could not run fast enough; her legs hurt from the endless roaming. One of the Omees caught her from behind. She tried to struggle, but the man was very strong. He used one of his hands to grab her bosom and the other to pull off her wrapper. The other two men were laughing. She dug into her wrapper, took out her knife, and stabbed him in his genitals, then she used her elbow to hit him. She ran toward the river.

The other Omee looked down to see his comrade dying, and took out his bow and arrow.

As she ran, she saw Obi running toward her and she knew she was safe. When Obi grabbed her, he felt a sting in his heart. He looked at his wife to see an arrow that passed through her chest.

"For you I die. I am proud," were her only words and she died.

"You live forever, I swear it!" Obi roared. He dropped his wife gently on the ground and when he rose his eyes were bloody red. He did not have the look of a man anymore.

The Omee tried to get another arrow, but the scene frightened him and his hands shook. Even when he got the arrow, he could not fit it properly. By the time it was well-fitted, Obi had already walked to him.

With an intense force, Amina's husband dug his hand into the bowels of the soldier and brought out his intestines. The pathfinder on seeing this took the Omee's knife and stabbed himself to death. Then Obi made a bonfire; it was an Omee code to show that the mission was accomplished.

The Omees on the other side of the river saw this and came back, but when they returned to the area, they did not see anyone. The general told them to spread out and look for the other Omees. They were careful because they had found one of their comrades dead on the other side.

As the Omees spread out, one of them saw his comrade sleeping and went to wake him up. As he shook him, he realized his comrade had nothing in his stomach, but it was too late. Death was behind him. Another Omee was roaming the bushes and saw a trail of blood, so he followed it cautiously. When he got to where the injured man was, his throat was sliced.

"There is something wrong. I am not hearing from the others," an Omee said.

If only he had looked closer he would have known that death dressed like an Omee.

The general was searching with another Omee. As they surveyed, they began to see dead bodies. The general went to investigate the scene properly, then he heard someone drop. He looked back to find out he was the only Omee alive. He put his sword into its compartment and reached for his bow and arrow. As his right hand reached for an arrow, he felt an arrow pass through his hand. He tried to pull his sword with his left and another arrow passed through his left hand.

Obi walked toward him while talking.

"Our people say, 'A lion that is not hungry will never disturb you, but if you decide to disturb it, it will disturb you.' Tell your King that there can be only one King in a kingdom."

Obi took out his sword and cut off the general's right hand at the wrist. The man screamed in pain.

"Give this to your King." Obi threw the man's hand to him. "Tell him it is my time."

Obi left the General still screaming in agony. He carried his dead wife with him.

When he entered Utagba Province, it was apparent that they were expecting him and they had heard the news. As he passed everybody, they all lay flat, giving the respect due to a king. He did not seem to notice anyone, including the Okpala, who was the highest authority there because they did not have a chief. Then he went to an open area and dug a grave all by himself. Nobody attempted to help him because they were not sure of his reaction. After burying her, he made an announcement to all the spectators who followed him.

"The cursed land of Ozuoba where my wife died I will make Utagba. On this spot where my wife is buried I will build my palace, and this province I stand in will be the capital of the whole kingdom, which would be called Utagba."

Every man, woman and child who was present started to hail their King. As he looked around him to see the people of every status in Utagba greeting him with great enthusiasm, his mind started to work. The day I was born, I forgot. The day my Aneaton died, I forgot. The day my Ifeanyi and Nneka died, I will forget. But this day that I stand on the grave of my wife—this day I will never forget.

Chapter 7

Okon had nine children, all girls. He was positive that the gods did not want to fill the earth with men of his flesh and bones. His three married daughters had sons, but they belonged to their father and his people. He needed an heir before he became chief. He was a very wealthy trader like all the members of his lineage. His father was not even an Omee, but was one of the wealthiest traders in the whole kingdom. He had only five sons and they were as good as their father in the trade. They sold to a province what it did not have and bought from it what it had in excess.

With time the trade extended beyond the different provinces to kingdoms near and far. Of the five sons, Okon was the youngest, extremely aware of every channel in their occupation. With the wealth they possessed, the Omees who respected them were the ones under their payroll. Although they were mainly traders, they indulged in different forms of business, making each son a specialist in different fields. The daughters in the family had no access to any of the transactions, but they were given anything they desired and most men that came for their hands paid a small dowry.

On a day bright enough for a bat to see, Chief Inyang of Ndemili came to the father's home, and the father ran out to welcome the lord of his province. The chief ignored the trader and walked into the man's home as though it was his own. Then the chief, who was younger than Okon's father, sat down without being asked. As a mark of respect, Okon's father sent for his youngest bride to serve the chief wine with all his sons present. It was very rare for even a general to come to the home of a commoner unless he came to bring harm or he had you in a good place in his heart. From the way the chief's eyes met with the eyes of the father's most cherished wife, Okon was positive they had met in another way. He was a trader and he knew when a buyer already had the goods and wanted more. The chief did not hide his lust for the trader's wife, and with time the girl grew bolder in the presence of the chief. It seemed only Okon was aware of what was happening. The chief requested in an authoritative fashion to be alone with the father. As all the men walked away, the brothers acted oblivious to what was going on.

When the two men had finished talking privately, they both came out laughing. Obviously, the demands the chief made were accepted. Okon was young, but he was not stupid and neither was his father. As his father escorted the chief out, he accepted that it was one of the things that came with his trade. Apart from his father taking all forms of insult from the chief, the man also acquired the father's prized possession—his wife.

He initially felt his father was a coward if he was aware of the atrocity, but he thought again. He analyzed the situation. The chief offered protection from criminals and greedy chiefs, both in their province and other provinces. The only time King Burobee was involved in the trade was when the trade was between kingdoms. He thought of his father killing his bride because in the custom of the land, if a woman wronged her husband in any way, he had the power to do as he wished with her, but the woman's family should be aware of the reason why she was being punished. Although that might eventually bring the story out into the open, such a move would have made his father lose ties with the chief. That was the day he made up his mind to become an Omee.

He never told anyone the reason why he made such a decision. Everyone from his family except his father felt it was a stupid idea because they owned and lived well in their world and Omees lived their life according to a chief, high chief, or king's world. They insisted that he was too old. They emphasized how he would have to start his training with children and how it would be difficult for him to start now because he has never been trained in that area. He listened to all their words, but he had already made up his mind. He joined in the training with ease through some strings he pulled. He learnt slowly, but he acquired everything.

It took him twelve years before he became an Omee. The way he was drafted to Ndemili and how he became a general could only be explained by a something his father used to say: At the right price the goods will not find their way past you.

Okon spent only four years as an Omee before he became the general. Inyang was at this time still the chief of the province and was strongly against Okon becoming general because he knew his father would die trying to make his son chief. None ever complained about Inyang being chief because he spread wealth to the province and the kingdom from a source and now the source's son was the general. He tried everything in his power to prevent Okon from claiming the position, but the elders fought strongly for him. The former general retired with a wide smile on his face claiming that a man like him was not worthy of a position that required hot blood. Inyang killed him personally, under the shadow of privacy, on the tenth day after he retired. When he killed the man he looked at the traitor, disgusted with what the world was coming to. As he left the dead man escorted by his most trusted Omees, he wondered why men didn't have pride anymore, what happened to honor. He was positive it was a cheap bribe.

Okon's time as general was always filled with different kind of traps that Inyang set around him, without letting any lead to him. Despite all these things, the general was up to the task. Physical attacks made on him by men who claimed to be criminals were fruitless because he was well guarded. Attacks that came in feminine form could not find their way to him; he had only two wives and he did not seem interested in any other women. Iyang kept sending him on death missions, but the general kept coming back victorious and his people were growing to love him deeply.

The general was asked to come to his father's house for a family meeting. It was obvious to him what they wanted to talk about, his second eldest brother. His brother had four wives. On the sixth day after his third wife's sister's son, Prince Nwosa, was publicity announced by the King to be his successor, his brother drove all his other wives away from his house, claiming they were witches. Then he announced his wife's year-old son, Okonjo, would become the sole heir to everything he owned.

If a man drove his wife away from their matrimonial home, she went to the oldest relative to report. In this case, the oldest relative was Okon's father. As he entered his father's home, the general apologized by lying flat on the ground because he was late and he did not want them thinking his position was going to his head. His father told him to get up; it annoyed him that a general would bring himself so low for a commoner like himself, especially for everyone to see.

His father's second son came very late and did not seem apologetic about it. He did not seem to worry that he was the reason why his whole family were there. Their father made a speech about husband and wives, asking and then begging him to take the women back into his home as they had done him no wrong.

Still the man was adamant. The old man's tone of voice changed and he gave his son an ultimatum of either respecting him as a father or walking away another man's child. The man got up and left.

About a year later, Okon's father died and he felt for the first time that feeling only a person in pain could understand. When Inyang heard the news, he did not know whether it was good or bad because now he did not have to worry about his general's influence. But now he had to worry about the general's powers because the boy was going to inherit a fortune.

Inyang called for the Omees he could trust who were not moved by greed. As the four men approached him, he told everyone in the room to leave them alone and shut the door. In less than five minutes they heard a man scream. When the Omees and servants rushed back into the room, they saw Inyang on the floor dead with a knife in his chest. Everyone in the room looked at the chief's most trusted Omees, who said in the most carefree manner that the man was tired of life and wanted to die.

Nobody argued with them because they knew the man to investigate the death would be the general and no third eye was necessary to know he was behind it. What disgusted the spectators was the amateur way they committed the crime and their uncalculated lies. Everyone thought it was Okon who assassinated Inyang, while in reality, these men were under instructions from the Head-of-Government. Even the

King knew a good investment when he saw one. With Okon as chief, the wealth of both his mind in trade and his inheritance went to the kingdom.

*

Okon was a chief accepted by every man in the province. He made Ndemili the richest province and paid the largest taxes to the King. As a great provider, the King loved him. Okon loved his third daughter most. He needed a son to carry his name and all the time he saw this daughter of his, he forgot the need for a male heir. She was always with him anytime she felt he needed her. Some of her younger sisters were already married, increasing the burden on her to get married. She was not single because she was ugly. Amongst all her sisters, she was the prettiest. Even ugly girls who were daughters of rich or powerful men easily got married. She was alone because she had a strong love for her father and she did not want him to ever feel lonely. At times the father went out of his way to bring suitors for her, but she refused them all. Whenever her father saw a father and his son, a pain scratched his heart and she could feel it.

One sunny day she told her father that she wanted to go on a journey. He asked where. She said she did not know. Her father ordered her not to go, but she still left. The father was angry when she left. He became scared for her and missed her. He paid different men to find her, but their search was to no avail.

She came back home after eight months. Everyone was speechless upon seeing her new figure. When Okon came out to where she was and saw her with a stomach swollen, she bowed and greeted her father. He wanted to hold her close to him and thank the gods for bringing her back to him alive, but he was chief and he had to set an example.

"Do you think you can just walk away from my house and come back here because you are pregnant?"

The girl did not say a word but her head was down.

"Answer me."

Her head was still down.

"Okay, where is the father of the child?" The Chief's voice broke; even in his words, the love he had for his daughter was evident. "Did anyone force you or cause you harm in any way?"

The girl shifted her head sideways.

"Then why did you leave and why are you back here pregnant with no husband?"

The girl remained motionless.

The chief now spoke in anger. "Do you realize what you have done? You have brought shame into our home."

The girl finally raised her head, looked her father in the eye and left the house.

Okon did not think before he made his next move, because if had, he would have realized that bringing his daughter back into the home openly showed that he welcomed the shame she brought.

The elders pressured him for the sake of respect of their people in the provinces that he should send the girl away, but he refused. They then offered to provide a husband who would claim her and the child to be his. He refused, because she did not answer him when he made the request. From the day she entered the home not a word had come out of her mouth, not even to her mother. On the day before she went into labor she kept a staff on one end of the room and a knife on the other. The general conclusion from the people in the province was that she had gone mad. The day she was in labor, she locked the door and did not let anyone in. Everyone knew she was in labor and kept banging on the door, but she did not reply.

Okon had to tell the Omees to force their way into the room before she did anything disastrous to herself. He felt guilty and swore to himself that if his daughter had harmed herself due to his constant pressure on her, he would kill himself. The Omees pushed the door open and found her on the floor covered with blood, with a crying baby. She gave birth to a boy and she finally smiled. Everyone started throwing white chalk and was happy, but her father still kept a straight face. When he spoke the noise ceased.

"Now that you can smile I want to know who the father of this child is."

The girl rose and picked up her child with blood all over it and with a smile she spoke.

"You are his father and his name is Oludu."

Everyone in the room seemed lost with incest on their minds. That was punishable by death of the parent.

"I don't understand what you mean," Okon said truthfully.

"I am an Omogor." As she spoke those words, everyone in the room gasped.

An Omogor was the single daughter of a man who had no son. She traveled to places far away where her identity was unknown. Every place she stepped into she slept with as many men as possible, not ever letting her emotions get in the way by sleeping twice with the same man. She would continue with this way of life until she was positive she was pregnant and there was no father to claim the child. Most girls who did such acts for their father never let anyone know what they did. If it was a boy, they placed a staff on the boy, telling the whole world what they did, so the child rightfully becomes their father's heir. But if it were a girl, they committed suicide. A daughter had to love her father extremely to engage in such. Up to this time, nobody believed daughters still made such sacrifices.

Chapter 8

Gbangba awaited the man who trained him personally to become an Omee. Throughout that time he had nothing but hatred and fear of him. The deadliest thing about the man was not his viciousness to his enemies, neither was it his acquired skill; it was the way he reasoned. His messengers told him that this high chief came to his province with only two Omees. If it were anyone else, this would have been the flirting of a deer with a lioness. But when Arubi made such a move, you had to stop and think.

Although Gbangba seemed to decode the power behind this daredevil move, the fact that he was an easy target tempted him. If there were an attempt on his life, the whole kingdom would be against him for making a move forbidden by the Omee code, thereby having a reason for all the other provinces to become stronger together. Then again, Arubi would expect him to think that way. That was probably why he came alone, because he was the key man to the King. Gbangba got up to welcome the fat yet agile Head-of-Government. After exchanging greetings both men sat down. They brought kola nut; he blessed it and chewed. They brought pounded yam; he laughed and ate. When he had finished, he praised the chief's wife for the excellent cuisine.

"There is nothing like peace within."

"Yes, my Head-of-Government."

"Please, Gbangba, I came to your Haku. I ate your kola. I drank your wine and I ate your food. Please call me Arubi when we are together."

"It's a title you deserve for every drop of blood you have ever spilled and every thought that has made our kingdom a better place. I am honored to call you my Head-of-Government."

"If you were a woman, I would have married you immediately for those words that come from the heart—yes, from the heart. Those are real and touchable, not the hypocrisy and lies that fill this generations."

Gbangba nodded in agreement without saying a word, but his gaze remained fixed at the Head-of-Government.

"There is a matter that pinches my soul. Come closer."

Gbangba left the seat he was sitting on from a higher level to a lower one. In a louder form of whisper, the Head-of-Government continued.

"Some people are planning to rebel against the King and destroy the harmony we have."

"Really?" Gbangba said, acting shocked.

"It even gets worse. Someone has come out claiming to be the son of the King." The Head-of-Government laughed and Gbangba joined him mechanically. "When the fool's wife died, instead of using his brain and disappearing, he sends an Omee's hand to the King. Our spies tell us he was crying like a baby when his wife died and I seriously feel they should check if he has a penis. They say he is a friend of yours."

"Yes, he is."

"Funny, isn't it? I don't think I mentioned who the person was, so how do you know he is your friend?"

Gbangba got up and turned his back to the Head-of-Government.

"You taught me that there were three ways to attack your enemies, either from behind his back, from within, or from the front as his enemy. I am tired of playing the fool. Everyone knows about him, so why don't you tell me what you came here for, Head-of-Government?"

"What I came here for is open as the skies above, as plain as the grounds we step on. Are you for us or against us?"

"What do I have to gain by being for you and what do I have to gain by being against you?"

"Life gives this complex illusion while it really revolves around simple theories. If you are for us, I promise you that you will succeed me and if you are against me, you will lose the battle. So which way are your leaves going to fall?"

"My honor dies with my King."

"I should be heading back to the capital."

"I am grateful for your presence in my home."

"Nonsense, Gbangba. I am grateful that you accepted me into your home. By the way, the King wants all the chiefs together, to know the people for him and those against him."

"When are we to meet with him?"

"Actually, he would like to see everyone immediately. He wanted to send the messenger, but I also had to know where you stood."

"Really, this is what they call bad timing. Can you imagine of all the times my sister's husband just died and I have to bring her to my Haku before she grows mad. When I do that, then I will dash down to meet the King."

"You will dash down. Your King requires your presence and you are telling me about your sister."

"I will make it as soon as I can."

"I am sorry, Gbangba, but that is not good enough. You are coming back with me."

"No, Arubi, I am the one who is sorry. I am not going back with you."

"Yes, the animal has come out of his cage. Only a fool will try and crack a coconut with his teeth."

"Before a bird can learn how to fly it has to jump," Gbangba retorted.

"But it is smart enough to jump from a height that it can still walk when it falls."

"Only a fool measures a height he cannot see."

"I take my leave, Gbangba, or should I call you Head-of-Government? You would be a smart man to kill me before I leave your province."

"And lose all my allies."

"Allies?"

"I think I spoke too much."

"You were always my favorite protégé, but your time has come. Your death awaits you."

Arubi left the Haku and the province with his two Omees without looking back.

When Arubi reached the outskirts of the province, he met his new general with two hands. He was ready for his first battle as general with their battalions behind him.

"Do we still strike tonight?" the man asked his master.

"No, not tonight; he is ready for us and he has allies. Or maybe he was lying. Let's go back to the capital."

Vacoura rushed down to where Gbangba was and with great enthusiasm reported, "They are retreating, my chief."

"I take it you are happy with this information you have given me?"

"Definitely."

"Did it not occur to you that they are going to come back and this time prepared? If they had attacked us, we would have had all the other provinces on our side if we had won or even lost. Please, leave. I want to be alone."

So all the provinces don't belong to the King. Arubi believed I had an ally, that's why he left. Beautiful. Going to war with Arubi is like digging to the middle of the earth, but it can be done. If I die at the hands of such a great warrior, I will be honored. My name will be respected. I have to make contact with Obi. The poor child lost his only wife.

Then Gbangba smiled—Obi gave the King a hand.

Chapter 9

Obi dwelt in the Haku of Utagba's former chief, still waiting to build his palace on his wife's grave. The general's daughter Ifrareta, whose left hand was handicapped, always attended him.

Three men came to visit Obi: the Okpala of the Province Utagba, the general named Ebikela and the envoy named Sagbe. The last time Obi came to the province he was bowing low to these men; now they were bowing to him. He looked at these men and realized a common goal amongst them.

Obi always had great respect for the people in the province. When their last chief died, he was to be replaced by Vokei, but King Nwosa sent down his general from the capital to become their chief because they were getting too powerful and they needed to be checked. The people of the province refused the chief and defied the King. The King sent his envoy to tell the elders that they had fourteen days to take back their decision and pay the fine for disobedience. The elders of the province sent their reply immediately, which made the King's rage increase. Arubi advised the King against an immediate attack because the people had more skilled Omees.

The province was initially made of a village near the sea. By an act from the gods, the sea started to run away from the land, widely expanding the area. Most retired head-of-governments, chiefs, generals and Omees settled in this secluded village so they would no longer be in the same environment with their successors, who now had power over them. They all came with their families and the land expanded with the people in them. This was about eighty years earlier, when they were under the Ozuoba Province. When they realized that they were too big to be under Ozuoba, they went to the King asking for a separation from Ozuoba. He agreed on grounds that the people of Ozuoba accepted their decision, though he foxily gave them the power to do what they had to do without his permission.

The people of Ozuoba initially disagreed and wanted to disgrace them in battle. When the men of Ozuoba saw the multitude and the fitness of their adversaries, they decided to let the people have their own province for the sake of the kingdom. The hate between these two provinces grew as the years passed.

King Nwosa did not attack the people in Utagba because they paid their taxes. However, they were still unable to make Vokei their chief because the ceremony had to be held in the palace and by the Headman to the Oracle.

Obi respected these men around him and understood their logic. He wondered what would have happened if he had not been taught about the strategies of war by Ifeanyi. He would have barked amongst the roar of lions.

"The news of your birth by Aneaton has spread to those near and far. I think it's time we make a decision," the Okpala said with a stern look on his face.

"What do you have in mind?" Obi asked, thinking how funny life was—the Okpala now answering to him.

"We should send a message to your father the King that you are rightfully his heir and that you intend on staying here until his death. We all know they will try to lure you to the capital or even make attempts on your life while you are still here, but our honor is to the death. I doubt if the King will want to attack here. If he wanted to, he would have done it a long time ago."

"There is a saying: 'A drunkard is a humble man to you as long as you continue giving him palm wine from your calabash, but when you decide to stop he will redefine the word humble to you.' I know you openly rejected him as your King, but you have always paid your taxes and still do not have a chief."

Obi then faced the general, asking him, "What do you have in mind?"

"I think you should surrender to the King because we are only strong enough to conquer at most two provinces, but not the whole kingdom. If you publicly surrender, you might be given amnesty and the whole kingdom would publicly acknowledge you as the first son of the King."

Obi looked at the general and nodded. He thought, No wonder you are still a general. He faced the envoy and asked, "What do you think?"

"The cat that comes out and looks the dog in the eye does not run away for fear. If you make any attempt to surrender, your body will decorate the grounds of the earth. It has passed the stage of forgiveness, the god of war screams for blood. Attack is inevitable because we have nothing to defend."

Obi was angry at the bluntness of the envoy but he knew that such a personality was necessary to wake him up to the harsh reality of everything around him. So he decided he would make him the King's envoy if they succeeded.

Just then a blind man walked into the room.

"Forgive me, Your Highness, I am late. The wind blew against my soul."

"How dare you come into our presence without announcing yourself!" the general exclaimed.

"Our presence?" Obi repeated, raising his right eyebrow.

"Your presence, Sire, forgive me."

"Who is that supposed to be?" asked the blind Ifa priest.

"Okpala, Vokei, and Sagbe, this is the Ifa priest."

"He is the old man with eyes that can see deeper than us," the Okpala replied confidently.

"Yes, I agree the Ifa priest was older and had eyes and could see, but he is dead. That is why I am here now."

Turning his head to Obi immediately, he said, "I have news for your ears only."

"Then it will wait. I have questions for these men," Obi said. "Vokei, how many battalions do we have?"

"Five, Sire, made up of eight to nine hundred."

"Sagbe, go to Ozuoba tonight with six Omees. Tell Chief Atani to surrender while he still has the chance, that we strike tomorrow night."

"I don't think it is honorable to go to war with them with only some hours notice, and such an act would make all the provinces have a reason to be against us," the Okpala said.

Obi continued as though he did not hear a word.

"Vokei, tell all the Omees to say goodbye to their loved ones for now. I want to see the women dance the war dance before we go to battle."

"We, Sire? With all due respect, you are not going anywhere," the Ifa priest said.

"Are you to tell me where I can go and not go?"

"Your Highness, Kings do not go to battle; they sit on their thrones and monitor what is going on from there," the Ifa priest replied.

"Look around you, does this place look like a palace? Have I seen all the chiefs drop their blood into a cup? Have I been crowned? No, I have not. So now if I decide to do what I choose, the law binding a King does not apply to me. I am not any man's King now," Obi retorted.

"You are my King," the Ifa priest responded with a bow.

Obi looked and wanted to do something to the blind man, but he did not know what it was. As he looked around him, all the other three men had their heads bowed. Then he started laughing and the other men joined him.

Obi directed the next question to the Okpala.

"How strong are the people of Ozuoba?"

"Compared to us they are like feathers against wings, but if they join the province next to them, then we have a real battle ahead of us. Maybe the people of Ozuoba would be ready to join us. Please don't forget they were your wife's people," the man replied.

"They were my wife's people—hear him talk. Was it not these people who gave the Omees from the palace permission to pass through and hunt us down? I will crush the place to the ground personally. Which province would they merge with?"

"Suyema."

"Sagbe, speak to me."

"The chief of this province is Otiotio, but the man to fear is his general, Shalebe. They have six battalions and two of these have never lost a battle and they are led by Shalebe."

"If Shalebe is the man behind the sword, then why is Otiotio still chief?"

The envoy looked around the room and spoke in a low tone.

"They say Shalebe is Otiotio's slave, that's why he chose him to be his general, because he can never be chief. Him being an Omee, and even a general, was due to the chief's and elder's influence. Till now, everyone in their province pretended not to know about it out of fear of the man."

"So do we review our plans and negotiate?" the general asked, pride in his voice for being right all along.

"You are right. We might have to review our plans. As of now the people of Ozuoba will not know that we expect to go to war with two provinces, so they will underestimate their predicament. We still strike tomorrow with two battalions, one led by—"

"Two battalions?" the general interrupted.

Obi continued as though he heard nothing, "—the general and the other led by me. Battle plans from Suyema will be drawn on site. The other three battalions will backup when the piper changes the song and the drums stop beating."

"Wherever you go, I go," the Ifa priest said.

"I knew you would say that," Obi answered.

"Whatever you do, make him think we are going to war with only him on our minds. Can I trust you, Sagbe?"

"This is one way to find out, Sire."

Obi looked into the man's eyes and saw they were clear.

"Go now and whatever time you get back in the night, come and give me the report." Obi used his fingers to invite the envoy closer and whispered into his ear. "Tell Odagwe, the general, that my door is always open to him."

The Envoy bowed and left. Obi faced the Okpala and general and told them to go and come back when the envoy arrived.

"Can I trust them?" Obi asked the Ifa priest.

"You did not seem to need that information when you were with them."

"That was not the question."

"He is already talking like a King. Is it amazing how the pompous nature of a position possesses anyone in power. They have not got any reason to be against you."

"So what did you want to tell me?"

"You have two provinces secretly for you and one that is openly fighting for you."

"Which ones?"

"Ndemili and Ahoda are secretly for you. Okon wants his son to succeed him and he does not want you to interfere when you are King."

"But his child can hardly walk. What about Ahoda? I can understand Okon joining because he was duped by the King over the Head-of-Government position, but I don't understand why Ihua would join us."

"Ihua was easy. I promised him he could conquer Ogbe and make it part of Ahoda."

"Are you telling me that he joined us because he wanted to go to war with Ogbe?"

"He has a deep obsession for Adesuwa, Ike's wife."

"How did you know?" Obi asked.

"I have passed from province to province in all forms and watched the ways and lives of these chiefs. I tried to be with them when the news got to them. Most of these chiefs had poor excuses for Tikpapas. I was tempted once or twice to kill them."

"You and I know the code of war: a king, chief or general who is killed by his enemy's Tikpapa during war has lost the battle," Obi angrily replied.

"That's why I used the word tempted."

"Get to the point and save your accomplishments for another day."

"Well," the Ifa priest grunted, "she used to be Ihua's concubine and then Ike came from nowhere and paid her dowry to the parents, who were more than willing to give their slave child to a normal man. Think of the humor of a chief asking her hand. So she became his wife."

"If he liked her so much, why did he not marry her?"

"She was a slave."

"You mean Ike married a slave? He must have really liked her."

"He didn't. It was all about showing Ihua that he could do anything he wants to. She is still treated like a slave."

"As much as he tries to deny it, she took a part of his heart away. He still tries to pretend that she was just sex to him. But she tortures his dreams and thoughts. Ike's and Ihua's families have been enemies for a long time. Ike feels the burn in Ihua when he sees him with Ugochi and he loves it."

"So what does this have to do with Ihua joining us?" Obi was getting impatient.

"Patience."

Obi looked at him with a wicked eye.

"Sorry, Sire. Well I realized that there was something missing in the story. Ihua asked the King to give him permission to marry Adesuwa. He refused, claiming it would be a disgrace for other kingdoms to find out that his chief was married to a slave. Later on Ike asked the King for the same thing and the King gave him his permission."

"Did the King know it was the same slave?" Obi was now engrossed in the story.

"That was the beauty of it—the King did not know it was the same girl. It was supposed to be a secret between Ike and King Nwosa. So as of now the King is not aware that Ihua's hatred extends to him."

"How did you...You know what I mean."

"I was in Ike's Haku."

"I hope they did not see you."

126

The Ifa priest answered the question in quick lilt, not to kill the flow of his story.

"No, they didn't. I was camouflaged." He continued from where he stopped. "Adesuwa's female cousins came to look for her. I did not have eyes to see her, but from the aura in the environment, I noted that the cousin was tall and she gave an Arabian impression by the way she dressed; she seemed to have covered herself fully. I was positive that she was a link to something Adesuwa was doing because she persuaded the Omees in the Haku with gifts not to say a word. I waited a while before entering the room they were in together and behold, right in front of me, I saw Ihua undress in front of me and grab another man's wife. He tore off her clothes like a wild animal that had not seen food to eat. She was licking the sweat from his neck and around his body. It was as though her clothes were like insects biting her as she threw the torn pieces away. When intercourse started she wanted to scream, but he stuffed the clothes in her mouth. The intensity of his thrust in and out of her making her act crazy. She used her nails and scratched his back. That was the time I made myself visible."

"If being a warlock allows a blind man to know when a woman is naked or dressed, I should consider being a Tikpapa. But more importantly, why could you not wait for them to finish?" Obi asked.

"Sire!" the Ifa priest exclaimed.

"Sorry, I got ahead of myself, please continue."

"So when Ihua saw me, surprisingly, he recognized me as the new Ifa priest. So I let him know I had no intention of spreading his secret, but I wanted to talk to him and I left to meet him in his Haku. So that was how I made contact with him."

"I have to admit that for a blind man you gave a graphic description of intercourse. Goodnight, my friend."

"Goodnight, Your Majesty. Won't you ask who is openly for you?"

Without looking back Obi answered, "I know who it is."

As Obi lay down, thoughts of his wife still filled his head. Each time he laughed or smiled, he was surrounded by guilt. As he fell asleep, he saw Amina walking around a field. He kept trying to catch her, but he was not fast enough. Whenever he was about to hold her, she moved faster, but still he kept chasing her until he seemed to catch her. As she was slipping through his arms, he held firmer. Then the ground opened and he fell. Soon as he landed, he woke up. This time, what he saw in front of him was no dream. He rubbed his eyes to be sure.

Standing in front of him was his wife. She was not talking, nor was she running. She was just using her hands to tell him to come. As he walked toward her, he was sure that no other human being could be as beautiful as she. Tears fell from his eyes. Wherever she was going, he would follow.

When he got to where she was, he stretched out his hands to touch her. In a flash, his wife transformed into an ugly man who grabbed Obi by the neck. Obi gasped for air as he tried to pry the man's hands from around his neck.

As the man tightened his squeeze, Obi punched his body. The man did not seem to feel anything. When Obi started kicking with his legs, he realized that they had ascended from the ground and were in the air.

All of a sudden the man dropped him and he landed heavily on the ground. On the floor, he looked up to see the old man and the Ifa priest in the air, looking each other in the eye.

"So it is you, the young Ifa priest, who wants to touch the waters that burn," the man said.

"I thought the code of war said Tikpapa's are not allowed to kill the adversaries of their liege. I wonder what kind of example the Headman to the Oracle is showing," the Ifa priest said to the Ishu priest.

"Learn your customs thoroughly, young man. The King can kill anyone he likes so long as his high chiefs agree. I will see you again, young priest. Remember that the King sets the rules," the Ishu priest said before disappearing.

When Obi was back on his feet, the Ifa priest reported that the envoy had returned.

"Why is it that it took them so long to come and get me?"

"It never occurred to them until Okonjo informed them."

Once they reached the Okpala, envoy and general, Obi asked for an update.

"Chief Atani gave me the impression he would come to battle without Suyema, but the lack of confidence in his voice proved he was lying,'' Sagbe said. "He said he, too, was going to attack tomorrow by daylight and he killed the six Omees who went with me. He said it took only one man to deliver a message."

"Is there another way to Suyema without passing through Ozuoba?"

"Yes, Sire, through the river," the envoy replied.

"As I said before, two battalions are going to battle while the others stay and protect the province. Nobody will know we have gone to battle from Suyema. The war songs will start by daybreak and the general will go to battle at the border where everyone can see him." Obi faced the Envoy again. "Do people always follow this way?"

"No, Sire, it's only the fishermen who use the route."

Obi told the general to prepare the battalions that were under him to move out immediately and silently. He also discharged the Okpala, leaving the envoy.

"What did he say?" Obi asked. The envoy looked at the Ifa priest.

"You can say anything about me in front of him," Obi assured him.

"He said nothing when I told him and he walked away from me."

"You should go and prepare. You are going with us."

The envoy nodded and left.

When Obi was prepared for battle and about to leave his Haku, the Ifa priest held him by the shoulder and said, "Your father...Ifeanyi taught you well."

Chapter 10

King Nwosa paced around his palace like a beast running from his prey. When his messenger arrived, he screamed at him. "Where are they?"

"Your Majesty, this is the middle of the night; they were asleep, but they are on the way. You are bothering yourself too much," the messenger replied.

"Okay, they have gotten to you."

"I don't understand you, Your Majesty."

"Well, I understand you. You have joined them to try to assassinate me."

"Your Majesty, I really am not getting you."

"Shut up, how dare you call me Your Majesty when you plan to stab me in the back and let me rot like manure on the earth?"

"But—"

"Don't but me. You think I could not smell your hypocrisy from the end of the capital?" The King called two of his Omees. "Take this disgusting excuse for a servant and make him die slowly."

"But Your Majesty, I have done nothing wrong!" the messenger screamed.

As he was carried away, Arubi entered the palace.

"Do you realize this is the fifth messenger you have killed this period?"

"They are traitors, all of them. I could see it in their eyes, they all want to become King," he said, using both hands to scratch his head. "This son of mine thinks he can destroy me, King Nwosa, the son of

Burobee. He is a dreamer. From now on, Arubi, I want you here at all times and—"

He stopped his tirade when he saw the envoy and the general.

"I think I should bow to you great men for making you come here faster than you should have."

"We were with you throughout the night," the envoy said.

"So you are ready for me now. They have sent you to face me eyeball to eyeball," the King said, pounding his chest.

"No, Your Majesty, what the envoy was trying to tell you was that he was with your words in his thoughts all night. Is that right envoy?" the Head-of-Government asked.

"Yes, Your Majesty, that was what I meant," the envoy said hesitantly.

The King did not sit on his throne; instead, he sat on the floor and rocked back and forth in an excited manner.

"So what is the...situation again?"

"I already told you earlier on," the envoy said.

"He wants to know again," Arubi screamed. "Even if he asks you a thousand times, you answer a thousand times."

"Okon and Gbangba have publicly denounced you and they both intend on attacking us from different directions," the envoy answered. "Ihua did not choose sides but he is going to war with Ike, whom we are

133

sure is with the kingdom. So Ihua is against us. Obi is attacking Atani today, but he is unaware that Suyema Province is backing them up. Akuna and Ezeonisha are both going to war and they both claim to be fighting for you. Till this very day none of them have set a date for battle."

As the envoy finished he looked at the King, who did not seem to hear a word he had said while rubbing his hand on the ground.

"All right, men, thank you for coming. We will meet again in the morning," Arubi said.

The two men did not bother to bow to the King as they left, highly irritated at being disturbed for nothing. When they had all gone, Arubi grabbed the King and raised him to his feet.

"What is wrong with you?"

"I have not been able to sleep or eat. I keep seeing that witch of a woman called Aneaton whenever I close my eyes," the King stammered, still rocking. "There is no point denying it—her son is coming to kill me and feed my flesh to the worms. I knew it was my son from the first time I heard her name again."

The King fell on his knees and sobbed.

"I did not want to kill her. I don't know why that stupid Ogun priest had to kill her. I always cared for her. I don't want to die. I really don't want to die."

Arubi again pulled him to his feet and warmed his face with a thudding slap.

"Look at you. You call yourself a King and you are scared because you are having bad dreams. Listen to me: This is one war we are going to win. Now stand like a King. Do you know what great men would do to be in your position right now?"

King Nwosa dusted himself, and looked the Head-of-Government in the eye.

"As King of Didasu, I accept the boy as my son, my heir, as I have seen he will be a better King than I."

"I am sorry, Your Majesty, that cannot happen. The boy is a criminal and that is the way he will remain. Why don't you sleep and you will wake up with your thought tuned properly."

"I have made my decision, Arubi, and so shall it stand," the King replied, still looking him in the eye.

Arubi looked down, raised his head back up, then said, "It has been a pleasure working with you, Sire."

Arubi pulled his sword and stabbed the King, and then immediately stuck his hand into his mouth so the King could not utter a word. As King Nwosa was dying, he looked Arubi in the eyes and Arubi looked back at him.

When Nwosa was dead, the Ishu priest appeared, watching the Head-of-Government drag the King to his bedroom.

"What took you so long before you killed him?"

"It's that limiting word called honor. Don't just stand there, help me before someone comes," the Head-of-Government said to the Ishu priest.

135

As they were moving the body, Arubi told the Ishu priest that the Ifa priest was protecting the son.

"I thought he was dead."

"He is, but he has a successor."

"He should not be a problem," the Ishu priest said.

"In the strength of these words, he is good."

"That is your problem, not mine."

"You don't have to worry. As long as I live, nothing can touch you."

"If I remember properly, those were the same words you told King Nwosa when he was alive."

The Ishu priest did not say anything else before he left.

After they finished clearing any trace of the assassination, the Head-of-Government told the King's personal guards never to disturb the King again or let anyone make contact with him, except through Arubi. The men were happy with the news because they were already unable to bear anymore of the King's actions. Arubi made them feel special by telling them the King was sick and they should keep it to themselves.

Akuna of Ogwashi and Ezeonisha of Abogima had agreed to meet on their boundaries for a dialogue. Such actions did not mean they wanted to settle. Most times chiefs came together in such areas to discuss the days that would be convenient for both provinces to go to battle. They were also there to warn off the other province and, on rare occasions, they came together when one of the provinces wanted to beg privately. In such circumstances, both chiefs had to have respect for the other's honor or else an arrow could come from any direction. As much as both chiefs gave the impression of respect, they took three-quarters of their army with them. The chiefs stood at different ends of the border with intense looks in their eyes. The expressions on their faces screamed blood.

Akuna's envoy told him not to agree on any date before the tenth, so their spies would give them better insight for their province. Ezeonisha's envoy told his chief the same thing, except he said they would be prepared after seven days.

The two chiefs walked toward each other alone. The Omees at both ends had drawn their swords, ready for anything. Only the sandy ground and blue sky witnessed them. When the chiefs met, they took a pace past each other and turned their backs to each other's province—a move intended to show their honorable motives. All the Omees wondered what the chiefs were saying because they were too far away to be heard by anyone.

"Ezeonisha, you are looking well," Akuna commented.

"See who is talking. You have immortality written all over you," Ezeonisha replied.

"So how are the wives, children and concubines?" Akuna asked, raising his eyebrows.

"Stop trying to make me laugh. My men are watching me."

"Okay, Ezeonisha, I know you arranged this meeting to beg for mercy before I crush your province."

"Akuna, I think you have been inhaling that grass in your province. You and I know that you are the one afraid to set a date for battle."

"I have never met an ungrateful man like you. I let your people feel the breeze of freedom and you are here telling me that I am afraid of you."

"If that be the case, Akuna, set a date—today, tomorrow, or even now."

"Why should I set a date? Why don't you set a date?"

"I am not setting a date. I asked you first."

"Thank goodness our men are not here to hear us talking like children."

"Let us open the bottom of the ass. I do not want to go to war unless I have to."

"Honestly, I was looking for a way to tell you the same thing all this time. Why do you think I never suggested a date?"

"So are you really with the King?"

"That is a private question. Are you?"

" Am I what?" Ezeonisha asked.

"Are you with the King?"

"I am not exactly with anybody. Let's just say I am with both of them."

"That's quite a heavy piece of information you just shared."

"I did not have a choice, Akuna, because whatever decision we make here has to end up with us fighting each other or forming an alliance."

"What do you suggest we do?"

"We have two choices: We either join this Nwosa's son, who has Gbangba, Okon, Ihua and the people of Utagba, or we join Nwosa and the rest."

"What if we keep delaying both parties until we are sure who the winning team is?"

"Take it from me, the winning team will not hesitate to attack us once they put their feet on the ground."

Both men spoke with a hardened look on their faces, giving their men the impression they were threatening each other. Akuna lowered his voice as he spoke, even though only Ezeonisha could hear him.

"I heard that Nwosa is getting mad and Arubi is now in full control."

"Are you sure about this?" Ezeonisha asked.

"Positive. So do we join King Nwosa as Arubi is in full control?"

"I don't know. I am beginning to feel suspicious about Arubi's situation. The last time the King's envoy came to my province, it was as though Arubi was politely asking me to join him."

"Yes, they approached me in the same way," Akuna said, still whispering.

"I have served him before and one thing is for sure, Arubi never begs."

"So, what do we do?"

"We join the winning movement, the prince," Ezeonisha responded.

"I have a problem with that selection because we don't really know the boy and there isn't any chance of the boy making me his Head-of-Government."

"You are truly a dreamer. You expect Arubi to let you take his place? That man is capable of killing even the King if he stands in the way of his power."

"So we are going to join the prince?"

"To death."

"Then to death we will follow our prince," Akuna said.

"But you are lucky it's not my province you are at war with."

"It's not too late. We can still go on with the former plan we had."

Both men laughed and they made it obvious for their men to see. The cheer from the Omees at both ends was a sign of concordance with their chiefs' decision. Both chiefs went back to their men and screamed all hail the prince. Not a single man from either side replied. There was dead silence and the look of amazement in their faces. They were all positive they were fighting for the King. Neither chief expected this response. It was as though, when they were conversing, a conspiracy was in the works.

Ezeonisha shouted again, "All hail the prince." There was suddenly a loud response from the Omees in the two provinces in honor of the future king.

Chapter 11

Vokei took only one battalion and left the other three behind. The Omees were all dressed for battle, with shells over their clothes, bow and arrows tied to their backs, swords at their sides, oval bronze shields in their hands, and scabbards tied around their waists. The commoners came out and danced to the beats of the drummer and the songs of the piper. During this short celebration, women with husbands mourned them in their presence; a woman never expected her husband to come back alive from battle, even though she was positive they were going to win. It made them prepared for the worst.

As they marched into the battlefront, the men divided themselves. The Omees who were very good at archery were placed in front; the next batch were armed with sharp double-pointed spears; and the last batch fought with their swords. These wars were carried out on foot, following the patterns of their ancestors who didn't have the luxury of horses.

When Vokei got to the battlefront—blanketed with dead leaves and hard rocks, and not a tree in sight—to his amazement he saw only Odagwe and the Ozuoba army. A smile crossed his face. He wondered what kind of coward would lead his men to battle and not be present. It was unusual for a chief not to come to battle. They normally did not fight, but their presence acted like a stimulant to the men. Vokei saw his adversaries and was sure they would not need reinforcement.

The piper in Ozuoba blew the horn for them to attack and the battle began. It started with the flight of arrows in both directions, then long distance confrontations with double-edge spears. The last group of Omees had not even attacked yet and they seemed to be winning. Vokei was exceptionally good with the double-edge spear and all the men who got in his way had a trip to death.

Odagwe was ruthless with the sword and he was the strong point for Ozuoba. His tactics in battle were different and lethal. When he saw they were losing, he signaled his piper who blew the horn and from everywhere they came.

Ebikela did not know his mouth was open.

The chiefs of Suyema and Ozuba appeared with the general, Shalebe, and the remaining troops. It was as though there was a pause in the battle. Everyone knew that Suyema had a powerful army, but these troops were five times greater than what the Omees in Utagba imagined.

Vokei ordered them to blow the horn summoning the remaining men. Even with all their men together, the Omees in Utagba were not as many as the two provinces together. Vokei watched his Omees die one by one, even with reinforcement. Tears fell from his eyes as he fought and watched the chiefs laughing together. For some reason Odagwe had stopped fighting; he seemed to feel guilt now that they were winning.

Meanwhile, Shalebe was killing the Omees of Utagba as entertainment for his chiefs. He also was a master with the double-edge spear. After he killed a group of Omees, he looked at Vokei and winked. The act burned Vokei and he could not take it anymore. Even if he had to die, all he wanted was to kill Shalebe.

However, before Vokei made it to the other side, he noticed an abrupt change—Utagba's enemies were now dying one by one. Behold it was his King and the remaining troops, attacking like a hawk on its prey. The Omees from Ozuoba and Suyema did not know in which direction to fight and their confusion lead to death. This time Vokei had a grin on his face and Shalebe bore rage. Vokei watched Obi fight and knew that the man was exceptional in battle, though there was similarity between Odagwe's and Obi's methods.

When Otiotio and Atani's Tikpapas saw the Ifa priest, they went for their own battle. The Ifa priest saw the two men coming and touched his King to let him know that he was on his own for now.

The three Tikpapas walked like brothers to a secluded area and sat down, crossing their legs and closing their eyes. They sat motionless without any form of bodily display, then from the center a fire ignited. The flames surrounded the Ifa priest like a snake. The fumes twirled around him. Thick sweat

144

poured from his head. The other two warlocks had smiles on their faces, their eyes still tightly shut. All of a sudden the fire went out and the Ifa priest got up, dusted himself off, and walked back toward the battlefront. The other two Tikpapas remained in the same positions, motionless—and dead.

At the battlefront, Odagwe had joined the war again but this time he was facing Obi. Obi knew Odagwe's strengths, so he dropped his other weapons and pulled out his sword. Metal clashed. Both men had sharp reflexes and were extremely flexible. When Obi looked into Odagwe's eyes, he saw a burning hatred. The more Odagwe fought with anger, the more the younger brother relaxed.

Odagwe felt the reality of a losing battle as he put everything he had into clashing swords with his brother. He desperately wanted to end the spectacle. He took a pace back and dug his leg under a dead Omee's sword, thrust the sword up, and caught it with his left hand. The general now had two swords.

Obi threw his sword in the air, which disconcerted the older brother, then kicked Odagwe in the abdomen and gave him a head butt. He caught his sword and held it to Odagwe's neck.

"Kill me!" Odagwe shouted. "I said kill me because I will always be your enemy."

"What have I done to you, to make you hate me so much?" Obi asked. "I am the one who is supposed to hate you."

From deep in the war zone Obi heard a distinct cry of death. When he turned, he saw Ebikela looking at him with a spear in his abdomen. Shalebe smiled, pulled his sword from Ebikela's body, and gestured for Obi to come. Obi left his brother on the ground and walked with his eyes locked on Shalebe.

It did not bother Shalebe that they had nearly lost the battle, his prize was coming toward him. Shalebe twisted his spear as though warming up. Obi walked over one dead man after the other en route to him. The Utagba Omees were all over the place, playing with their enemies because it was evident they had won the war. They could easily have interfered with the two men's private battle, but something about the confrontation made it clear that would not be necessary.

Obi picked up another spear and they began. Shalebe made sharp attacks, but his opponent was as flexible as rubber. Shalebe swung the spear at his head, but Obi dodged it then caught it in the air with his left hand. Shalebe looked at his adversary with a spear in his hand and realized that death was near. He charged at Obi empty handed.

Obi just stood in the same stance, watching him. Immediately the General got to where Obi was, Obi turned swiftly and used one of the sharp edges of the spear and pierced Shalebe's heel. When he was down with a serious cut on his foot, he tried to tell Obi something, but the prince was not interested. Obi stabbed his heart.

Chief Atani told his partner to get ready to flee, but he did not hear a response. He glanced back to see Chief Otiotio dead with an arrow in his neck and he started contemplating where to run.

All the Omees started hailing, not because they had won, but because of Obi's encounter with Shalebe. As the warriors celebrated, a spear flew from nowhere headed toward the prince but nobody saw it—except Odagwe, who deflected it with his elbow. The Omees scouted for the man who had thrown it, only to find Chief Atani already dead and the Ifa priest by him.

"Did I miss anything?" the Ifa priest asked.

Obi did not say a word to Odagwe, but he freed the prisoners of war in the battle and put them under his brother. These were the men who followed Odagwe to the Ekpona Hills. Obi then merged the Suyema and Ozuoba provinces.

*

The four men in the palace were quiet when they heard the news from the messengers. Arubi was short of words. When Ogwashi and Abogima provinces said they were for the prince, they felt it was a minor issue that could be fixed when they began winning the war. When Utagba Province defeated Suyema and Ozuoba, their hopes were still alive. Immediately after Ike killed Adesuwa on grounds of infidelity; Ihua annihilated the people of Ogbe and Arubi's hopes still existed. But with the sudden reality that Alloida and Ndemili Provinces announced their attack this night on the capital, it dawned on them that something was wrong.

The Ishu priest derisively started, "At least they were nice enough to tell us they were coming."

Arubi did not find humor in the Ishu priest's statement.

"We will divide ourselves into two groups: The first group will be led by me to where the sun sets to battle with Okon, whilst the general will take the other team to face Gbangba. When we have conquered both provinces they will all come back on their knees to be part of the kingdom."

The men he spoke to did not say a word and they had no expressions on their faces.

"Can you men smell it?" the Head-of-Government asked, raising his head high, as though he were going to fly. "Believe me, if you can't smell it now, then you will smell it when it splashes on your faces. It is the smell of victory."

The King's envoy interrupted him, saying that the elders were demanding to see the King.

"Why are they asking for him and in fact why are you looking at me like that?"

"I was not looking at you," the envoy replied.

"Yes, you were. I know what you are thinking. I feel it in your bones. I have no intention of letting one stupid wretch of a child ascend to the throne. When

148

everything smelt like roses, you were all fully behind me."

All three men acted confused.

"Don't use that old trick with me. We all know what happened to the King and it was even you three who suggested it."

"What do you think I am talking about?" the general asked.

"What do you think I am talking about, you son of a baboon, or are you all deaf? I am talking about the death of King Nwosa."

"Are you trying to tell me our King is dead?" the Ishu priest asked.

"What do you mean by that stupid question? Were you not the man who helped me hide his body here?" The Head-of-Government faced the general. "Was it not you who helped me discharge the body? And the King's envoy, did you not tell the elders that you were with him while we burnt his flesh?"

"You have an iron heart to face us and tell us you killed the King," the Ishu priest shouted.

The Head-of-Government wanted to say something, but the words would not come out of his mouth.

The envoy spat on his face and said, "You don't deserve to see another day."

Arubi, in anger, reached for his sword to kill the Ishu priest and the envoy, but he wasn't fast enough. The general sliced off Arubi's head, then looked at the

149

body and said, "Who looks like the son of a baboon now?"

They reported to the people how the Head-of-Government killed the King and offered peace with the two provinces. But both the provinces pretended not to get the message and attacked anyway, killing everyone they believed to be a threat and dividing the capital into two—one part for Ndemili and the other for Alloida. The body of the Ishu priest was never found, nor was he heard from again.

Chapter 12

Obi was crowned King immediately after Okon and Gbangba took control of the Didasu capital. The capital was moved to Utagba. As of that time, Ndemili was the smallest province, yet one of the richest. Even with half of the Didasu capital, it was still the smallest. Obi made Okon an offer, either he became Head-of-Government or he took the other half of the Didasu capital that was given to Gbangba. If he wanted to let his son succeed him, the kingdom would not get involved in the decision.

Okon chose the latter, not because the other half of the capital would have made Ndemili as large as any other province. Neither was it because as chief you were the lord of your province and the King could not easily get access to what you were doing. It was because of Oludu, his heir, his grandson and adopted son, who deserved to be in his place now that he was getting old.

That was how Gbangba became the Head-of-Government to King Obi, the Ifa priest became the Headman to the Oracle, and the Okpala of Utagba became the Okpalaukwu.

The King married Vokei's daughter, Ifrareta. Notwithstanding the fact that she was handicapped, he still made her his First Queen. The elders who were handpicked from the different provinces did not approve of his marriage to the disabled girl. The major reason he married her was to show a sign of gratitude to the dead general's spirit, wherever it roamed. Although she was not the greatest lover to him, she was a good wife. His brother, the late King Nwosa's other son, remained a royal with no position of power.

When Obi was fully settled as King, he made two visits. The first was to the missionary he called Michael and requested his tooth. In exchange, he gave him permission to teach about his God to anyone who wanted to listen—and constant access to the King. The second visit was made two years later to Okonjo.

When King Obi went to the home of the man who caused all his problems, he found out the man ran away, leaving behind his wives and children. The only person he begged to follow him was his latest wife, Weruche, who was determined to stay. After he ran away, his other wives and children disappeared because they were aware that the man of the house was the person who revealed Obi's identity to the world. Okonjo was a rich man and he spent two years at an unknown address, but he came back to the house as often as he could to see his fourth wife and cover all her needs.

The King entered the trader's home with death on his mind. He did not notice how splendid Okonjo's home was; all he was interested in was taking revenge on anybody who played a part in his wife's death. The only people in the house were his slaves and servants. His Head-of-Government told him the man had run away, but he was not satisfied. He still wanted to see the house of his enemy.

As the King looked around, he noticed a hidden passageway. When Obi opened it, it led to a stream behind the trader's house. The King walked down the passageway made of granite rocks and all the Omees followed him, including the Head-of-Government.

They saw a woman swimming in the stream. She showed an indifference to the presence of the men around her and got out of the stream naked. At this time all the men were positive she was a mermaid. They had never seen this kind of beauty in a woman, from the top of her head to the sole of her feet. She majestically walked to where her clothes were, put them on her shoulders, and then walked back into the house. Every man seemed to be in a trance. No one made a move or said a word for some time.

All of a sudden, Obi walked back into the house and started searching the rooms for the girl. His men did not follow him as they usually did. Obi finally found the room she was in and closed the door.

"I don't care who you are, but do you know who I am?"

Weruche slid down the bed, still naked, and with a wickedly seductive voice she said, "I do. Is that the reason you came back here like a bull?"

"I can snap my finger and every bone in your body would be pulled apart, or even a hundred of my men would ravage the beauty that infects your mind."

"But you would go first. Do you honestly think you could give me away after that?" She had a husky voice and wicked attraction to her expression.

Obi could not take it any longer; he grabbed her from the bed, raised her to the wall, and started licking every part of her like an animal. Weruche locked her legs around his waist, using her hands to grab and scratch him at the same time.

He entered her, making extremely fast thrusts with his lower body, as though they were running out of time. The more she called his name, the faster he moved. The passion was diabolic and the electricity endless. Even after he ejaculated, his lower self still wanted more and he kept looking at the wickedness of her beauty.

Obi got up, got dressed and then he asked, "who are you?"

"I am the wife of the man you want to kill," Weruche responded in her seductive voice, still naked on the floor.

"So he left his wife behind to simmer me."

"I did what I did because I want to. My husband has been impotent for about four months now. He said his other wives met a Tikpapa to make him lose it because of their jealousy for me. Anyway, I still care for the man."

"Tell your husband when he comes that, till he dies, he is now a labeled criminal for collaborating in the plot to kill me. He is free to roam the kingdom as

154

he wishes, but from this day all his children will share the name with him. You should know that this is the last time we will ever meet."

Weruche wiggled her fingers as a gesture to say goodbye. Obi looked at the naked body and the pretty face, knowing it was not going to be easy. Even the way she made him forget the torture he had planned for Okonjo was a miracle.

With time Okonjo was no longer an issue to the King. On the day that the queen gave birth to her second daughter, Okonjo brought the most expensive gifts to the King and he accepted them. Four months had passed since the King paid the visit to Okonjo's home and his daughter was only a month old when Weruche sent a message to the King, telling him she was pregnant by him. Obi ignored her message until the day Ifrareta told him Weruche had given birth to a son.

They both lay in bed when she told him. His eyes were closed, yet he was widely awake when he replied her.

"What does it have to do with me?"

"It's no secret that you entered her. That son she bore could be your heir, your only heir," his wife answered.

"She has a husband who is a criminal. The child could be his."

"So long as the child is yours, who cares about the man being a criminal? She also told me the man has been impotent for a while now."

"She told you?" Obi's voice deepened.

"Yes, my King, she was here and she told me her predicament."

"Can you not see with both your eyes? The woman is a liar and she is desperate to climb higher than she already is."

"Yes, my husband, I might be handicapped, but I can see. The woman is beautiful and there is no point denying it. Even a blind man will bow to her just by touching her skin. I have tried everything as a wife, but that hole your former wife left behind is getting wider and it consumes me as it increases. I know you went out of your way to marry me."

Obi cut into her speech saying, "I married you because I wanted to."

"With all due respect, I am still talking." Obi opened his eyes and saw the seriousness in his wife's face as she spoke.

"I know I am not beautiful. As many times as you try to deceive yourself about it, I know the truth. I wanted to make it up to you by giving you a son, but my two children are girls."

"They are just your first two, more will come."

"Yes, you are right, more will come and they may all be women. In your family lineage it's no secret that sons are not easy to come by. Nwosa had only two sons and his home was swarming with women. First of all, as King you have the power to marry many wives, yet I am the only one you have. Yes...yes...I am grateful. As long as you are King, I will forever be the most powerful queen in the whole kingdom, but I don't want to be the only one."

Obi wanted to say something, but Ifareta continued without giving him a chance. She knelt beside him and continued.

"Even if she can't fill the emptiness that is in your heart, your son might cover it a little as your daughters have."

"Ifareta, I married you because you were smart. Don't tell me you believe her story about her husband being impotent."

"Look deeper into it, Obi. A wild animal goes to war with any of its offspring that was raised by another, but any offspring that were raised by it, whether it be for another, it feeds and teaches this offspring its way of life, as though it was its child." She came closer to her husband and her voice softened. "I know there is a possibility that the child might not be your own, but you can accept the child as yours temporarily, to prevent assassination attempts on you. The chiefs and elders are still hungry for power. As long as there is no heir, they will look forward to the day you die so they can tear the kingdom apart and be gods in their provinces. You will marry other wives and she can still give birth to other children.

Immediately after you have another son, how would I put it, accidents happen."

"She already has a husband."

"That is the easiest part. You and I both know that you haven't forgiven Okonjo. You tell him to divorce his wife and offer him triple the dowry he paid. From what I know of him, he is going to refuse. Then you kill him publicly, letting everyone know that the criminal defied the King."

"He might not refuse the offer if it means clearing his name as a criminal."

"Take it from me, Weruche is positive that he will not agree."

"It seems to me that you and Weruche have already decided everything, but do you realize that you are inviting a cobra into our home?"

"I know, that is why we have to suck out its poison."

"The elders are not going to agree with the decision."

"If the pressure they put on is strong, we will let the world know that you have a son, but you don't have to marry her. But if you still have not gotten a son after a time, then you marry her, with or without their consent."

"Do I take it that you have no faith being the mother to the heir?"

"My faith has grown slim, but I swear to you, if I give birth to your son, even if he is the tenth son, he will become King."

"Strong words for a woman I thought had a soft heart."

The King grinned and they slept alongside each other.

*

Okonjo refused to give his bride to the King despite the offers that were made to him and he chose death as his option. The elders were strongly against the King marrying the wife of a criminal, but none of the elders disputed her child being the King's son. Queen Ifrareta gave birth to another girl and she found a second wife for her husband. It was a conventional rule that the First Queen scrutinized and picked the other brides of the King; that is why the King picked the First Queen personally. .

Chapter 13

The King summoned Chief Odagwe, and as much as he tried to lie to himself, the chief knew why. His contempt for the King was solid. They grew up together and between them there was a bond. He had been there for his supposed brother all his life. The only time he ever asked Obi for anything, the boy refused him. The excuse that he was a child was not acceptable; he had made his decision with the heart of a man.

Obi was not the only one the chief's fire of vengeance burnt toward. His entire family had forsaken him the day he walked out of the house. All the things Odagwe lost because of his father's Ikaza status couldn't be substituted by being trained by an Omee. Even by one who was good like their father was not enough; he needed the respect that went with it. Every time he passed a particular status, everyone mocked the son of the Ikaza and he hated them for it. Most especially he hated every member of his family for it.

Odagwe looked around the palace; there was something different about it. The King might kill him on this day, but he did not care. He saw him sitting on his dirty throne and he bowed down to the man they called King, but to him was an insolent pig.

"Odagwe, my brother, I am sorry for bringing you out here in these gory times."

160

"For my King it is my duty to be within your presence at anytime you request."

"Do you think this battle we are in is necessary to us?" the Head-of-Government asked.

"The Yeres refuse to accept our King and their soil is fertile," Odagwe said.

"They are not in the vicinity of our kingdom. They have every right not to accept me as King," Obi said.

"But their land flourishes crops of all forms and they breed healthy livestock."

"Omees from the Yere land are very fierce in battle, especially in water, and their land is bounded by rivers."

"I do not intend to enter into a battle which I cannot walk away from with my head high."

"How high your head is, is not the problem. If your head is still on your body, is what we're talking about," said the towering Gbangba, bouncing a mango in his hand.

"So you guarantee me victory?" the King asked, ignoring his Head-of-Government's mockery.

"I would settle for nothing less, my King."

"Gbangba, give me some time alone with my chief."

"At you request, Your Majesty." The Head-of-Government bowed to King Obi and left the two men alone.

"It has been long since we have had the chance to talk alone, Odagwe."

"Destiny has a way of covering the good times, Sire."

"Anyway, we are here together now like the old days."

"There cannot be anything like the past, Sire."

"Our father used to take us to see the lions when they were mating."

"With all due respect, Your Majesty, he was my father, not our father. I have known you since your birth; you were never good at small talk. Please, what is the purpose for me being summoned here whilst my Omees wait patiently for me to give orders for them to blow the horn for battle?" He spoke more confidently as the Head-of-Government was not anywhere near to punish him for his fraternal attack.

"You take advantage of my position. You fail to realize that the only reason you are alive is because we have the same mother."

"For the last time, we do not have the same mother. We were raised by the same woman, which you realized was not your mother. I have never taken advantage of your position. I am a chief because I earned it. If you decide it is time for me to die, do not expect me to beg."

"You are jealous. I feel it through the echo of your voice. I find that feeling you carry completely unnecessary."

"There is nothing to be jealous of, Obi."

"If you wish me to treat you as a King, so shall it be. On your knees while you address me. I want to see maximum respect."

Odagwe went down on his knee slowly.

"I heard you are betrothed to Onyela, daughter of Imasuen."

"Yes, I am."

"I cannot hear you, Odagwe."

"Yes I am, Sire!"

"How much dowry have you placed on this girl's head?"

"Enough."

"As you are leaving meet the Head-of-Government, he will refund whatever price you feel you deserve for letting go of her."

"I am sorry...I cannot concur."

"Do I detect defiance?"

"No, Your Majesty, but the girl is unworthy to be your queen."

"That is for me to decide."

"She is not a virgin."

"Imasuen said she was raised from the shadow of men. The only outsider who got access to this girl was you."

"I never said it was not me who took away her innocence."

"Another lie. Everybody knows this girl lives for purity."

"Again, I never said she gave in willingly."

163

"When?"

"Two nights ago."

"I could order your execution on the grounds of rape."

"Then start a war with the people of Ekpona Hills."

"You flatter your people. I would rather say annihilation of the people of the Ekpona Hills."

"She was betrothed to me. I had every right to do what I chose with the woman who belonged to me."

"You were betrothed to her since she was crawling. Why did you have to wait till now before you broke her innocence? You might as well have married her first."

"You really want to know?"

"I wouldn't be asking if I did not want to know."

"I saw your messengers bring gifts for her parents and I wondered why the King would send gifts to these peasants. I thought of their assets. The father is a very good palm wine tapper. They have a perfect family background and they have a daughter who is almost an angel, gracious in her every move. I was positive the only reason you scouted her was due to your spite for me. Then I heard you invited her to your palace. I hoped you would just look at her and notice that she was not exceptionally pretty. Unfortunately, you discovered that her beauty was in her heart. I watched your guards escort her home. The look on her face told me two things: you did not rape her, which I knew was your motive; and she no longer belonged to me. So I stood looking into the sky wondering why I should lose such a gift created by heaven. But there was something about this girl that I did not understand. My two wives are more blessed with beauty than she. So I sneaked into her room. She tried to scream, so I put a cloth over her mouth, held her firmly to the ground, and raped her, not once, not twice, but over and over again. She seemed to have fainted before I had finished. I was extremely disappointed to notice that you did not rape her and she was virgin. So that's about it. My apologies if I prevented her from becoming your concubine."

"I never intended for her to be my concubine," the King retorted.

"How stupid of me to think my King would think of such a thing with a girl like her."

"Anyway, you asked why I sent for you."

"Yes, Sire."

"To invite you to my wedding to Onyela on the tenth day from today. The Head-of-Government will meet you on your way out of the palace."

"Why?" Odagwe asked with his face looking strained.

"Because I can."

"Revenge for Ikpong's daughter."

"I wish it were, Odagwe."

"Onyela has enslaved my heart," he sighed on his knees. "Don't look at me on my knees as a mark of respect for a King, but look at it as a man who begs a King to let go of a woman he loves."

"Why, Odagwe? For love or your ego?"

Odagwe thought, then rose with renewed ego. "I will not miss your wedding."

"By the way, Odagwe, Onyela told me everything."

So he knew everything all along and he had an excuse to torture me, Odagwe thought while walking out. I am a fool in his eyes. It seems he forgets the vulture is a patient bird. I am backed by destiny. The time for reckoning will arrive.

King Obi married Onyela, who gave birth to a son. Thus, the elders no longer bothered the King about his getting married to Weruche. She eventually became the King's fourth wife and her son was finally a prince because his mother was no longer a concubine.

Chapter 14

Chief Vacoura of Alloida was inflexible and distinctly simplified. He had a normal life for a chief and his people didn't expect him to rule like his predecessors. His people begged him to trade with the Portuguese, but as a man of strict traditional principles, he was not interested in touching anything that violated the morals of the land.

His people gave a general cry for the slave trading with the Portuguese; they always went through the elders because they were not allowed direct contact with the chief. The elders of Alloida were made up of six of the oldest men in the province, all past warriors.

One stormy night, there was a meeting between the elders, the Tikpapa and Vacoura in his Haku. Vacoura entered into his conference room and saw the faces of the elders and knew exactly why they came. As he entered, all the elders bowed, including the Tikpapa. He gestured with his fingers urging them to proceed.

"Vacoura, your people cry out that they are being left out in this new world. They see the coconut of the other provinces bringing out sweet waters and they wonder why their coconut is dry," said the oldest of the elders.

The tallest elder continued. "The duck that decides to spread its wings and fly has done no man harm. Vacoura, your people want to hatch from their shell."

The youngest elder spoke next. "What the Portuguese are ready to provide we need and what they want we have."

Vacoura spoke slyly. "And what do they have that we want?"

"They have luxurious items that sparkle in the moonlight," the youngest elder immediately responded.

"That is pure vanity of man. It does not make the land we live in a better place," Vacoura replied.

"They have stallions that stand firmer than an elephant and move as fast as the wind," the oldest elder said.

"Horses are vanity that the Arabians have spoilt us with and even then, Chief Odagwe's stallions are just as firm."

"But the price we have to pay is more than what the Portuguese are offering," the youngest elder blurted out.

"We will manage what we have to be stronger within."

"How about salt? You expect us to keep trading with Oludu?" Irritation was growing in the youngest elder's voice. "We all know that the traditional salt that we get from our akanwo roots isn't as good as those provided by the Portuguese. Yes, the kingdom is getting stronger, but all the other provinces are ahead of us."

The oldest elder spoke again.

"What they ask for, we have in excess quantity: beads, cloths, ivory and…slaves. In this province a commoner has at least one slave; these are people who do not know what it feels like to conquer an opposition, or carry a wounded warrior during battle. We used to be a very great province. We used to be able to stand and every other province would stretch to look at us. We used to—"

"You used to be able to what? You ungrateful snakes," the chief interrupted angrily. "In the days of the past you walked in fear. Now you walk on the roads with laughter on your faces. You sip your wines without the thought of a spear coming in your back. Do you think I don't know what you people and all the market women gossip about? 'He is a poor imitation of his predecessors.' When the King gets to hear about us selling slaves to other kingdoms, do you think my head alone will be taken? He will execute all of you. He will make our women and wives concubines to people of the lowest niche in society. Our Omee and sons will be auctioned as slaves."

"But nearly every province is into slave trade," the shortest elder said.

"It is against the law to sell slaves to anyone outside the kingdom, that isn't my law but the King's. And even if the other provinces sell slaves in the shade of the night, you all need to remember, this is not every province. This is a proud and great province," the chief shouted.

"The tortoise walks because he has no reason to run. It's time for us to run or else everyone will leave us behind," the youngest elder said.

"Even if the tortoise wants to run, it cannot because it is not its nature," the Tikpapa said.

With a venomous riposte the elder said, "You answer me only when I talk to you and till then you shut that contaminated mouth."

"The Tikpapa sounds with my voice," Vacoura said calmly. "His words are my words; his thoughts are my thoughts; his reply is my reply. So if you tell my Tikpapa that his mouth is foul in my presence, then you are telling me that my mouth is foul. I will pretend that nothing of that nature occurred as soon as you send your apologies to my Tikpapa."

"Chief Vacoura, the patient one, if I, the son of this soil, have offended you my chief, I apologize," the elder said. "But for me to apologize to a man of lower respect than I—even worse is that he is of a younger age than I—I cannot."

"Even if I, Chief Vacoura of Alloida, asks you to?"

"Even if you asked me again, I cannot apologize to a man lower than I."

"Don't push my hand, old man."

"I am of the old breed. I will not dampen my pride." The older man had his head low and eyes set to that of the chief.

Vacoura waited for seconds, minutes. No response, not even an attempt of response.

170

"You will be executed by the peak of the day tomorrow in the middle of the town square on the grounds of treason. I will take care of the execution personally to give you the respect you deserve as an elder," the chief said firmly, then he clapped his hands and the general approached. "Escort the elder to prison. Stay with him till the sun shines. Give him everything he desires, but let nobody see while he prepares for his execution."

After they left he turned to the remaining elders, discharging them and telling them to converge during the execution.

The chief was now alone with his warlock.

"Well?"

The dwarfish Tikpapa spoke carefully, not due to the vicarious act that had been done on his behalf, but more because now he was sure he had been serving the right man for over a decade.

"If you decide to execute him, your people will no longer respect you. They will fear you and vilify you behind your back. But if you decide to forgive him, your people will adore your forgiving heart and your words from then will be as dangerous as a snake with a goat in its mouth."

"Pardon me, Great Chief," the announcer said, "but the market women of the province stand by the gate screaming amnesty."

"Tell them I have poor self-control and my blade is hungry."

171

"Your elders fight against your decision." The announcer said.

"Until tomorrow." The Tikpapa gave a slight bow to the Chief and walked off.

There was a knock on the door and the chief knew it was time. He dressed himself in his chief's outfit and walked out with his eyes straight. As he mounted his horse, the crowd kept screaming, "Amnesty!" This he heard continuously till he got to the town square. The warriors created two straight lines that formed a path up to the town square for protective reasons. As he passed each soldier, the soldier bowed.

When he got to the town square he was greeted by his elders and his Tikpapa. He looked up at the platform and saw the elder tied down on his knees. At this point he was ready to let him go, but the congregation kept shouting, "Amnesty!" Derogatory statements started coming from the crowd. Spontaneously, he picked up his sword climbed up the platform and sliced the elder's head as though it were a coconut.

From within the crowd an arrow flew toward the chief's skull. The Tikpapa stood out, blew white chalk in the air and shouted, "E JEKE EBE." The arrow stopped right in front of the chief's skull and exploded into ashes sprinkling onto the floor. There was silence in the whole town square.

"If anyone has a problem with my authority, let him come now and settle it with me, man to man. I promise you nobody will touch a hair on your head," the chief said.

The silence remained except for the birds that sang. In anger the chief returned with his party. He craved to polish a man's blood on his sword in battle. I am totally surrounded by cowards, he thought as he rode away. From that day the assassination attempts proliferated, all to no avail, and his word became as hard as a rock.

Chapter 15

Chief Akuna was receiving pressure from his elders to hand over power to his general, Pokzee. General Pokzee of Ogwashi was an abnormally big man. They said his mother died during his birth because there was only space for one of them to survive. Since he was eleven years old, he represented his province in wrestling fights and was still undefeated.

The chief kept deferring the matter until there came a time that something had to be done. So during the Feast of the Ikenga—attended by people from all over Utagba—Akuna told Pokzee to sit by his side. Men and women performed their folksongs, plays, and cultural dances. Masqueraders with canes chased after children and blessed anyone of respect.

During the cultural dance of the Alloida people, Pokzee was mesmerized by one of the dancers and Akuna saw the lust in his eyes. He asked Pokzee as they sat on the sandy floor underneath palm trees, "Do you like her?"

"How can anybody not like that body of fire?" Pokzee replied, loud enough to be heard over the drumming of the musicians.

"Things might not be what they seem when you take a closer look," Akuna said, looking into his eyes.

"If she is a cobra, let her bite me, but she will bear my children as my second wife."

When the dance was over, Akuna asked his envoy about the girl.

"Her name is Nkiru, daughter of our late envoy. She has not been touched by any man before."

"Then why has she not married by now?" Pokzee asked.

"The suitors who came for her hand could not afford the dowry."

"When the day is over, tell her to go to Pokzee's hut with her party."

"Chief, that is a shrewd request," the envoy spoke carefully.

"Are you trying to tell me that my general cannot afford her dowry?"

"No, Chief. But there is a slight possibility that she may refuse."

"Then if she is not interested to take the hand of a great man in marriage, let her not come to his hut when the moon is full and she will never step into this land again."

"Chief, this is a simple issue. If she does not want to come, it's not a problem. The whole place is packed with women looking for suitors," Pokzee pleaded.

"Go and deliver my message to her," the chief commanded the envoy. He turned to Pokzee, talking as though his pride was at stake. "If she does not come with her party to see you, tell me first thing in the morning."

He rose and marched over the sandy ground, through the huts, and out of the feast with his entourage.

It was the full moon and Pokzee awaited Nkiru and her party. He was alone because during the introduction to a woman for the first time, nobody in his party was allowed to be there. He began to wonder. How much bride price will they request? I have not really investigated her background. She could be a slave. May the gods forbid. When I marry this girl, I will not waste energy with any other woman for at least two weeks, but there is a possibility that she might not come.

There was a heavy rap on the door. That son of mine thinks he can keep knocking on my door anytime he feels like. I will teach him a little respect. This is a ploy by his mother to prevent me from getting a new woman.

He opened the door and instead of his son, he saw her. He stood amazed at her coming alone, then she walked past him and with every step she took she dropped a piece of clothing. Pokzee was still facing the door. By the time he turned around she was naked on the floor. At this point the only thing in his head was that if this was temptation, he was only human. With a fierceness he could not control, he grabbed her close to him and started to suck on her breast like a calf feeding from its mother. He held firmly to her hips and looked into her eyes. Then he penetrated her and she grabbed tight to him until he ejaculated.

When the intercourse was over, he looked at her with a smirk on his face saying, "I thought they said you had not seen a man before."

She smiled. In a sudden flash she got up and ran to the wall, pounding her head continually against the hardened clay. With blood on her head, she dashed out of the door naked, screaming, crying while running like a lunatic.

"People of Utagba, I came to Ogwashi to dance for the Ikenga. Was it evil that I should come to dance here? The people of Ogwashi have taken my innocence away from me. What wrong did I do to make Pokzee capture and rape me? What have I done to be punished like this?"

Pokzee immediately put his clothes back on and went to find out exactly what was going on. By the time he came out, a multitude awaited him by his gates. Nine heavily armed warriors told him that the chief requested his presence.

"Let us go. I am ready," he said.

Pokzee's wife grabbed her husband, screaming, "Nobody is going to take my husband anywhere!"

He reprimanded his wife, telling her to go back and prepare food for him to eat. He looked at the warriors and apologized for his wife's actions. As they walked to the chief's Haku, women started spitting and insulting him, but all through this, his head was still high.

He got to the conference room to find the chief, Akuna's Tikpapa, the envoy, four of the elders, and Nkiru. They were all seated except the girl and him. Akuna looked at the girl, now covered with a wrapper, and instructed her to speak.

"I was informed by my envoy that my presence was required by Pokzee, but I said I was not going to go because I felt I deserved to be a man's first wife. If I had to become a man's second, he had to be of great standing."

Pokzee thought about the situation. Why would she go out of her way to do this? I might have offended someone in her family line. But the envoy told me she has not been touched by any man. He even told the chief. She did not wait to hear what I intended of her, but what have I done to this vixen to breed such intense hatred?

"When the different provinces had presented their dances, I decided to go to the stream to have my bath with my friends. In the bushes I saw a glittering light, so I decided to take a closer look," she said, stopping to wipe the tears from her eyes. "As I went nearer to it, I felt a firm blow on my head and a strong grasp covering my mouth. I tried to scream, but he was too strong. He was just too strong."

At that point Pokzee, the chief and the elders made no expression. Only the envoy had tears streaming down his cheeks.

178

"He took me into one of his huts and took away my innocence. He said if I told anyone what happened, he would destroy my life. I told him my life was already destroyed. That's when I started to scream in the town before your men brought me here."

Akuna looked at Pokzee and asked him with authority, "Did you sleep with this woman?"

"Yes, but she came out of her own will."

"So, I am to understand that she just walked into your hut to get raped?" Vacoura's envoy asked.

"I am not obligated to answer to you," Pokzee replied.

"I am the envoy, a representative of my chief, the questions I ask are the questions Chief Vacoura asks you. Or am I to understand that you cannot answer the questions of my chief?"

"She walked into my home and had sex with me, not rape," Pokzee said through gritted teeth.

"Then where did the blood from her head come from?" the chief asked with disappointment all over his face.

"She... hit her head on the wall by herself."

One of the elders got up and spat on the ground, anger in his every word.

"Do you think we are goats that you kill and eat with our eyes wide open? The man is as guilty as the devil. Give him the punishment he deserves," the elder yelled.

179

The chief looked at the other elders and they all nodded in approval.

"Do you have anything to say?" he asked Pokzee.

"If the Oracle has opened the gateway of my death through this deceptive snake, then let it be."

"Pokzee," the chief now said paternally, "is this a deliberate attempt to have us at war with the people of Alloida?"

"She lies," he said, his large burly form, straightened.

"I, Chief Akuna of Ogwashi, put you on exile from this land and if you—"

"A great apology, oh Great Chief," the envoy interrupted, " but if this man roams the kingdom, it might set an uneasiness for my people because the girl's life cannot be secured. Not to mention that my chief might feel you are preserving him somewhere, as he happens to be one of your respected Omees. It's not as though I believe that a man of your integrity would engage in such a thing."

The chief rose, looked at his elders and then he said with a heavy heart, "I sentence one of the greatest Omees in my time to death by noon. Until then he will be confined to prison."

They escorted Pokzee to prison to await his execution. He spent the whole night in a six-by-six clay-bound wall, trying to unravel why he was in this predicament. A light appeared in front of him and he

180

saw a lizard, which transformed into a man—the Ifa priest.

"Am I to be honored with the presence of the Great Ifa during my execution?" Pokzee asked, bewildered.

"Honestly, young man, I did not know of your existence in the past, but as of now the oracle has labeled you an asset to the King. Chief Akuna has violated the laws of the land."

"So it was the chief who put this dilemma on me."

"Are you trying to debase me so I will come all the way here to settle such a trivial issue as your rape case?"

"Sorry for my uncultured interference, Great Ifa."

"Your chief has broken the laws of the land. He has been trading with the Portuguese and purposely forgot to ask the permission of the King. Upon the wealth he claims, he still sheds tears of poverty when asked for his taxes, and most especially, there is a disloyal approach to his character. I came to take his life and install you as chief, but this situation manifested. As you said, you were put in your predicament, probably to prevent an early succession. As of now there is nobody else worthy of taking the title."

"What must I do?"

"You will chew these leaves as they lead you to the platform. As you get there, spit them out and shout, 'AGAM OBODO OZO.' You will disappear to a safer distance. You have twelve days to clear yourself of

181

any allegations. If by that time you have not returned, I will not hesitate any longer to take the life of your chief and replace him with who I see fit."

"What if the people reject your choice?"

"Then the people of Ogwashi will go to war with the kingdom of Utagba and every Omee who exists on this land will be slaughtered, every commoner and child will be made slaves, and all the women of this land will be distributed as concubines to the masses."

"Is this what you foresaw or a threat of what you are capable of?"

"It's not what I am capable of, but what your King is capable of."

"But you are aware that they would never accept anybody you choose."

"That I am aware of. It is probably the reason why the King chose you before this predicament, but notwithstanding, there is a contingency plan."

"May I ask what it is?"

"If I tell you, it might prevent you from coming back."

"I do not have a choice. I have to come back or else my wife and three sons will be executed."

"It is to put a man from Abogima to govern your people."

Otuturex, the name echoed in Pokzee's head. I wonder what his attachment to the King is based on that he is ready to destroy our population for him. He is positive that the people would reject his decision and the King is positive that no chief is going to come to our aid.

The door unlocked and three Omees entered telling him it was time. He looked behind him to find out the Ifa priest was not there, but the leaves were on the floor. He picked them up and started chewing as they led him to the platform.

Why does the Ifa priest want to help me? It would have been more convenient for the King to let me die. If the King squashes the land, he would be able to suck the sweetest fruits from the land, increase his slaves, put in the kind of chief he can trust, not to mention how fertile our land is.

Every step he took seemed steep. Pushing the cursing spectators with tears in her eyes was his wife, not missing a pace of his journey.

"I am still here,'' she shouted as she followed him. "I am not going anywhere. If it be my destiny that we cannot be together in the land of the living, then I will wait for you in the land of the dead."

Tears nearly fell from his eyes looking at this woman, but he believed that men don't cry. Watching her as he was escorted, he knew his wife did not deserve this humiliation. I promise to come back to you, my sweet wife. Everything will be as it was and I swear to you I shall have no other wife till death. These were the words he wished he could tell her through the horde.

As he climbed the platform, he looked around to see the people who were there to celebrate his execution—an angry mob that despised rapists more than their enemies.

As they placed his head in the wooden framework, he spat the leaves. Before he could say a word, from the crowd he heard those words that haunted him throughout the days of his life: AGAM OBODO OZO.

There was an explosion on the platform. The three Omees on the platform ran down. Everybody started chattering, with only the Tikpapa walking cautiously toward the scene.

Pokzee looked around, unable to run with his neck locked. The noise from the crowd started to fade, and there was clearer visual on what was behind the smoke: It was his wife.

"People of Ogwashi, you have the wrong suspect. The person you should be punishing is me. I am a witch," she declared.

"She is lying. She acts from an untamed love," Pokzee screamed.

Nkiru cut in asking, "Am I so stupid that I don't know the difference between a man and a woman?"

"I changed into a man and grabbed you from the stream," Pokzee's wife replied.

"She lies. It was I that raped her and took all her innocence away. Do not listen to a word my wife says!"

"If I tell tales, how do you explain the scar I put on her face."

"You did not do anything to her face. She did it by herself. If you attacked her, how did you know I had asked her to come?" Pokzee said, still screaming.

"I did not know she was coming."

"But I was at the feast and I saw the way he was looking at her when she danced. That's why I attacked her at the stream."

"She speaks falsely. She is a liar. She is trying to protect her husband," Nkiru said.

"What makes you so sure she was not the one?" the Tikpapa asked, his eyes fixed on hers.

"Well, I should know. I slept with him…I mean he raped me."

"I know my wife. She is no witch. She is trying to take my burden."

"Or it is you trying to carry hers?" one of the elders asked.

"I tell you on the lives I have fought and died for, my wife is not a witch."

"Then how do you explain her entrance to this platform? Whatever she did, it's magic," another elder said.

"It was the Ifa priest who cast that spell, not her."

"You lie. Nobody witnessed the Ifa priest arriving," the envoy said, hoping he was right.

"He lies to protect his bride. That was why he refused to defend himself properly during his trial," another elder said.

"I said nothing because I knew I was guilty of the crime committed."

"My husband is a fool to die for a crime that I committed. Today it is Nkiru, tomorrow it could be your wife, your brother, or your only son I will possess."

"Please do not listen to her, she is lying," Pokzee said with tears in his eyes.

"Watch my husband cry like a woman. Does he not know that men do not cry?"

The oldest elder stood up and said, "I am not worthy of being an elder in this province. How could I have been a party to the execution of a man who brought pride to our land?" He dropped his staff and walked away.

"No, no, that's what she wants," Pokzee screamed from his enclosed wooden framework.

Chief Akuna rose with indifference on his face and spoke with an air of command. "Release the great Omee and prepare the witch for an immediate execution."

Two Omees walked toward them—the first went to tie his wife up and the other released Pokzee.

As soon as he was free, he grabbed the Omee by his testicles and neck and threw him over the platform. The other Omee used his clenched fist and hit his back.

186

Pokzee staggered, but not before using his elbow to bang the Omee's jaw. A taller Omee climbed the platform and threw a punch. Unfortunately, he missed and received half a dozen across his ribs before he was thrown over. Another charged at Pokzee like a deer. He fitted the man's neck into a jab from his elbow. The next Omee was bigger than he was and immediately squeezed him in a bear hug. Pokzee head butted the man, but the Omee refused to ease the grasp, so he used his knee to continuously pound on his testicles until the man fainted.

During this time, his wife was tied by her hands and feet. All that crossed her mind was that if there was a greater man to die for, she would never see him and if that person existed, she did not want to live to see such a person because she was proud of her man—her only man.

Pokzee looked at the crowd and saw more than three thousand Omees waiting in line to hold him down. He rushed, untied his wife, put her up on his shoulder, using his elbow to hit the next Omee who entered the platform and then he ran and jumped into the crowd of spectators. They didn't call him the bull for nothing. As they landed, there was chaos amongst the crowd.

The Tikpapa shouted, "NODI YADI BA FO YEH JEKE EBE OBONE."

The crowd parted in the middle, where Pokzee was frozen in a spot with his wife on his shoulder. The

Tikpapa waved his hand and both man and wife collapsed on the ground, unconscious.

Pokzee opened his eyes to find himself in his hut along with the Ifa priest, who was drinking palm wine from a calabash.

"Where is my wife?"

"They have executed her by burning her on a stake. I could have sworn she was laughing during the execution."

"You could have saved her."

"Yes, but she chose her destiny. A sacrifice was required. This palm wine is still sweet after two days."

"Why did you not take me instead?"

"You are important to the kingdom."

"I cannot help you...you could have saved both of us. Now I will wake up never to hear her tell me I worry too much."

"You can find people to replace her. It's no secret that you change your women as fast as the days change to night."

"I can never find a replacement."

"She had to die to appease the oracle. She was a good woman and she even begged to sacrifice her life so you could live...probably she wanted you to recognize she existed."

"Then why did you end up telling me to do things that were unnecessary?"

"At that point it was necessary, but I changed my mind."

"Do you think I really care for these people anymore?"

"You might not care about these people, but you care about your descendants and most especially revenge."

"I have to clear her spirit by proving to the people that she was no witch."

"You can do that when you are chief."

"Then they will say I used the power bestowed on me to clear her name."

"You have till the fifth day after that. I will not wait any longer. Take these leaves with you, they might come in handy."

Pokzee walked out into the main town to see the burnt corpse of his dead wife on a stake. Nobody had touched it, not wanting to be infected by her evil spirit. He picked her up in his arms and took her to his home, where he buried her in his compound. He then climbed on his stallion and rode as fast as the wind without resting at any spot until he got to the Alloida boundary.

He immediately went to the Haku of Chief Vacoura. One of the two Omees at the gates answered with sarcasm.

"And who might you be?"

"Tell him Pokzee, son of Wadunko, General from Ogwashi."

There was a flicker of respect from the two Omees when he introduced himself. One of the Omees went to inform the chief.

As he waited he observed that Vacoura's quarters were nothing compared to Akuna's and he did not even see a single white man as he arrived, not even Arabians. The horses in the province were not as strong as their horses in Ogwashi. Women carried baskets on their heads to go to the market with their children on their backs.

Mother and child, he thought, my children will have no mother. Somebody is going to pay with blood.

The Omee returned. "The chief will see you tonight, but till then, I will lead you to where you will eat and rest."

Pokzee wanted to insist on seeing him immediately, but he knew there was a level you cannot cross with a man of higher respect.

As they walked away, Vacoura watched them from his quarters and told the Omee next to him to bring the envoy to him.

The envoy walked into the chief's conference room knowing something was wrong.

"My Envoy, how was your journey to Ogwashi?"

"My Chief...The Patient One." He bowed very low to show extended respect. "The feast was grand. With all the Ikas present, it could be the best I have ever participated in since I became envoy."

"You are wasting my time."

"A girl was raped, sir."

"Who was she?"

"Nkiru."

Vacoura burst out laughing. "Tell me it is not the barren woman who dances the fire dance and has slept with everybody I know."

"It is her, sir."

"Who is the fool who does not know that a dog in heat does not choose her man or he could not afford her?" the chief asked with laughter in his voice.

"It was Pokzee's wife."

The chief stopped laughing. "Are you trying to call me stupid?"

"No sir. She was a witch, so she turned into her husband and raped her out of jealousy. She confessed it."

"Envoy, I heard about the flamboyancy your wives are portraying. They put on glittering coral beads."

"They were given to me by Chief Akuna during the feast."

"But your wives wore them when you were away to let the market women know what coral beads should look like."

"I sent it for them during the feast."

"Let me see, you were away for four days. You went with a convoy of people so that should be at least a day's trip. So which day exactly did you send them to bring these beads? Because your last wife wore them on the day you left."

"My mistake, he gave it to me before I left," the envoy said, nodding as he corrected himself.

"You and I both know Akuna will never give you anything for free. I initially thought it was for transporting goods to him so he could sell to the Portuguese, but it seems there is another reason. So the choice is yours. Confess and save yourself being tortured to get everything out of you. Then you will be removed as envoy. You and your family will, of course, be banished from the province, or you make things easier for all of us."

"Chief Akuna gave me the beads for a favor."

"I do not have all day. What was the favor?"

"It was a personal favor, sir."

"I understand." Vacoura snapped his fingers and two guards came forward. "Cut my Ika's thumb and his middle finger."

"The Patient One, what are you telling these men to do?"

The two Omees pinned the envoy on the floor, brought out their knives, and sliced his fingers from his hand while the envoy screamed at the top of his lungs.

"Stick a cloth in his mouth. He is blocking my ears." The Omees immediately stuffed a rag in his mouth.

"Look at what this avaricious fool has done to my floor. Do you not have any sympathy for the people that work here? Just imagine him allowing his blood to pour all over. In fact, cut the whole hand off."

The envoy was kneeling and trying to beg with words, but his mouth was full. The Omees had pinned him down again as they wanted to slice off his hand.

"Wait! I think he is trying to say something. Remove the rag from his mouth," Vacoura ordered.

"Chief Akuna sent his messengers to me before the feast. He told me to bring a girl to Ogwashi who would announce rape publicly regarding Pokzee to inhibit his succession. He gave me horses, beads, and other gifts and due to my weak heart, I fell for the temptation. Everything was going well until his wife claimed the crime."

"So what happened to her?"

"She was burnt alive, but the woman was really a witch. Everyone saw her appear from smoke."

Vacoura looked him deeply in the eye and then faced his messengers and told them to bring Pokzee to his presence.

As Pokzee arrived, he bowed to the chief in the conference room. He saw the envoy on the floor with blood all over his hands and he was not positive, but it seemed like he was crying.

"I know why you have come and we accept the shame that our envoy has bestowed upon us," the chief said. "I have thought of over a hundred ways to replace your loss and this is the best I can do. I give to you Okonpoli, son of Aghinere, now the former envoy of Alloida, to be your slave, along with his wife and children. From now on they will be recognized as your slave."

"That is too much for me, Patient One. All I require is the envoy...I mean the former envoy."

"Then he is yours. Relax and enjoy the pride of Alloida."

"I wish I could, but my time is short. I have to leave now with my slave, with your permission."

"Take my staff so everyone you talk to will know that you speak with my blessing. When you come back, I want to be talking with a chief."

Pokzee put his slave on the horse and rode to Ogwashi without slowing down to breathe.

Immediately after he got to Ogwashi, he went to the chief's quarters. As he tried to pass through the gates, the Omees blocked him and ordered him to wait while they alerted the chief.

"I require you men to do me this favor as your friend, comrade and chief: Summon the elders. Tell them their presence is required by the chief, whilst my slave remains here."

"First of all, Pokzee, you will have to kill us before you pass these gates and secondly, you are not the chief," the Omee said fearlessly.

"I initiated you before you became an Omee. I saw the pride of the pain when you passed through it. I have no intentions of passing through the gates, but I am giving you a direct order as your Chief to go and call the elders. You are either for me or against me."

The two Omees stood looking at each other, then they faced Pokzee and said, "As our Chief requests." One of the Omees went on the errand.

The other Omee heard a scream, "AGAM OBODO UZO," and he saw smoke where Pokzee stood.

As Akuna was sleeping, he kept hearing his name and each time it got closer. When he opened his eyes, he saw Pokzee.

"How dare you come into my presence without announcing yourself."

"You took away my priceless gem."

Akuna bounced to his feet and walked toward the exit as he replied to Pokzee's biting words.

"Your wife was a witch and she got what she deserved."

"I never did you wrong. Why give me this pain?"

Akuna had gotten to the door and was trying to open it, but was locked.

"I don't understand what you are talking about."

"Confess. I brought the envoy with me."

"So what am I supposed to do, beg you? You are nothing. I faced great chiefs like Ezeonisha in gory times, and now you expect me to be scared of a baboon like you," the chief said with extreme confidence.

At that time there was banging on the door.

"The envoy has told us everything," the elders shouted through the door. "The soul of your wife will rest in peace. Open the door."

Pokzee looked at Akuna and walked toward the door.

"I know what is in your heart, Pokzee. You are grateful I helped you get rid of that pathetic excuse for a wife. I thought chimpanzees were ugly creatures until I met your wife."

Pokzee just stood there looking at him, but the fume of his anger heated the room.

"Thank goodness you are here. I always wanted to ask you, was your wife a chimpanzee?"

Pokzee roared. He couldn't take it any longer. He wanted to pounce on Akuna, but his legs were stuck to the floor and they could not move."

"You have to take life in small paces," Akuna's Tikpapa said while laughing.

"What is wrong, Pokzee? Do not tell me that the earth is too heavy for you," Akuna said, laughing heavily.

The banging on the door got louder.

"We do not have much time, Akuna, kill him."

"Why am I not surprised that even a chief has to put a spell on a fellow man like himself to kill him?

Would you not want to take me down and have it on your conscience that you dealt with me like a man?"

"Do I look stupid to you?" Akuna asked, picking up his knife.

"It is too late for you, Akuna. The envoy has told everyone what happened."

"You do not understand. If you die, the envoy will conveniently change his testimony on grounds of imposed confession through brutal force. The elders can't complain because I do not have a replacement, and if that archaic Vacoura sticks his nose into my business, then we go to war with his people. Is life not sweet, Tikpapa?"

There was no answer to the chief. Akuna turned around to find his sorcerer's head separated from his body.

"I hope I am not late," the Ifa priest spoke with his normal coolness.

"Your timing is impeccable."

Pokzee pounced like a cat on Akuna. The chief stabbed him in his shoulder before they fell on the floor. They grasped each other's neck, trying to choke one another.

"Pokzee, feel free to invite me when things get a little too rough," the Ifa priest said while eating a watermelon.

Akuna used his knees on Pokzee's groin, then stood up and hit him with a chair. Pokzee rose with the knife still in his shoulder and walked toward Akuna, who

197

ran to his sword. He pointed it at Pokzee, but the man kept coming at the same pace.

"My death will never be at your hands," were the last words Akuna spoke as he stabbed himself with the sword.

Pokzee stood for a while looking at the dead body of the chief. There was no sorrow, but worst of all, there was no joy in the revenge. He turned to thank the Ifa priest, but he had vanished.

Chapter 16

Chief Okon died ten years after Obi was made King and his grandson Oludu became the Chief of Ndemili. In the years Oludu ruled as chief, the province continued to prosper in the same way it did, under his predecessor. The King, knowing how independent he was, invited him to the palace to watch his first daughter, Ugonwa the Ada, perform The Dance of the Seven Fire Stars. Before the dance, there were other forms of entertainment like folksongs, feasts, and jocular acts.

Oludu knew this was definitely a ploy by the King to match him with his daughter, from whom most men seemed to run away. Some questioned how a woman so beautiful could choose to be alone. Others said she believes herself a man and fights like one, thus why her father loved her the most. A few said she was alone because she insisted on being the only wife.

People also whispered she was an Ogbanje, a possessed girl with psychic powers. They belong to the spirit world from birth and lived for a short time. Their link between the spiritual and reality is a package made up of anything they find precious and this package is hidden by the girl in a place where she will never remember. As long as the package was not found, she stayed alive.

Oludu did not believe in making wives out of women, instead he believed in loving them as concubines, so they were free to bring out their animalism. Most times he wished there were other species that could replace them. He knew they had the power to make the land of man a better place, but instead they gave birth to jealousy, envy, sorrow and tears. The only thing he could not understand was his greed for their touch, their body, their comfort, and their offspring. He had five children from different women for whom he provided everything they required except marriage.

A notable group of guests assembled around the room. Everyone squatted on mats placed over the animal hides as the beat of drums filled the room. A contained fire started to burn in a passageway, but nobody noticed. From nowhere Ugonwa's legs flowed through the fire. Every step she took followed the beat like a lioness seeking its prey. Every turn she made was like the earth turned with her.

As she twisted her waist and let her braids create their melody, it was as though an explosion was about to occur within every man. Her every curve stung the lust of every man watching. She began to sway like a drunk looking for his way home. All of a sudden the beat changed and with a rejuvenated firmness, she danced toward Oludu, watching her steps like a peacock. At that point, Oludu was looking into her eyes, but in a flash the beat ended, there was a large applause, and she rushed away.

Then Oludu understood why men traveled from afar to see her dance whenever she chose to, for her father. He turned to the King and said loudly for the remaining guests to hear, "I son of Okon, Oludu, Chief of Ndemili, would like to take your daughter Ugonwa to be my first wife."

As though he was talking to a child, the King said, "Sit down and stop shouting, you are blocking my ears."

With a stroke of shame, Oludu sat down reluctantly to aggravate him. In the most indifferent manner the King continued softly.

"Did you think I invited you all the way here to come and screen my daughter and see whether she is worthy to be your bride? I could snap my fingers and she would have over a hundred suitors."

"Then what brings me to such a beautiful land we call our capital?"

In a deep voice Gbangba said, "You never question your King. If he tells you to walk, you run. If he tells you to keep quiet you, cut your tongue. You are here to answer to commands and questions that are asked of you."

"Gbangba, try to relax. These are flexible times," the King said.

"I beg your forgiveness, oh Great King, if I altered my obeisance. It's the animal in my age." Oludu said, lying with a straight face.

"Forget all that rubbish. The Head-of-Government is still living in the past. Anyway, I didn't call you here to see if you would accept my daughter. I called you here to see if she would accept you. She happens to be a very stubborn human being and seriously raised out of the laws of tradition. It was due to her constant relations with the white missionary and his wife, who have infiltrated all kinds of crazy stories into her head. The gods knew why it had to be her of all my daughters to give me such pain in the head. If it was someone else I would have...anyway are you still interested?"

"More than ever, Your Majesty," said Oludu.

"My servant will take you to her. We await your reply," he said softly.

Oludu bowed and left.

When he had gone, the King turned to the Head-of-Government and said, "What do you think?"

"The boy is as dangerous as the Ifa said; his eyes did not leave mine when I spoke. The boy does not know what fear looks like. He is protected by a greater force than he can imagine. What makes you think your daughter will be able to control such a man?"

"Do you believe there is anything that walks and crawls on this earth that can make me do what I do not want to do?" the King asked.

"Unless the man with six legs," the Head-of-Government said.

"Well, Ugonwa doesn't have six legs and she does it to me all the time."

The closer he got to her house, the faster his heart beat. He wondered why he would be shivering to meet a common female, and he didn't understand how they duped him into begging for her hand in marriage. He was positive of it then—she was a witch.

As the servant knocked, the maid received them and asked them the purpose of their meeting.

"I, Chief Oludu, have come to see if your princess is worthy to be my wife."

"I am sorry sir, I will not be able to deliver that message."

Immediately a voice from behind the door said, "Don't worry, I already got the message. Let him in."

As he approached her quarters, the room was crowded with all sorts of women of all ages as it was the custom not to meet with a spinster with less than a dozen women present, unless she was a woman of high position in the society.

As he entered, she waved her hands to show him where to sit—an un-wifely characteristic. It was the woman who drew the seat for her man. As he sat down she said, "Yes." Another gaffe. A woman shouldn't speak to her man until she was spoken to.

"I know you are looking for a man who can look through your voluptuous body and love your tumultuous mind. You seek the powerful emotion of the white man, giving your man your dress to wear. I just called to say your dance was imposing and good luck in your quest."

"You are scared of me rejecting you," the princess said, grinning.

"What would give you that impression? I am a man of defined views and, as of now, I am positive you make my wine taste sour."

"Really? I might as well tell you anyway, my father had already told me to accept if you asked."

"If you listened to your father, I am sure you would have married any of your former suitors."

"Do I detect interest in the Great Chief Oludu?"

"Don't flatter yourself. It's that little word they call curiosity," Oludu said, walking toward the door.

"For your curiosity's sake, he has never asked me to marry anyone before. He just showed them the way to my place."

"Then what makes me so special?"

"That is what I want to find out," she said congenially.

"So, left to you, you would refuse any man who asked for your hand," Oludu said from the doorway.

"I never refused any of the men, I just had a little chat with them." Spontaneously, she clapped her hands and everyone in the room started leaving. "You seem uncomfortable; the seats are there to be sat on."

He knew that was exactly what she wanted, but he was not ready to flirt with custom because of this juvenile and be left in the room alone with her.

"Don't tell me the almighty Oludu is afraid to be alone with a little lamb like me. If it will make you feel better, I don't bite."

It was not as though anything would happen to him if he decided to alter such a law of minimal power, but if she decided to claim that he made an indecent approach to her, her word would be taken over his. He sat down anyway and said, "Talk, I am listening."

"I know people have been saying things about me, like the only person I answer to is my father, that I am an Ogbanje, I choose the flexibility of a man whilst I am a—"

Before she could say another word, Oludu interrupted.

"I don't participate in rumors."

"Well, I just wanted to let you know...they are not rumors, they are true."

He tried hard to resist showing surprise, but it showed in every inch of his face.

"I am an Ogbanje, a daughter of the spirit world. I am possessed with powers beyond my control. The only reason I have not returned to the spirit world in death is because my father holds me down here with a force greater than the one that wants to take me away."

"Then why...please continue," Oludu said.

"Then why does he not tell the Ifa priest to find the package that makes me return to that other world when they call?" she said, finishing his question with the same grin on her face.

He was no longer surprised, now he was more cautious.

"You should know by now that people like us read your mind and see your future just by looking through your walls. The Ifa priest could not find my package because the spirits that led me to where I dug the package are the same spirits that lead him to see what he sees even without his eyes."

"So where is this package?"

"You intrigue me, Chief Oludu. It would require a great force on me to reveal where I dug it because even I cannot remember where I put it."

"But you said your father had a greater power than what holds you here."

"The power he had that I was referring to is the type," her voice lowered, "that makes a dove fly through all the skies and still comes back to its nest. It's the power that makes a bat enter a cave with hundreds of other screaming bats and yet it still knows which cry belongs to its offspring. It's the power that makes a chicken go after a hawk that took its chick. The power I said he had cannot make my tomorrow better, but it can make me go to bed at the end of every night and appreciate the day I am about to let go of. Chief Oludu, I think you better go back to your quarters for the night, you have an early journey tomorrow."

She got up and opened the door for him.

"I thought you read minds. Why don't you know that I cannot leave here without you?"

"I can be an expert at words from a man's mind, but I am an amateur at the words from a man's heart."

"Am I to understand that as long as I ask your hand in marriage, you cannot reject me?"

"Yes."

He made a slight bow and said, "I am yours if you will have me."

The words started running faster as though their time to talk was limited and danger was knocking on the door.

"You realize that you can never marry any other woman apart from me, or else you will die along with the first son I bear for you."

"When I saw you dance, I realized that my life was empty. The time I have stayed with you I have experienced a fullness not of this earth. With you I will need no other to fill the emptiness I feel within."

"You realize that my life is transient. I cannot live for long," she explained.

"Then we make the best of every day that passes us by." The firmness of Oludu's voice intensified.

"Maybe you don't understand: I will go to the land beyond immediately after I hear that call in my dreams. It could be after thirty years or tomorrow. You do not deserve that kind of torture."

"Let me be the man to choose the torture I can or cannot take. The question here is whether you want me or not, because if you don't, the King will never know that you refused me. I will just walk up to him and tell him that your voice was louder than the echoes of a cave," Oludu said with a smile.

She looked at him with all the seriousness that he did not believe she could exhibit and said.

"I crave for you more than the sun wants to shine," she said. "You touch my soul in places unreachable to any man. I never believed I could look at another apart from my father and feel I was a female, but you make me realize that I am a woman. And the scary thing is, your stories are all that drew me to you. Now is the first time I have seen you, but not the first time I have known you."

He stretched his hands and said, "Then come with me. This is no longer your home."

She held his hand and they walked away, together.

BOOK
2

Chapter 1

After the twentieth year of King Obi's rule, the Okpalaukwu died at the age of ninety-two. During the burial of an Okpalaukwu, an initiation ceremony of his successor is carried out simultaneously. People danced on the grave of the dead high chief while his successor was locked in seclusion until the ceremony was over.

King Obi mysteriously died the day after, with the Head-of-Government and the Headman to the Oracle by his side. For the King to be buried, his successor was to be the first person to pour sand on the body in his tomb. The longer it took for a new King to be crowned, the more people died and the easier it was for neighboring kingdoms to attack, so the people always cried for a new King.

The kingdom at this time had two princes who were contesting the throne. Such circumstances could only be allowed if the high chiefs permitted it. The first was Weruche's son, who had the dilemma of being born an unofficial prince and, by the time the king married his mother and he was officially a prince, another had already been noted as the first. The second was Onyela's son, who was the first acknowledged prince of the kingdom, but not the first son. The high chiefs in such circumstances acted like watchers, waiting till the eighty-second day for a unanimous decision from all the province chiefs. After that, if they all didn't choose the same King, the high chiefs killed the chiefs and picked whomever they wanted to be King on that same day.

During those eighty-two days, if a King wasn't chosen, the chiefs were exempt from the ruling of the high chiefs. They had the power to battle and conquer a province, putting whomever they wanted to rule. It was an opportunity for the lords to give their sons a chance at power, beating the inability of passing the chieftaincy position to their children, which only occurred when the King and the people of the province agreed. That was a very rare occurrence. Everyone knew the chiefs would take advantage of this time, when gods bleed.

There were six provinces at this time and six chiefs— Ihua of Ahoda, Otuturex of Abogima, Oludu of Ndemili, Vacoura of Alloida, Pokzee of Ogwashi and Odagwe of the Ekpona Hills. All the chiefs were supposed to come together to the palace on the seventh day after the death of the King.

In such a quandary where there were two contenders for the throne, the princes had their Hurdenes draw up any political scheme. The Hurdene was usually the person the King candidate trusted the most. The Hurdene always went out of his or her way to make sure their candidate became King. The Hurdene had powers overriding his or her candidate when he became King, unless the candidate was over fifteen years of age. The Hurdene could be his brother, his friend, his relative, his wife, but most kings always chose their mother. If one of the contesting princes was not chosen, both the prince and his Hurdene were immediately put to death by the high chiefs to prevent any form of treachery, so the Hurdenes normally fought till death to get their candidates crowned.

After the King's death, the fastest messengers were sent to the six provinces to invite them together for either a quick decision to be made about the King's heir or a longer one that could extend for not more than eighty-two days.

On the seventh day the palace was drained of all its vitality. Every woman in it had her hair shaved as a symbol of disowning her beauty with the death of the husband. The King's palace was still with its flawless panache and the structure awaited its new master. Most times a new King built another palace at a site where he would feel safer, thereby creating a new capital province.

Everyone in the palace was expecting the high chiefs and the chiefs to arrive. It was evident that they were taking advantage of the death of the King to exercise the flexibility of their powers. The King's first wife, Queen Ifrareta, was preparing the palace for their arrival. Due to her slightly bulky nature, her pregnancy was not too obvious. She was a very ordinary looking brown-skinned woman and she loved her position. She could have sent over a hundred maids to prepare the palace, but she chose to do it with them, notwithstanding the fact that she was six months pregnant. Throughout her preparation, she still did not let anyone know that she was in the vicinity.

Chapter 2

The first to arrive was Chief Ihua of Ahoda, who was still firmly built and unusually agile for his age. His people always complained of his age and each time this occurred he conquered a new village to rekindle their trust. To those whose voices were too loud, he sweetened their throats with the finest palm wine from the forest of the black sky. Once in a while he put a little poison in it. He had seen over sixty years, but he could not imagine giving up his chieftaincy to do anything else. He couldn't become Okpala because he wasn't the oldest man in the province. Neither could his son take his place, as only an Omee of great respect could take that position and it wasn't hereditary.

Why should I give up my title to become one of the elders of Ahoda, not even Utagba? To imagine that the elders are not allowed to sleep with other women outside their wedlock. May the gods forbid me that punishment. I know what to do. After this King succession problem I will go and get that enthusiastic warrior, that bloody son-of-a-palm-wine tapper and I will deal with him personally. Imagine the peasant wants to be a chief. Come to think about it, this succession thing might be to my advantage, but those old dismantled, dirty elders of the King's court might bring up this chief issue. Why am I bothering myself? By then I should be talking to the King.

He saw a calabash of water and went to wash his hands. His reflection flashed before his eyes and he realized that it was not only his youth that had passed away; the heart of the Omee that became the chief had sailed to a place he could not reach. He looked around at the emptiness of the castle, and it sent chills down his spine in fear that it could be a trap.

Someone might have told the King about the slave transactions I had with the Portuguese. Then he makes me believe he is dead. I doubt that. They were too few for him to have noticed. It could be that palm wine tapper's son who went behind my back to set me up. Anyway, if they want to attack us, my Omee and I will fight to the end.

He sighed and scanned the room.

I should stop deceiving myself. With only two hundred men, my bones would be fed to the vultures.

When he heard the sound of horses, a relief grew upon him.

Thank goodness, it is not a trap. I wonder who it is. It's not as though it prevents what is going to happen from happening. I have seen their voracious eyes over the pride of my land.

The next to arrive was Otuturex of Abogima. When he entered, there wasn't the crowd of hypocrites that normally surrounded him, or the dance of a thousand coquettes. It was accepted for now because this was a time of death. He was a big-boned man with a thick beard and he had a sluggish way of walking. Although the quietness of the palace made him realize that anything could happen, he wasn't called Otuturex the Conqueror for nothing and he didn't carry over a thousand men for decoration.

Why would they want to kill me anyway? I send them my normal taxes, which happens to be larger than what I am supposed to give. Probably their eyeballs want to stretch into to the vastness of my land. They were always jealous of my attachment to the King. They probably want to bring up that issue about that mysterious death of former Chief Ezeonisha. How can they even think about suspecting I killed a man who was more than a father to me, the first man to show me how to hold a spear? In fact, let me hear the first person to utter a word about it; I will bite his tongue out of his mouth. Then they will know that those who stick their fist in dirt usually get their fingers dirty.

The deeper he walked into the palace, the stronger the reality of the death opened to him, and he thought back to the first time he saw the King.

*

216

He was only eight years old. A man ran into the house soaked with water from the sky and blood from the flesh. He searched all the rooms as though he was looking for something in his own home. The child wanted to scream for his stepfather to throw this intruder out, but the look in the man's eyes, even for a child, was fearsome. Otuturex took it personally that his presence as a child made him not worth noticing. The intruder suddenly started climbing to the top of the room. The boy at this time was positive of two things: the first was that he hated their moving to this isolated place at the boundary between Ozuoba forest and Utagba; and secondly he made a mistake by not following his mother out.

The boy watched as the man climbed to the rafters, holding firm to them with a knife in his mouth. When the man noticed him, they studied each other from different heights. Suddenly, the home was surrounded by six Omees armed with swords, knives, bows and arrows.

His stepfather ran to the door of the room with bewilderment in his face.

"Great warriors of good fortune, what brings you to my humble home?"

"We are in search of a rebel and we have reason to believe that he is seeking refuge here."

"Honorable Omee, do you try to soil my name? I am an honest trader between the two boundaries. Why would I want to take a man who wants to rebel against an Omee? It seems you are not aware that my brother is Chief Ezeonisha."

"He is a rebel against the King and our orders come from the Head-of-Government. Please step aside, we want to search the house."

With disgraced humility his stepfather moved aside and the Omee searched everywhere on the ground without looking above.

"Where are the other inhabitants of your home?"

"My wife and her sister went to see their mother and I am alone with the boy."

"You mean you have only one wife and a child?"

"My other two wives couldn't give birth to children and they convinced themselves that I had problems, so they left."

"Why would they think so when you already have a child?"

"The child was by another man."

The warrior grinned and continued.

"Have you seen anyone around here?"

"Not a soul."

"How about the boy?"

"I don't know. I was not with him."

"What is his name?'

"Otuturex."

The Omee walked toward the boy and asked, "Have you seen any stranger recently?"

The boy used all his willpower not to look up because the man they sought was hanging horizontally above him with a knife in his mouth.

"Is that supposed to be a jest? Nobody ever comes to this area and I am sure my mother is not coming back here again," the boy said.

"Would you shut up," the stepfather snapped.

The Omee laughed.

"If I were you, I would not talk to the little one like that or else he, too, will leave you for more fertile soil."

Everyone laughed except his stepfather, who burned with rage.

The boy, meanwhile, had spotted blood on the floor; above him, the strange man was trying to shield his cut hand. The boy knew that sooner or later the warrior would notice, so spontaneously he grabbed the warrior's knife and cut the Omee's hand.

"Is something wrong with you?" his stepfather shouted.

The Omee held his hand, speechless and shocked.

"It seems you are not man enough to raise a child. Let me teach him that manners are part of our custom," said another Omee, who gave the boy a slap on the face.

The boy got up and stuck his tongue out to the warrior. With anger for the child's unrepentant response, the Omee used his large palm and struck him again on his face. This time the boy landed on his back and slid on the floor. The boy shed the kind of tears that came from a mature man, but a sound did not come from his mouth. He got up again and pointed the knife at the Omee.

"I am so scared. The boy has a knife and wants to kill me," the Omee said.

Everyone laughed.

There was a burning look in the boy's eyes, then all of a sudden he started laughing and everyone else stopped. He took the knife and cut his own hand, still laughing. Then he turned in circles.

The Omees watched the apparently possessed child with a combination of pity and fear. An Omee was trained to face anything physical, but anything of a spiritual nature always scared them. They tried not to walk out of the house too quickly, or else rumors would spread that they ran from a child.

His stepfather, with the last paternal strength in him, said to the boy after the Omees had quickly walked away, "It's time for you to go to bed."

To his amazement, the boy went to bed with blood dripping from his hand. From that day he watched every word he spoke to the child. As the boy went to bed with finger marks on his face, he was impressed with the act he had pulled. He re-enacted how he saw a possessed girl turn in that cyclic manner when he went to the market with his mother.

In the dead of the night while the young Otutrex pretended to sleep, someone woke him up. The man untied the cloth around his palm to show a bleeding hole and then took the boy's hand that was bleeding and merged their blood together. With a final glance he disappeared into the night.

To imagine that the man he helped was the King—King Obi.

*

"Otuturex the Conqueror!"

"Who is that man who calls my name and stands on his feet?"

" It is I." Ihua banged his chest with his fist. "Ihua of Ahoda."

"The Immortal, you stand firmer than I."

"Stop flattering me. I am an old man."

"You insult the ancestors that a man with such juvenile vitality calls himself old."

"Anyway, how are your people?"

"They are all fine. I hear that the immortal is still expanding."

The stupid pompous fool could not even wait till we finished with the matters of our beloved King before stylishly bringing up the issue of his third wife's village. I thought he said she was a witch.

"Forget all that rubbish people are saying. We are still a small province, but it doesn't stop any of these ambitious warriors from wanting to take my chieftaincy title from me. Do they realize what it is to kill a rhinoceros with your bare hands?"

This old monkey is beginning to cross the line. Prove to me that you have four heads to speak what

222

dangles in your mind. Let me polish your skull with my sword, the younger chief thought.

"I have a couple of them in my province, men who dip their hands in fire knowing what the pain feels like, but wanting a possession that they cannot afford to handle."

This fool is getting on my nerves. I should bend him down and give him twenty lashes from a tangerine cane. He is lucky he came to the capital as though they called him for a battle, or else I would have dealt with his young blood. I should be careful though, if I say too much, they might decide to end me here.

"Forgive me, I forgot to congratulate you on your new born son," Ihua said with a rejuvenated smile on his face.

Who does the old monkey think he can seduce with that kind of woman-talk? Does he care about his own children before asking about mine? If I were the old fool, I would have disappeared from the face of the earth. Apart from that, I am positive every other Chief has his eyes on the salt of his land. During the meeting I will publicly declare war on Ihua first, before someone else beats me to it… I am good at what I do.

"Otuturex, are you okay? I inquired about your son and you were lost in thought."

"Please forgive me. It is just dawning to me that we lost a great King."

"Who has arrived?"

"I really cannot see." He tried peering down at the battalion. "But from this distance, the man carries the flamboyance of a peacock. It could be The Python."

Chapter 3

The Python was Chief Odagwe of the Ekpona Hills. His province was the largest and estimated the strongest, and the inhabitants of his province were known for their heartlessness. When he was told the King was dead, he wondered why he was not filled with bliss instead of a slight trace of sorrow.

Walking into the palace, passing the empty rooms and mourning faces, he thought, It is not as though I was ever in Obi's favor.

The ungrateful son-of-a-fool. I still remember how I saved the fool's life in battle. My blood stretched through the fields of the lands he called his kingdom and what did he repay me with. When the war was over, he says to me with that evil grin, "Odagwe go straight forth to where the sun touches the end of my kingdom at the Ekpona Hills. Your province extends to that point to replace the land I have taken from you."

If I didn't have any respect for him, I would have spat in his face. But I, The Python, went to the end of Utagba and stretched its tentacles to areas over the hills, where men feared to step. I proliferated the kingdom into extensive power and what did I get in return—my taxes were increased over tenfold. Did I complain? No. Did I plan a coup? No. Instead he sent his despotic friend who exacerbates every inch of me to be my envoy. Imagine the conceited bastard having the audacity to think I did him wrong because he was the King. He took my sweet wine that came from the fruits of goodness away from me. The thought still pierces my heart till now, the satisfaction he derived from what was rightfully mine.

Chief Odagwe surveyed the palace like an eagle seeking its prey. The farther into the palace he went, the more the environment disgusted him. He hadn't seen any of the chiefs. Can you imagine this vagrant group of chiefs? They have not arrived. They are expecting me, The Python, to sweep the floor they will sit upon.

"The Python of the Ekpona Hills," Chief Ihua called out.

"The Immortal of Ahoda," Odagwe replied.

"The feathers of your gayness radiated the skies before you arrived."

"If there was a man that had a sweeter tongue than yours, he hasn't yet been born."

"You flatter an old man."

"Otuturex."

"Odagwe."

"They should have informed me that we were coming for battle and I could have brought my wives."

"Your sarcasm still grows with your age. They came to give sacrifice to the Okonta shrine."

"I wonder what is happening these days. The bat thinks he can see with the sun; now he tells me 'my sarcasm grows with my age,'" Odagwe said in a resonant tone.

"Do I tell a lie?" Otuturex asked.

"You hide behind your legion of females who call themselves Omee. If I have to listen to another single note of disrespect coming from your arrogant lips, you will not see the next sunlight."

"I shiver with fear. Maybe the thought has sailed through your memory, but I am chief and that means there is nothing that walks and crawls on this earth that I pay allegiance to except my King. Even when I was an Omee, it was solely to my chief. So don't think you can come over here, look me in the eye, and expect me to be mollified by anything you say."

"Remember what we came here for," Ihua said.

"Otuturex, I hope your blade is as sharp as your tongue."

"That is for you to find out."

As swift as a panther, Otuturex drew his sword. Odagwe stood wickedly looking at him. Both sets of Omees in the palace protecting their chiefs also pulled their swords. The entire scenario was just a show of ego. Otuturex wanted Odagwe to know he was mortal; the only blood that could drop in the palace had to be at the hands of the King.

"Otuturex, that will cost both of you two herds of cattle," the Ifa priest said in a soft tone, appearing from behind the throne.

High chiefs had the power to invoke an authority on any of the chiefs if they disobeyed any of the laws. The Ifa priest despised hedonism, as was expected from a man of his position. It was believed that he was ubiquitous, so people with abhorrent thoughts about the King always watched their tongues. Usually, in his free time, he did a little spiritualism with the dead. The slightest glimpse in his direction let him see into a person's soul.

All the chiefs had heard the same story of how he became the Ifa priest. They were told that before taking the place of his predecessor, he was ordered to hunt down and kill every single member of his lineage—men, women and children.

At night he came in the form of an eagle and claimed those who fled. Some tried hiding under the protection of freelance warlocks. After he had killed everybody with direct contact to his bloodline, he took out a knife and removed his two eyeballs. He burnt them and gave them as sacrifice to the oracle. Myth or reality, none of the chiefs had heard any other version. One thing was for sure, with the blindness, nothing passed him.

"The great Ifa, you should forgive my actions in your presence, but the puppy thinks he can bark like a dog," Odagwe said stoically.

"Ifa, even in your presence he called me a dog," Otuturex responded, fuming.

"But Ifa, I didn't see you come in through the door," Ihua purred.

All the chiefs looked at Ihua with disgust. Nobody ever knew where the Ifa priest appeared from and nobody ever asked. It was the Ifa priest's way of telling them they had no secrets. Most times the King sent him to act as his personal hit man in case any of the chiefs stepped out of line, but for the King to kill a chief required an agreement from all the high chiefs. In order to prevent the perilous movement of a king's or chief's warlock, they always showed only their liege the loophole to their destruction.

Ignoring Ihua, the Ifa priest said with the same indifferent manner, "I want them in the shrine after the coronation. Where are the other chiefs? Do they expect us to wait for the sun to go on holiday before they arrive?"

"I thought the same thing myself when I arrived," Odagwe said.

This High Chief title is beginning to get to this aging ape's head because Obi is dead, Odagwe thought. First I had to listen to this infant-born-yesterday insult me. Now this blind man is talking as though he is God. He is lucky I came for something that required my presence, or else—

"I hope that they did not collide with an unfortunate accident," Otuturex said with a suspicious stare at Odagwe.

Then Chief Oludu came in and said, "What are we waiting for?" as though he was there all along.

Oludu was average size, with small eyes and wide nostrils, a slim face and dreadlocks. Chief Oludu ruled over Ndemili with a subtle manner and a dangerous mind. His true self was incognito. When the King was alive, it was Oludu whom the Ifa priest said was not palpable. He gave an insouciant impression, thus no one really knew. He was the only chief in the past hundred years who took the position from his father.

When Oludu was eleven, he went with some hunters in the forest. During their chase for their prey, they left him behind. By the time they returned he was in the same spot with a dead boar in his hand. Nobody ever asked him how he did it, not even his grandfather, the late Chief Okon.

"Am I surrounded by men of respect who are supposed to lead men through the dark, or bats that don't know the way home?" the Ifa priest exclaimed.

As the Ifa priest spoke, Otuturex thought, He should know.

In a flash the Ifa priest turned to Otuturex. "Or are my words too small to be heard, Otuturex?"

"Only a fool would believe that your words are not strong enough to hold an ocean," Otuturex grunted.

"By the way, Chief Vacoura is on his way here. We were both held up by the muddy soil from the Choba Lake. His party was immediately behind ours," Oludu said.

"Correct yourself, Oludu, I am not on my way here. I am already here. The Great Ifa, The Immortal Ihua, Odagwe the Python, Otuturex the Conqueror, Oludu the Untouchable, men of the King's court, I greet you all."

He gave them the traditional handshake, which involved the men hitting their hands sideways twice before a firm grasp at the elbow; Vacoura did so in order of age. The Ifa priest was exonerated from the chief's handshake because only people of equal respect and those of lower authority participated.

The Okpalaukwu entered the conference room unaided by anyone. Everyone rose and bowed to give respect, except the Headman to the Oracle who pretended not to notice him. Left to himself, the Okpalaukwu would have distributed a handshake, but he knew that liberty required him being at least ten years younger, so instead he just gave a slight wave as he was helped to sit down by his men.

"Are we all here?" he asked.

"The only people absent are the Head-of-Government and Chief Pokzee," Ihua responded.

"The Head-of-Government is with Queen Ifrareta. When we are all complete he will join us," the Ifa priest said.

So they don't want to kill me after all, Otuturex thought.

"So where is Pokzee?" Okpalaukwu asked.

"I am here, Immovable Okpala of Utagba. I got held up by my in-laws. You know how these things happen," he said, smiling.

When he looked around, he realized he was the only person with a smirk on his face. He begrudging hailed chiefs Okpala, Ifa and Vacoura. He did not bother to greet any of the other chiefs because he wanted them to realize that they were of no use to him and, if they wanted to start a fire burning, he was ready. After the Akuna incident, he didn't care what anybody thought.

Chapter 4

The tall, wide-shouldered, one-eyed Head-of-Government walked to a spot where everyone could see him and began to speak.

"Now that we are all here, the egg can hatch. My fellow high chiefs, the chiefs of Utagba, it is my solemn duty as Head-of-Government of Utagba to address you men as our King is dead. The wing of the eagle has been cut down and it is time for it to grow another. We are all aware that there are two Hurdenes. Even our late King knew this would be. I am sure that you men are aware of the custom, but due to the etiquette of the land, I will repeat the laws governing the coronation.

"For the coronation, only the chiefs are involved in the decision-making. You have from now until the eighty-second moonlight to tell us your unanimous decision. If, by any chance, a general conclusion is not reached by the six chiefs, you will all be executed, whilst we choose whomever we see fit. From now till the eighty-second day of the King's death, you are kings in your land. Do not abuse the powers laid on you. When the goose hatches more than one egg, who are we to ask it why? If the same sky that wets us with waters from the heaven opens up and scorches us with rays from the sun, do we dare ask it why? Let me tell the tale now and leave the folksong for storytellers. There are two Hurdenes with qualified candidates for the succession and both of them are here to address you. The first will be Onyela, daughter of Imasuen, the palm wine tapper."

Odagwe smiled and made himself more comfortable as she came into the room. Onyela grew prettier as she grew older and the gracious aura was still with her. She knelt as she spoke.

"Infallible high chiefs, I humbly come to address you, the great Chiefs of our time. With optimum respect I come to your presence."

"Rise and speak," the Head-of-Government gestured to her with his hands. All the eyes of the seated men were on her.

"Honorable men of the King's court, I am in your distinguished presence in lieu of the apotheosis of our King. For men of your esteem and caliber, I apologize in repeating the customs of the land to you. We are all aware from the first time the sun touched this great kingdom of ours that the man to be King has to be the first prince accepted by the capital and kingdom. The prince I gave birth to belonged to me for only nine months and that was when I carried him in my belly. Immediately after his eyes opened to the world, he belonged to the people of Utagba. He was raised fed, dressed and trained to be your King since he was born. This other child that is infected with a criminal's blood—"

"Watch your words, woman," the Ifa priest reprimanded her.

"Forgive me, oh great Ifa. My son may have seen only ten years of harvest, but his heart is that of a King. When the King first summoned me before I became his bride, I wondered what he would want from the daughter of a peasant and palm wine tapper. He asked me to cook for him and I was perplexed because he did not know me well enough to trust me with such a deed. When I had finished, he did not even ask his taster to taste the meal, he just started eating and asked me to join him. When he finished eating, he asked me if I would give birth to the next King. I said no because I was betrothed to another and he escorted me to where his guards were and told me he would continue asking every day until I got married to my betrothed. I went home with respect for a good King."

The grin in Odagwe's face had disappeared and at this point a very edgy feeling was tickling his spine. He knew that every chief would derive satisfaction from what she had to say. She is probably going to say it is because she knows I will never let her son be King as long as I am alive. Probably that is the reason she seeks my death. I am impressed.

"I was under a force that was greater than I and then I knew it was my destiny to bear your King. The gods gave the King only two sons and from the two only one can be King. Search deep into your hearts without losing the slightest details because the choice you make does not only affect you men of the King's house, but the commoners, peasants, women and children, not for now, but with the length of time.

"Yesterday I was the daughter of a palm wine tapper. I could run in the fields of the earth and nobody would ask me why. Now I am Queen, and I have to watch what I say because people listen. I have to watch where I go because people follow. If my son is to become King, for the rest of his life he has to always look back, or else someone will be there, waiting for him. The problems of every single person in this kingdom will become his. He will not be able to hold his children like a father, but like a King. I am sure you wonder why I am here then. I chose to be Queen because it was my destiny and my son shall be King because it is his destiny. No matter how you try, you can never run away from your destiny."

She bowed and left the room.

The grin on Ihua's mouth continued to stretch as his thoughts dangled.

Sweet words. They could not have been better said by anyone else, but the antelope will not go and seek refuge with the lionesses in their den. If only Weruche did not come from Ahoda, I would have chosen Onyela's son to be my King. I am not getting any younger and the mother of a King with the same background as myself is the best token for better days, especially if she knows I voted him King.

"We have heard from the first Hurdene and now we will hear from the second, Weruche, daughter of

Isagba," Gbangba announced, and an Omee echoed it to her outside the room.

She walked in with an immortal combination of beauty and power notwithstanding her shaven hair. She bowed genteelly and began.

"The great high chiefs of our time, the stable chiefs of our future, I have a story to tell and I hope you will open your hearts to understand that it involves a primordial law that goes back before the birth of even the Okpalaukwu.

"Our late King had sixteen children and only two sons, of which we are bound by law to observe our customs. It is no secret that I was married to a criminal, but it does not change the fact that the first-born son of the King is the rightful heir. Forget all the alterations that changing generations have created. What has made us great has been the tradition that was passed on to us from generation to generation. Nowadays our customs have to be altered because I became a queen late, or probably politics is reconstructing our traditions. We never ask ourselves why things are the way they are because it would destroy those little things that we take advantage of. I am not in denial of the fact, both in my mind and heart, that my son is your King, but even if he is not to be better than his competitor, who is two whole years younger than him, has anyone thought of the wrath of the gods for such an attenuating action? Let us all think about it. If there was to be a tilt in the succession, why has the oracle not sent a message down to us on the alteration?"

"You should stay away from statements regarding the oracle because even when King Obi ruled, the oracle stopped sending messages to us," the Head-of-Government directed her.

"But the oracle always opened the way for the King, if there were scales blocking our eyes," she continued talking, not looking at the Head-of-Government.

"Well, woman, you have a point, but have you not noticed that the oracle also neglected your son? Do you have anything more to say?" the Ifa priest asked.

She nodded and continued. "I was married to a criminal I cherished and respected, but I slept with and married the King when he asked me to—not because I wanted to sleep with and marry him, but because custom demands I obey my King. That is why you men of our time should put my son as your King because our custom demands it."

She bowed and walked away.

When she left the conference room, she was directed to another room to await the chiefs' decision. Onyela was seated in front of her.

"Weruche, how is your day so far?" Onyela asked with a wicked grin

"Onyela, believe me when I tell you today smells like roses in the stars. How about your own day?"

"My day flows in the direction of perfection. It seems we both have a confidently good day so far, but by the end of the day one of us will not be smiling."

"I am sorry to break your shortsighted illusions, but there is no way those men will make a decision today."

"That I know, but my heart will pump like this until they do⌐—be it days, weeks, months."

"You cannot blame them. This is their chance to build their colony the way they want to, without the intervention of the King and the high chiefs."

"I have to admit, if I was a chief, I probably would do the same and tell the Head-of-Government to eat my feces." The two women laughed.

"Onyela, forgive my directness, but what makes you imagine that your son can be King?"

"Weruche, Weruche, Weruche, you are missing the message. There is nothing to imagine—my son is King."

"I admire your optimism but the frog enters water because it knows it can swim. You have a chief vouching for your son."

"I am impressed by your tactical deduction. Am I supposed to believe that you don't have a chief on the inside vouching for your son?"

"The touch of power has always tangled my spine, and now I have the chance to hold it in my hand."

"Weruche you are diving too deep into your dream. May I remind you that even if your son is the chosen one, he becomes King and not you?"

"Don't play naive with me, Onyela, both our sons are children under the guardianship of their Hurdene."

"Let's not drift away from the facts. From this day, these chiefs are going to distribute blood on the grounds of the kingdom and their wars might proceed to the last day. We both have secrets we deny, but this war that will come is neither between the chiefs nor the princes. It really is between you and me."

"Now that we are open with each other, I might as well tell you, I hated you then because of your subtle manipulative manner and I hate you now even more."

"I am flattered and may I add that I feel exactly the same way about you." They both laughed again.

"So what do we do now?"

"We wait for the men to realize they can't make a decision today."

"Chiefs of this great kingdom, we have heard from the two Hurdenes and it is time to reach a conclusion. You men can give a unanimous decision and prevent yourselves the problem of catching a snake by the tail. As of now we, the high chiefs, will excuse you men so you can have your privacy," the Head-of-Government said, then left with the other high chiefs.

"Fellow chiefs, I feel it is better for us to get to a conclusion now because by the time we leave here without a general decision, we might get to understand that it is not easy for an ostrich to fly," Ihua said, standing.

"I wish it could be as easy as you put it, Ihua, but the fact that you want Weruche's son to be King does not necessary mean we all share your opinion," Vacoura responded.

"Vacoura, are you trying to imply that I came here with a biased mind? We all are aware of how your bark softens to the roar of a lion. Weruche is from the same place as you and we all know your—"

"Shut up, you archaic excuse for a chief. Before you knew what an Omee was, I was a chief," Ihua spat back with a rejuvenated ego.

Vacoura is beating me to it. I have to look for an excuse to declare war on Ihua before he does, Otuturex thought as the men bickered.

"Are you, Ihua, telling me, Vacoura, to shut up? The moonlight at night! The burning sun in the sky!" Vacoura said, hitting his chest.

"Chiefs, there is no need for all this hostility. Whatever you men have in mind, settle it amicably. By the way, Otuturex, please choose the day you will prepared for battle so I can attack," Odagwe said indifferently.

"You seem to have prepared your decision before coming here. Or is there something I don't know?"

"Do I make you quiver, Otuturex?"

"You amaze me, Odagwe. What makes you think I would allow you to attack? As the moon goes to bed on the fourteenth day, we will strike at the Ekpona Hills."

Otuturex's words came out as fast as his heart pumped and his head kept trying to understand what made Odagwe speak with conviction.

"Young man, I advise you to let me attack because your men cannot know the hills of our land. I would not want to defeat you flawlessly, or else Ezeonisha will be angry in his grave that he was killed for nothing," Odagwe said condescendingly.

"The anxiety to taste your blood on my sword is making me thirsty."

"Now that we are aware that we are not going to get to a unanimous decision, I would like to know when we go into battle Ihua, or else you choose to apologize for your abrupt words," Vacoura said.

"Will the thirtieth day from now be okay for you?" Ihua said with a pride lacking strong foundation.

"Unquestionably perfect timing," Vacoura replied.

"I do not intend to hide my intentions, but Vacoura's enemy is my enemy. Who plans battle with him, plans with me, so I declare myself initiated in this war against Ihua," Pokzee said.

"I see Vacoura is too weak to fight alone, so he needs help from Pokzee to fight like a man. As they say, the stronger the war the greater the battle," Ihua said, still with a smile on his face.

"Is it not amazing that today you smile and very soon I and Vacoura will witness the tears of an old man?" Pokzee said.

"You do not seem to understand that I need more spaces of power to fill in my offspring and I am grateful for you participating. I would have liked the world to know that I can deal with both of Vacoura and you alone. But Oludu and I will do it," Ihua said.

"Oludu never mentioned that he was involved in this battle, old man, so if you are looking for a means to beg, we would understand that you are old and your time has passed," Pokzee said, staring at Oludu's resistive look and Ihua's wicked smirk.

"Unfortunately for your naive mind, Oludu and I are now involved in a joint trade opening our borders for items like salt, iron, beads, ivory and gold."

Immediately, Oludu's expression changed from awe to assuredness.

"Let me understand this. Is the great Pokzee scared of Oludu? Okay, if it will make you feel better, I will battle with both of you alone," Ihua said with a sarcasm that could cripple any ego.

"How can I be afraid of a man who lives under the voice of a woman? I will defeat him anytime he is ready, whether it be thirty days from now, tomorrow, or even right now," Pokzee responded angrily.

"No rush, Pokzee, thirty days will be sufficient. Now that we have reached a conclusive phase in this meeting, I think this meeting is adjourned," Oludu said.

All the chiefs got up and left the conference room with dark expressions and audible curses. Leaving the palace, Oludu took Ihua's arm and whispered into his ear, "How did you know I would go into battle in the interest of this trade?"

"I didn't. It was the only option I had before I dipped my hand into suicide."

"If there is anything you need for your battle with Vacoura, remember my borders are open to you," Oludu murmured.

"I will keep that in mind and I hope you remember that my own borders are open to you, just in case. But by the way, which Hurdene are you backing?" Ihua asked as they approached their carriages.

"I have not made up my mind yet," Oludu replied and left with his Omees.

As the chiefs left the palace the three high chiefs sat nearby under a palm kernel tree, drinking palm wine.

"Fools," the Head-of-Government said as he watched the chiefs depart.

"What happens now?" the Okpalaukwu asked, holding tight to his walking cane.

"We wait to see when gods bleed," the Ifa priest said, picking up sand and rubbing it on his palms.

"I know I am supposed to be the wisest man here but how can a god bleed?" the Okpalaukwu asked.

"That's the point, a god is supposed to be the highest power," the Ifa priest answered. "In our culture where we believe in multiple gods, when men go to war putting their entire faith in their god and they lose, it means their god has lost, it means their god has failed, it means their god is human—"

"It means their god can bleed," the Okpalaukwu cut in.

"It means they are not gods," the Ifa priest said as he rose and poured the sand in his hands onto his feet.

"So what you are saying, as the Headman to the Oracle, is you agree with the missionary," the Head-of-Government said looking intently at the Ifa priest.

"Agree with what, Gbangba?" the Okpalaukwu asked.

"That there is only one god," the Head-of-Government replied and walked away.

Chapter 5

Oludu arrived at his Haku when the night was its fullest. From the time he left the capital he had not uttered a word. His wife welcomed him, but he still did not say anything to her or anyone around him who came to register their presence to him. They were expecting a sign of appreciation to acknowledge their waiting up for him. The chief seemed only to recognize the direction ahead of him. Nobody could unravel what was playing in his mind, but they were positive it had something to do with the coronation of a new king.

His wife, Ugonwa, always ignored the protocols that followed the traditional rites of marriage. A wife typically only came to her husband when she was asked to or after she had asked permission from him through her maids. But Ugonwa gave her husband a bath and then she knelt down by him to massage his feet, even though he still hadn't spoken. Throughout the act, she still could not squeeze a word from his impermeable mind. She watched him lie down on the bed then she left him alone. As she walked away, a pain pierced her heart because she didn't know what was bothering her husband. There were times just by merely looking at him she could tell what he was thinking. But on this day the man had a world of his own that no matter how hard she concentrated she could not enter.

Am I worthy to be a Chief? The grounds cry for the blood of the people of Ndemili. I wonder what my father would do if he carried the staff as I do. Are lies not beautiful when you need them most? If they had let the world know, I could have been the man who listened to the horn instead of blowing it. My general thinks I am blind. I see the hatred in his eyes for pledging his loyalty to a man younger than he is. I feel his dream of ever becoming chief slip away. The fool sings loyalty as the vulture preaches hard work. Keep singing, for I need you alive.

As they say, the man you know will stab you in the back is your most trusted comrade because you always put him in front of you. The pressure in the play is rising. I can hear the laughter of the gods. They know the more I use what they gave me, the darker I become...I will prove to both man and gods that I don't need to be beyond the limits of man to win a war. Pokzee, I see death in my face if I don't play with your weakness...your logic.

*

The seven-foot general's name was Boodunko. He was older than the chief, but at the ripe age for the position of general. From the day he started to understand life, he wanted to be chief. As much as he tried to deceive himself, he knew that honor and power were two words that were born together but lived separately. He waited for the chief to discharge him before he could leave the Haku and, from the look of things, it seemed the chief was not coming out from his shell. As he waited, Ugonwa came out of the room where her husband was and told the general he could leave. The uncaring attitude she used to talk and walk away from him ignited his anger.

Still, watching her as she was walking away the anger seemed to transfer into a fierce lust. I know what is punishing her. She lacks a real man to take care of her inner needs and desire. It's a pity that she is bodily deprived. All she had to do was ask and I would take care of her desire anytime and anywhere. Boodunko's thoughts seemed to give him an inner redemption because his grin was connected to his heart.

For an enigmatic reason, Ugonwa stopped and started walking back toward him. The general felt that maybe when he grinned, he must have made a sound that was disrespectful. She was coming toward him like a warrior seeking vengeance for an unforgivable sin. He did not know when he instinctively stretched his hand toward his sword. As she approached him, she started walking around him like a creature she had never laid eyes on. The general was still in the same position.

With a smile and a seductive voice she began, "How much of a man are you?"

"I am sorry, I do not understand you," the general replied.

The servants and Omees in the room did not know what was going on, but they were aware that something was about to happen.

Her voice was getting slightly louder.

"Please do not tell a poor lonely woman like me that you are not ready to fulfill the desires that my husband cannot reach."

"What are you talking about?"

"The desires you want to help me reach, which my husband cannot handle."

"I never said that."

"But you thought it."

"With all due respect, I think your words lack sanity."

"Really? Or is it that your stupidity deflects you from our present circumstance?" She smiled at his exposed anger. "With all due respect."

"Watch it," he said as he started to leave.

"I take it you just handed me a threat, or are you threatened?" she said with a sly smile.

"I would never threaten the wife of my chief." He walked away from the Haku finally knowing why the chief never had a Tikpapa after he married the late King's daughter

Chapter 6

Otuturex got to his Haku by dawn. He stayed a day extra in the capital because of the feast he attended with his men. His envoy escorted him, along with his general named Adu and his Tikpapa, to a private chamber. Before he sat down, he started giving his general orders.

"Appoint Omees at all the boundaries of the province. Recruit as many commoners as possible. Get rid of anyone who has contact with Ekpona Hills. I especially want you to find as many people who know the Ekpona Hills. All the slaves we have should be made Omees."

"Why?" his Tikpapa asked.

"What do you mean why? Do you intend to be at the battlefront?"

"Sorry."

"How about the elders?" the envoy asked.

"Yes, how about the elders?"

"I mean, what do I tell them?"

"Those old men have been on my back since I became chief. Go and ask them if there are any volunteers to go to battle."

"I get the message," the envoy replied.

"Tell me about the physical features surrounding the Ekpona Hills," the chief asked the envoy.

"There are a number of small villages, but the major settlements start from over the hill and its elevation is high. Our horses aren't used to climbing those steep heights. By foot it's a day's journey to Odagwe's Haku."

Directing the next question at the general the chief asked, "How many Omees do we have?"

"We should have four battalions."

"That was not the question. I asked how many men do you have in each of your battalions?"

"From seven hundred to a thousand."

"Take your worst battalion and divide it into four parts. Send the first bunch tonight to the Ekpona Hills and the others will follow with day and night. They should not be dressed in Omee outfits from this province, and they should capture those little villages."

"Odagwe is no fool. Those are the first places he will guard and any attack in any form will be connected to you."

"How can I explain this to you? Desperate times cover honor. The victor, no matter how dishonorable he is, still gets the glory. Yes, I said that I would attack on the fourteenth day, but even Odagwe knows that is fiction. The war starts today, but there will be no war song or dance until I leave here for battle. These men will leave with the turn of the days and nights. Let them know their mission is suicidal and, if they don't want to go, place them in the final battlefront."

Otuturex sighed, looking at the men around him. The beauty of war was that it exposed the people you could turn your back to and those you could not risk such an act with. There were a lot of ways to prevent your enemies from attacking you from within, but the best method was by starting your war from the most important direction, from within.

Odagwe knew he was going to battle with me soon as he stepped into the palace. He has someone on the inside. I have nothing on my general to be sure of his allegiance to me. All I have is his honor and the good name that came from the loyalty of his father and the generations before him. Well, I am a lucky to have let my Tikpapa tell me how to screen through some of his supernatural arts. I have to admit, if I was a Tikpapa even to a King, there are some secrets I would never tell.

Otuturex faced the three men standing and waiting on him.

"Please sit down."

With a grin he asked the Tikpapa, "Where are you from? I keep forgetting."

"Are you talking to me, sire?" the Tikpapa asked.

"Yes I am," Otuturex answered in an unusually polite manner.

"I am a Yere. My people are slaves to the province at the Ekpona Hills. You are aware of this, my chief."

"With this war, things are getting a little blurred in my memory. I remember you were at the Ekpona Hills on the day the King died."

"Yes, I was. My people are there and I asked your permission before I left."

"I did not mean to make you edgy. The thing bothering me is that Odagwe seemed to have made up his mind to go to war with me even before he arrived."

"I tell you, my chief, my hatred for Odagwe is deep and my loyalty to you is to the extreme," the Tikpapa said, bowing.

"Yes, but if I understand the code of war, if slaves decide to join a province in war, their people become free."

"So what are you trying to say?"

"I don't trust you. Adu, kill him."

The general drew his sword and struck the Tikpapa's chest. The sword bounced back as though it hit a stronger metal. The Tikpapa brought out a powder from his fist and blew on it. Fire surrounded the boundary between them.

Otuturex stretched his hand under his seat and brought out an egg. As he raised his head, he saw a spear coming right for him. He swayed, but he was not fast enough, the spear pierced his shoulder. As he fell to the floor, he crushed the egg on the ground and the fire was extinguished.

The Tikpapa ran away as the general threw his knife at him. It struck the Tikpapa's neck before he got to the door. As he turned, there was a pained expression on his face. He was trying to say something, but the general was too disgusted to give him a chance, so he used his foot to bash his face.

Then he took the knife from the Tikpapa and went to attend to the chief, who was already with the envoy.

"We should be able to treat him," the envoy said, pulling the sword from the man's shoulder. "I am sorry, my Chief."

"Why should you be sorry? These are the reasons I am chief."

"I will go and call the herbalist," the envoy said.

"I am also sorry, Otuturex," the general said before stabbing the chief in the chest with the same knife he used to kill the Tikpapa.

The general then turned to the envoy with a demonic look.

"You killed the chief," the envoy said, stumbling backward.

The general walked toward him.

"I did not see anything. Please, I beg you. I will tell them I did not see anything. What am I saying? I really did not see anything," the envoy pleaded, now on his knees.

"Will you get up. You are so disgusting. If I kill you, who else would be my envoy? You are the most qualified and if you are a little smart you might become the King's envoy."

The look on the envoy's face transformed from fearful into that of a mercenary.

"Did you say the King's envoy?"

"I see I have touched a part of your spine that dances to my tune."

"Talk, Adu, I am listening."

"Correct yourself. From now on you address me as Chief or my Liege."

"Forgive me, my Liege. I was carried away."

"All we have to say is this: The Tikpapa attacked the chief with a spear when we were not aware. I attacked him with my sword, but it did not pass through his chest. Then he cast a spell and appeared in front of Otuturex and stabbed him again in the chest. That was when I jumped on him, took the knife from him, and stabbed him with it."

"I don't mean to sound pushy, but I don't think the elders will believe that story."

"They don't have a choice. As of now, they are all bothered about the war we have with the Ekpona Hills," the general said, moving the Tikpapa's body close to the chief's.

"Yes, that's a point. What about our war with Odagwe?"

"There isn't going to be any."

"What do you mean?"

"Who do you think planned all this?"

"I hope I am confused. Are you trying to tell me that Odagwe planned all this before now?"

"About six months ago."

"But the King was still alive then."

"Honestly, I really don't care because now I will become chief and not answer to this dead piece of rubbish anymore. The animal is not even close to my age and I had to take his order because he was the King's boy."

"So what do you have to do for Odagwe?"

"Nothing, just vote for whosoever he wants me to."

"Then who was the Tikpapa working for?"

"For me. Let me explain. I convinced the Tikpapa to join forces with me because I did not want him using his power against me. I promised to help free his people in the Ekpona Hills. He was a smart man; he didn't believe me. So I organized a meeting in the Ekpona Hills with Odagwe. It was a coincidence that the time Odagwe asked for him was about the same time the King died. So when we were coming back from the palace, I told Otuturex about my distrust for the Tikpapa and the puppy assimilated everything I said. My striking the Tikpapa with the sword was pre-planned. The spear I threw was supposed to end him."

"You threw the spear."

"Are you deaf? Yes, I did. You were too busy running to a safe place when I did."

"Then why was he running toward the door?"

"When Otuturex squashed the egg on the floor, it seemed his defense mechanism broke, making him completely vulnerable. Tikpapas feel naked without some form of a force around them. He was not running out, but he was looking for a safe place to be until I killed Otuturex."

"Then if Otuturex had not counteracted his spell, what would you have done?"

"I would have gone with the first plan."

"What was that?"

"Tell every man in the province that you killed the chief."

"Nobody would have believed you."

"With the Tikpapa backing me up and not to mention them continually thinking we are going to war with Odagwe, believe me I would have glided through smoothly. Now, the Tikpapa killed the chief because he has an alliance with Odagwe." He looked up as though expecting a prize from heaven. "Am I not brilliant?"

The envoy looked at the man with a fake smile. This is the biggest fool I have ever been engaged with. First he tells me everything I can use against him, then he lets me know that he can get rid of me as easily as he did with the Tikpapa. And to top it all, he thinks Odagwe's plan is his. Amazing grounds we stand on. Everyone knew the man was a dunce, but Otuturex still chose him to be his general because of his time of service. This is how the man repaid him.

"So what do we now, wise one?" the envoy asked.

"Wise one. I like it. Open the door and start screaming for all the Omees while I pull the knife from Otuturex's chest."

The envoy walked toward the door as the general went to where the chief was and pulled out the knife. As he did so, Otuturex's eyes opened and the envoy started screaming outside the room. The chief gripped the general's neck. Adu was trying to free himself while the envoy screamed louder. As dozens of Omees approached the envoy, he pointed toward the general, then the words from his mouth became clear.

"The general has killed our chief along with the Tikpapa."

The Omees ran toward the general; when they got there, both he and the chief were dead, next to the Tikpapa. Otuturex had twisted the general's neck the way he used to break the shell of coconuts.

Chapter 7

Ihua had spent days thinking, calculating what he was to do and what he could not do. He gave specific orders for no one to disturb him, not even his wives. The only people worthy of sharing his momentous time were his concubines. On the ninth day after his meeting with the chiefs in the conference room, he asked his messengers to summon five people—his general, his Tikpapa, two Omees named Ikenna and Tunde, and a shrewd white trader named John Anderson.

Four of the men came at nearly the same time. He asked John to wait while the others were led into his chambers. He watched the general approach and he could see in the man's eyes that he felt degraded for not being asked for before now. When finally asked to the chief's presence, he had to be summoned with the two radical excuses for Omees. Ihua wondered why he never accepted the man as his general, and the only time he either mentioned or thought of him was like the son of a palm wine taper. The general walked in acknowledging that the chief wasn't looking at a palm wine taper's son anymore but a general.

Well, well, well, you finally realize you need the palm wine-taper's son, now that there is war. Old fool, your retirement age has overflowed. It's time for new blood to flow in the people of Ahoda. I can't wait to tell to the over-grown monkey that the elders have all agreed for him to go. How stupid can a man be? The wrinkled man knew that his people want him out and he still went along to agree for battle with the people of Alloida. I can't wait to tell him the time is up and this time there is no king to carry his ancient soul, the General thought with a smile.

Ihua looked at the other two Omees who approached him bowing. The two men were excellent choices, both descendants from generations of Omees, generals and even chiefs. The only problem was that they were deep-rooted enemies. Everyone was scared of leaving them together because one of them would kill the other. They were supposed to be generals, but the elders did not know which one of them to pick so they did not choose either.

The hatred the two Omees had was passed on to them from generations. Families of both claimed they stole one another's land.

The problems started eight generations back, when an Omee wanted to marry a girl who had lots of suitors. The Omee promised the girl's family the dowry they requested and his land that belonged to both his lost younger brother and himself. They immediately gave him their daughter to marry. After some years, his lost brother appeared and demanded what was his. The older brother gave him a million excuses why he gave them the land and offered to replace it. The younger brother killed his brother and married his brother's wife. It was custom that when a man's brother died he married his wife to keep the dowry within the family. If the man was not interested in marrying her, he was free to refuse, but the woman did not have this privilege.

The younger brother took the land from them, claiming his brother had no right to make that decision alone, but gave it back to them after a year as his in-laws. Eventually his wife had six children—a girl and a boy for his elder brother and three daughters and one son for him. The two boys grew up to be sworn enemies and the generations after them fueled the hatred.

Ikenna and Tunde stood with their heads down like they were born together. Ihua looked at his general seated on the wooden bench.

"Are you comfortable?"

"Not exactly, but I will manage," the general answered with a trace of sarcasm.

Ihua smiled and faced the two Omees.

"I have heard about the two of you always attempting to kill each other. Are you people not ashamed of yourselves? If you could bury this dirty hatred you men have, our province would have proliferated. I will say this once: One of you will be under the other and until then you both have to impress me. If either of you hurts the other, then take it that you have hurt me. I will not only deal with you, but I will make sure that your generations will end. Do you understand me?"

"Yes sir," both men shouted together.

"Touching speech, Ihua, but I think I am wise enough to give the elders my nominee for general. As sure as the sands of the earth, these two radicals won't come close. Old man, make this thing nice and quick and tell us you are stepping down as chief...I have people to lead."

"As for now, there is something both of you will do for me. You—"

The chief was interrupted by the general. "These matters you discuss are of no relevance to me. I would like to talk to you about more serious issues."

"Take it from me, this next issue has everything to do with you, General." A smile grew on the chief's face as he spoke.

The general also grinned. Finally you want to speak my language.

The chief turned to the two Omees. "I have heard a lot about the two of you. Now prove to me how good you are. Annihilate this man."

It took the general a second to realize that he was the man they were to get rid of. He quickly reached for his sword, but Ikenna was faster. Ikenna cut off the general's hand, and Tunde gave his head a clean slice.

Ihua wanted to scream flawless, but he knew better than to praise an Omee when he started an assignment or else he might feel he had reached the highest standard. Now he knew why they did not know which Omee to make general. What did he have to lose, now? He had two generals. The only thing was that they could not bear the title. In this situation, both men were now his best protectors, especially against his most unpredictable enemies.

The two Omees still stood, heads bowed, awaiting their next order. He offered them seats, but the men chose to stand.

Ihua told his messenger to ask John in. Upon seeing the general's head separated from his body, fear took the white man's composure. He had trade transactions with Ihua. He gave Ihua everything he asked for in exchange for anything valuable in his home like ivory, gold and, on rare occasions, slaves.

"John, take a seat. You are acting like a pregnant woman about to have a miscarriage."

John tried to smile, but his face could not handle the forced expression.

"Sorry about the place." Ihua called for his servants to clean up and then continued. "You are aware that the King is dead."

"Yes, I am."

"We are going to war with Vacoura and I need a favor from you."

"Anything, Chief. Have I ever not answered your request?" John's confidence rose.

"The kingdom is supplied two types of salt—the local salt from our land and the white man's salt. The local salt comes from Ndemili and Ahoda, and the white man's salt is supplied by a white man who knows his way around the kingdom better than our own people. Let me cut this story short: I have always known you were the major supplier of this salt."

"Ihua, how can you think I would be involved in such a transaction? We have worked together for over a decade and there is no dark secret I have not exposed to you. Believe me from the depth of my soul. If you want me to swear by your gods, I will. I am not involved in any form of trade apart from the transactions both of us have."

Ihua grinned.

"I knew the source of my information was not trustworthy. They are trying to break the bond we have. They said you are planning to take advantage of the war so you can trade your salt strictly for slaves in the provinces that don't have this merchandise."

"Who…" John stammered, "who are these people who want to spoil my bond with you?"

"I know you are the one, John, so stop playing with me because the next question you get will come from these Omees."

John looked at the two Omees eyes and they were screaming blood.

"Ihua, I am a businessman and I do what I have to do to make profits. I spend months coming here by sea, not to make friends, or eat what your people eat, nor to drink your wine. I prefer my own drinks, my own food and my own lifestyle. Yes, I am the major supplier of the white man's salt, but I have never been less than a noble subject to you."

"John, what do you take me for? You have not done anything wrong and I was surprised that you denied it initially. Anyway, for now you will be my guest in the Haku and anything you need will be brought to you here until the war is over."

John wanted to say something, but Ihua continued.

"Take it from me, it's for your own protection."

Ihua called three other Omees and told them to take John to his new confined home. When john left the chambers, Ihua asked the two younger men, "So what just happened?"

"You want to stop the traffic of salt around the kingdom, so you can stretch the war," Tunde said.

"Then again, the people of Alloida will end up attacking faster than they were supposed to," Ikenna added.

Ihua got up from where he was seated and asked them, "A man crossed a river to pluck a paw-paw fruit. When he got there he plucked four and he could not cross the river with all four fruits. He could only swim across the river with one of these fruits. So what should he do?"

Ikenna answered. "He takes the fruit one at a time across the river."

"Good, then what happens if this continues?'

"He starts getting tired as he swims back and forth," Tunde answered.

"Get every man, woman and children with strong hands and tell them to start digging on the borders a wide trench, deep enough to cover over a thousand standing men. When this is done, assign a battalion to guard the boundaries."

"As much as Vacoura is a lot of things, he has honor. When he says thirty days so shall it be."

His messenger returned, talking with his head to the ground.

"I bring you dreadful news."

"Speak," the chief commanded.

"Your Tikpapa was found dead with his head buried in his feces."

Ihua angrily told his messenger to get out. He faced the two Omees again a little confused.

"You were telling us of Vacoura's honor," Tunde said.

Ihua could feel the echo of the two Omees laughter hidden in the serious faces they pretended to put on. He was even beginning to wonder if the men were really enemies. It is terrible what war does. Imagine honorable Vacoura organized the death of my Tikpapa while I am here waiting for thirty days. Only the gods know whether the ancient pig has already planned my death with someone around me. One thing I am sure of, it cannot be either of these two. The bastard had to kill the only man I could trust.

Ihua sighed, then faced his two general's without the title.

"Start organizing the digging now."

The two men were filled with youthful joy. They were going to war to kill people and probably get killed. Ihua realized these men were crazy and dangerous; he was lucky they were on his side. As Ihua discharged them to do his task, Ikenna looked back at the chief.

"You did not have any informant. You just tested the white man to see if he was the one supplying the salt."

Ihua ignored him and left, now knowing who would be his successor. He regretted that none of his sons had the fire of an Omee, but even so, he had to take care of at least one of them.

Chapter 8

It had been nine days since the meeting at the conference room and Pokzee never mentioned anything about the battle with any of his men, including the elders. Although he did not get married again, he was still living in the bosom of pleasure with different women. One night the elders came to his home while he had a female guest. He asked them to come back at another time, but they insisted on waiting. When he finally met them in his chambers, he greeted the four elderly men then sat down.

"So what brings the four anchors of our province to my humble home?"

"Only a fool will see a stone coming into his eyes and not react. Pokzee, we have been fools for about nine days, but our hearts are as heavy as yours. There is a war coming and nobody knows what we are planning to do," the oldest man said.

"Is it not Oludu? I will take care of his province on my own," Pokzee said, his mouth full of roasted antelope.

"Our forefathers who have served us kola nut with blessing had nothing to gain by this gesture, but even today we do it and so shall the generations after ours," the darkest elder said.

"Forgive me. Please take some kola nut," Pokzee said.

"This is not about Kola nut," the elder continued. "How can you estimate the height from the heavens to the earth?"

"Let us hit the ground, Pokzee," said the elder with a scar across his face. "We are all aware that the war is in twenty-one days from now. We know we are a powerful province, but Oludu's chronicle is not something we should ignore."

"What chronicle? Is it that he killed an animal when he was young or that he is the son of an Omogor?"

The shortest elder finally spoke. "No wonder, he does not know."

"Know what?"

"I was beginning to wonder if they had settled," the scarred elder added.

"Know what?" Pokzee shouted.

The darkest elder started, "Okon sent his general and Oludu, along with about fifteen Omees, to the village of Asuqo."

"Correction, there were only ten Omees with them," the scarred elder cut in. "Okon sent them to the village head to collect the taxes."

"Okon never sent his son to places he felt were sensitive. Upon the death of an animal at the boy's hands, he still treated him like an egg," the shortest elder said.

The darkest elder continued. "Asuqo was a village that had no Omees and everybody there was a farmer. They were not up to a hundred people in that land."

"So Oludu, the general and the other Omees got to where the village head was and asked about it," the scarred elder added.

"The man walked to where the general was and spat on his face, ran out and shouted a signal," the shortest elder said.

"It was GBOWE," the darkest elder reminded him.

"Thank you," the shortest elder said, not even caring who he was telling the story to. "From nowhere Omees, all pretending to be criminals, appeared in the scanty environment. They were about a hundred."

"Stop exaggerating; they were about fifty," the scarred one said. "All twelve men ran toward the exit away from the village. At that point they formed a straight line prepared for battle."

"When their adversaries saw the blockade," said the shortest elder, "they stopped chasing them and stood side by side with their prey. At this time the twelve Omees were looking the fifty men in the eyes with traces of fear. Then their leader appeared. It was obvious that Oludu did not know who he saw, but the general recognized him and let the boy know that the man was his father's second eldest brother."

"Since Okon's father disowned him, the two brothers had never met again," the scarred elder added.

"So Oludu's uncle told them he didn't want to waste the lives of honorable Omees and all he wanted was Oludu," said the shortest elder. "The general told him never and screamed for Oludu to run back to the town. Their adversaries attacked and the boy started running. All the Omees prevented anyone from passing through but their enemies were too many and they started dying one by, but they still kept the blockade."

"When he was close to the town, Oludu turned and started running back. The general always said to him, 'Only a boy runs from the battles of a man.'" The darkest elder seemed proud to have remembered the statement and continued. "At this time Oludu was still quite young, although he already was an Omee. When he got back to where his Omees were, he saw only his general and three other Omees still fighting with over thirty Omees or criminals. The boy entered the battle like a hawk grabbing its prey. His hand was his shield and the sword was passing through anything. At a point, they said his sword dropped and he started using his bare hands. He did not seem to feel the arrows they shot at him and at that point they knew the man had protection from a great god. The few men alive ran away. His uncle tried to escape, but the general shot him in the foot with an arrow. Oludu went to his uncle, pulled the arrow from his foot, and told him to bury the Omees that had died while protecting him. He then made him burn his clothes and go back home naked."

"Is that why you have all come to my Haku?" Pokzee asked, playing with his fingers.

"No," the oldest elder said. "We have a visitor for you."

One of the elders went out of the chambers and brought in someone with the face covered.

"You may unveil yourself. You are in the most discreet grounds."

Pokzee could not hide his shock; he was not expecting this. And they said victory was not on his fingertips.

"Is this a social visit or you have something for me?" Pokzee asked, knowing the answer.

"Oludu will attack you on the twenty-first day from now as he said, but he will pass through the black-eyed swamp because he knows you won't be expecting him to pass that way. I suggest you wait for him at the edge of the swamp in the forest in three day's time," the person said.

"Why three days?" Pokzee asked.

"You know why," the person replied, covering the face that was not meant to be seen.

Pokzee watched his spy walk away and did not know what to believe.

Chapter 9

Chief Vacoura was in his Haku with his Tikpapa, envoy and general. They were all quiet, waiting for something. Vacoura was agitated; he could not sit anymore. He paced around the chamber, rubbing his hands together. Then he abruptly faced the envoy.

"This was all your idea."

"My Liege, the day has not ended," the envoy replied.

"How could I have listened to you? My honor will be disintegrated." Vacoura said.

The envoy glanced at the other two men to bail him out, but all of them pretended not to notice his signal.

"How could I believe a Wovamee would be able to kill a Tikpapa? My useless Tikpapa could not even advise me not to play in troubled water," the chief continued.

The short Tikpapa tried to explain, but words would not come out of his mouth.

"I don't understand what is going on. The general was supposed to have thrown out Ihua from the chieftaincy position. The spies we have are no longer sending any messages back to us and to top it all we paid a Wovamee to kill a Tikpapa and I have heard nothing. I feel like killing someone."

A messenger ran in. "An old beggar requests to see you."

"Do I look like I am ready to waste my time with an old man?"

"He said I should tell you that he has a gift for you from Obi."

"You stupid boy, can't you for once get things right? Send him in."

The old man came in. He was not as old as he was pretending to be, but he was good at acting it. He bowed to the men in the room, but he was more concerned with the chamber as he surveyed the area with his eyes.

"You don't have to feel uneasy. Nobody can hear or see anything in this area of my Haku, so I guarantee you maximum discretion."

"Ihua still refuses to really put me in the picture."

The old man still felt uneasy talking with the Tikpapa and general in the room, but the envoy was acceptable because he was the contact man.

"Listen to me, I trust these men with my soul, so what you say in front of me you can say in front of them. That's why they have their positions."

"That is easy for you to say. Am I not Chief Ihua's envoy? As I came here, so also any of these men could do the same," the man replied.

"Are you trying to categorize me with you? You?" the general asked.

Vacoura ignored his general. "You have a point and I am sorry. When next we meet, we do it alone. What do you have to tell me?"

"The elders had already agreed to impeach Ihua and replace him with the general, but as of now the general is nowhere to be found," the man said. "Ihua came out in public and announced that he would find his general by any means necessary, even if it meant taking him from your Haku."

Vacoura grinned. "So I killed his general. Continue."

"His most trusted comrade died with his head in feces." They all laughed and the Tikpapa asked who it was, even though they made it obvious they knew the answer. "It was Ihua's Tikpapa."

"What took you so long before you could report?" Vacoura asked.

"These are war times and I have to be very careful. Also, they are digging this trench between the boundary of Ahoda and Alloida."

"What trench?" Vacoura faced his envoy. "What trench?"

"My Liege, I am not aware of any trench. I have not been able to get information from Ahoda until now. Their security is tight."

"Are you deaf? The man said they were building the trench on the boundaries."

"Chief, I really think it's the general's job to scout those areas, not mine," Vacoura's envoy said, defending himself

Automatically, everyone in the room faced the general.

"The boundaries between them and us are extremely large and they belong to none of the provinces, so we did not have any cause to check those areas."

When he finished the statement, everyone was still looking at him. He tried to hide his face, but the rays from all the men touched him. He dropped flat to the ground.

"Forgive me, my Liege. I was incompetent in my duties."

Vacoura ignored his general and talked with his spy.

"How long have they been digging this trench?"

"Over eight days."

"How many people are digging it?"

"Most people in the province."

"How deep and wide is it?"

"It's the height of a man and about a thousand paces wide."

"How could you pass through this wide hole without anyone seeing you?"

"That's why I came at this time of the night and I am disguised."

"Do you have anything more for me?"

"I heard he has locked up his business associate, the white man. That is about all."

"The land you require at the Ijeska falls is yours to collect when the war is over. Now go before they realize you are gone."

Ihua's envoy bowed and left, walking over the general who was still on the ground.

When the spy had gone, Vacoura gestured to the general to get up.

"Let us review what the envoy spoke of from the beginning," the chief said, rubbing his chin. "The general is dead, so our initial plans for impeachment can't hold. Luckily for us the Wovamee killed the Tikpapa, although I felt that was impossible. So they could probably send one of those women to kill my Tikpapa."

"He was weak, that was why they killed him. Let any of them come near me, I'll bury my foot in their vagina."

"Just in case, Envoy, have you settled the Ikaza who got the Wovamee?"

"Yes, I have and I gave him a little extra to let us know if their next hit would be on us."

"Beautiful. Now why would he lock the white man up?" Vacoura asked the men around him, but they seemed lost. "What kind of people are you? Can't you ever think of anything?"

"Okay, what does the white man do for Ihua?"

"He engages in trade transaction with Ihua," the Tikpapa answered.

"What does a foreign trader provide that Ihua does not have?"

"Salt," the Tikpapa answered.

"Who provides the salt for the whole kingdom?" Vacoura asked the envoy without looking at him.

278

"Oludu was the major supplier to some provinces and other kingdoms. The white men provide the other provinces their salt, but they don't come near us. The closest was a group of criminals who were involved in the trade, but they have been eliminated by you," the envoy replied.

"You used the word was all over. Next you will be telling me we don't have any salt in the province...or do we?"

"We do, but it can't last us up to ten days."

"And you just decided to share it now?"

"At that time I felt it was something we could easily get access to from the white man. We can easily get it from Ogwashi."

"Ogwashi is in this war because we are in it. They have their problems and we should not burden them with ours." Vacoura bit his lips then he continued. "Ihua is forcing us to attack before it is time."

"Let us go now. We are ready for them," the general shouted.

"It melts my heart to realize that you want to succeed me with this naïve approach to confrontations. Someone should help me. Why are they digging a trench that wide?"

"To prevent us from importing salt," the envoy answered.

"It goes beyond that," the chief said.

"They want us to delay the war. With the trench, it makes it more difficult for us to enter Ahoda. With time we are going to get desperate because they have cut our supply of salt," Tikpapa answered.

"Now the Tikpapa has told us their motive, what do we do?"

"If we stay too long, we fight desperately and stupidly, but if we attack now, we could escape the hindrance that the trench would cause."

"Finally, you speak like my general. We attack now when they await a war at a later date."

"But the men are hardly ready for war today," the envoy reminded him.

"If our men are hardly ready today, then imagine how lost Ihua's men will be," the general answered.

"But there is no honor in such an action," the envoy murmured but everyone ignored him.

"I will go and tell them to start singing the war songs," the general said.

"No need. That may cause unnecessary attention. Let us go and bring back victory then they will sing the victory song instead."

They all went preparing for war except the envoy, who was not an Omee and went back to his bed. The dwarfish Tikpapa walked out of the Haku with the men, then he returned under the guise he left something behind. He met Vacoura dressing for battle and asked, "What about Bugadashi?"

The question seemed to have taken the chief by surprise. He took his time before he replied.

"He will stay behind and guard the Haku, with the Omees over here."

The Tikpapa nodded in agreement and was leaving when the chief called him back.

"Do you think I am being a weak chief by hiding my only son from war?"

"As you said, my Liege, he is your only son."

"What does he want?"

"What he wants does not matter, only what you say."

"That was not the question. What does he want?"

"He hungers for battle like any Omee. He hates you for shielding him from the different quests that makes an Omee recognized."

The chief sighed and the man's age showed on his face.

"He does not have to go anywhere. We will make him guard the Haku and let him know the seriousness of that position."

"You and I both know that is the position of coward. When I was younger than he was, I had seen death pass me a hundred times. My son...my only son is not a coward and if he chooses to fight in battle alongside his father, then let it be. But, my friend, this is what you will do for me: I want you to be with him every step he takes during war."

"That I cannot do. Every man will notice that I am with him and not you, making him a greater coward."

"Okay, then tell the general to do it. Get out of here. I want to be alone."

The Tikpapa left, leaving the father to worry about his son.

*

Ahoda's envoy had climbed over the trench separating the two provinces, but the area was unusually empty. Even though it was late in the day, they had to put people around the vicinity. When he left there were some Omees on guard, so he disguised himself. He was positive they did not recognize him. He did not care anymore; all he wanted to do was just leave this area. He tied his horse far from the trench so there wouldn't be any connection between him and the trench. As he got to where he kept the horse, it wasn't there. He then walked farther wondering if he forgot where he left the horse. He walked farther and the dark was making him very nervous. Then they appeared. What scared him was not his recent actions, but the normal fear that he got just seeing one of them, not to mention both bloodthirsty radicals.

Tunde talked with a grin on his handsome face.

"Envoy, I have to admit, if that is a disguise then I ought to look like the King."

"I was just surveying the area to see if there was anything abnormal going on. I used the disguise so nobody will recognize me."

"The guards recognized you a thousand paces before you reached the trench," Ikenna said. "They pretended not to recognize you."

"Someone even followed you until you met your escort at Alloida," Tunde added as he was breaking a nut. "By the way, Ihua will be here any minute now."

The envoy knelt down crying and begging.

"Forgive me. I went see a friend of mine at the...I mean in Alloida, he is extremely sick."

"Do we look stupid to you?" Tunde asked.

"No, I didn't say that."

"Look at you oozing fear in your every word. And you expect us to let you go with those lies."

"They are preparing to attack as we speak."

"You are still lying, but anyway my comrade here and I are both men with certain issues to settle, so you have the count of ten to run before we fire," Ikenna said.

"What do you mean fire?" the envoy asked.

"One...two...three..."

The envoy started running with all his might, deep into the bushes so he could have deflectors.

"Four...five...six...seven..."

The spy ran faster than he ever imagined he could.

"Eight...nine...ten..."

The men fired; both of their arrows hit the envoy at the same spot on his back and the man died. Both men walked toward their prey and admired their work.

"If you look properly you can see my arrow penetrating deeper, but don't get me wrong, you fired a good shot."

"Tunde, I think you are mistaken; that arrow you think is yours is mine."

"I was not referring to that cheap arrow."

"The only thing cheap here is you."

"Why don't we just settle this problem once and for all?" Tunde said, drawing his sword.

Ikenna was just as quick with his sword.

"All right, let's do this, you son of a thief."

Tunde and Ikenna faced each other with their swords, going round in a circle.

"See who is calling me a thief. You and the generations before you were all born criminals."

"What is happening here?" Ihua asked.

Both men stood at ease, swords by their sides.

"We were checking who is faster at drawing the sword," Tunde replied.

Ihua was disgusted by the lie and he was now positive that one of them was going to kill the other if they were left alone.

"So what information did you get from the envoy before you killed him?" Ihua asked, surveying the body.

The two Omees looked at each other as though they were communicating with their eyes. "He told us everything as you said it," Ikenna replied.

"So how did I say it?"

"He said they are attacking immediately," Tunde said.

"Perfect, get the troops ready."

Ihua walked in another direction in the bushes. When Ihua had gone, Tunde whispered to Ikenna with Omees all over the bushes, "Do you realize the problem we are in if Alloida does not attack us now?"

Ikenna whispered back, "We will claim they gave the envoy false information. By the way, this is all your fault. You were the one boasting you were better than me with the arrow."

"It was not as though I did it alone. You joined me."

"What are two of you doing over there? Come here!" The chief screamed.

*

Vacoura and his men approached the trench and were all amazed at how large it was. They saw there was no way into Ahoda except to pass through the trench, which was deeper than they expected. They had to leave their horses behind and go down on foot. Descending into the trench, they did not encounter anything other than the silence of the night. When climbing out of the trench into Ahoda, it all began. Attacks deluged them from every corner. The Omees from Ahoda attacked Vacoura's men, who had climbed up the trench; the others shot arrows of death at the Omees below. The Omees from Alloida were dying in plentitude. It was a massacre.

Vacoura expected his general to tell the Omees to fall back, but the man was probably trying to be stupidly brave, so he called for his men to withdraw. The Omees ran back, climbing through the trench. Even at that, death met most of them at their backs as they tried to flee. The Ahoda Omees did not follow, knowing it would put them in a disadvantageous position.

Vacoura lead his men back into Alloida with his head down. Walking alongside him was his dwarfish Tikpapa, whose sorrow was deep in his facial expression. Vacoura looked behind him to see less than a quarter of his Omees returning. He talked with his Tikpapa as they walked to their province.

"Ihua's envoy betrayed us."

The Tikpapa did not reply.

"Ihua knows we are handicapped now. He might attack us soon, so we should allocate men at the edge of the trench and use it to our advantage until we are strong again."

The Tikpapa said nothing. The chief was still talking in order to encourage himself.

"The only problem we might have will be the issue of the salt. You don't have to be so gloomy, we haven't completely lost the battle."

The Tikpapa was still silent.

The chief stopped and all the men behind followed his footsteps.

"Where is the general?"

The Tikpapa finally spoke.

"He is dead."

Without looking back the chief asked, "Where is Bugadashi?"

The Tikpapa tried to say something, but the words were stuck. All he could do was use his hands to tell the Omees carrying the chief's son to bring him forward.

The chief watched them drop his dead son on the ground. Vacoura froze. The wickedness of disbelief hit him and he began shaking, then clenched his hands together, looked into the sky, and yelled out in sorrow.

"He looks good in an Omee's outfit. Handsome man, like his father," Vacoura said, using his shirt to clean the blood on his son's face. "I always knew he had the blood of a warrior...Real men die in battle."

Pointing at his son for all the men to see he said, "Look at his hands. He still holds onto the sword. I remember when I told him to trade, he said, 'No Father, I am born to die in battle.' I can't believe I wanted to limit your destiny, my son. I wanted to tell you so many things, but now I have to get to where you are to tell you."

He squatted down, holding his son's hand. "Tikpapa, you won't believe this...but I have never known your name, I only know you as Tikpapa."

"It is Osas, my Liege."

"Osas, how insane do you think it will be, to go back now?"

287

"Insanity is in the mind. The people of Ahoda will believe only an insane group of people would come back after such massacre, so they celebrate their victory because they are at war with a sane group of people."

"Great Omees of Alloida we fought an honorable battle and lost. I really do not care what anybody believes, but I have been proud to have you men by my side. Our people say, 'The man who sees fire and touches it knows the pain he wants to feel.' My people, I am entering that fire with my eyes open and I am not inviting any man to come with me, but if you hunger for that pain you may follow."

The chief headed back to Ahoda. The first to follow him was the Tikpapa and then the other Omees all followed, with a few remaining behind.

The people of Ahoda were dancing and merry. Palm wine flowed through the gullets of the Omees in the province, the men gyrated to the beat of the drummer, coquettes swung their hips, and women threw praises at the chief. In the heat of the celebration, men started dropping silently and rapidly.

This continued until a drunkard screamed, "Sabotage!"

The Alloida Omees attacked fully in open. Commoners ran back into their homes with their children and the Omees of Ahoda found it hard to organize their troops in the mayhem. The infiltrators were equalizing the deaths of their comrades in the trench. Tunde and Ikenna appeared from different directions and fought like hungry beasts. There was a wickedness that both commanding Omees displayed in battle. Vacoura knew that their chance of victory was very slim, but his priority was having vengeance for his son. The Ahoda Omees were too much and it was impossible to detect who in particular killed his son, but the perfect man to take the blame was the chief.

Ihua was weighed down by the age of time and could not engage in the battle, while Vacoura fought with a passion. Any man who gave him a tough time, the Tikpapa was there to deal with the obstruction. The more he fought, the closer he got to Ihua's Haku.

Ihua stood in front of his Haku watching the mayhem, watching the splotches of his men's blood stick to Vacoura's skin as he got closer.

As Vacoura was getting to where Ihua was standing, an Omee from Ahoda attacked him with a double-edged spear. The chief did a maneuver around the Omee and stabbed him with his sword, but before he died the Omee spat something into Vacoura's eyes. The chief could not see. He rubbed his eyes and moved in the direction he last saw Ihua with the intention of killing the man, with or without his sight. The Omees guarding Ihua wanted to make a quick kill on the blind chief, but the Tikpapa threw something on the floor and a fire surrounded his chief as he moved. The

Tikpapa fought the battle in front of Vacoura as the chief advanced.

Ihua saw death coming toward him, so the old chief fell back.

The Tikpapa was Vacoura's eyes as he advanced fiercely, swinging his sword at anything.

The older chief began running back to find himself trapped in the enclosed passageway. From what Ihua saw of the battle they had almost won, but what he did not understand was why he had to run. He grabbed his sword, but it burnt him so he dropped it. He watched Vacoura's Tikpapa kill everyone who attempted to protect him, using diabolic methods.

Vacoura was following the feeling from the fire that burnt in front of him and did not know what was happening, but he knew his Tikpapa was ahead of him. When Ihua was trapped, the Tikpapa said to his chief, "His life is yours for the feud on your son."

Vacoura could not see Ihua, but he felt his presence. Ihua at this time was angry they had to kill his own Tikpapa. He wished they had killed his wife and children instead. What got him angrier was that his two Omees were not anywhere near.

Two arrows passed through the heart of the Tikpapa at the same time from two different directions. The Tikpapa didn't understand how the arrows pierced him. He touched the blood on the metals and realized it was his. He chose to die silently so his chief would complete his task and not be disturbed.

Vacoura could not see now, but he knew something was wrong and he quickly pounced on Ihua, bringing him to the ground, pulling out his knife to feed it with his enemy's blood. The older chief was not strong enough to hold the blind chief. Vacoura struck at Ihua, but Ihua shifted away and Vacoura raised his hands to try again before two arrows were fired at his back from a distance by the same commanding Omees who killed the Tikpapa—Tunde and Ikenna.

Vacoura was adamant despite the two arrows deeply buried in his back. He struck at Ihua again, but the older chief used his hands to grab the knife of the dying man. The blind chief kept pushing the knife into Ihua's heart. With time, the call of death was stronger than Vacoura's vendetta; he died on top of Ihua. The Omees came in time to push Vacoura away from their chief.

"My Liege, I have to admit, you truly are in good shape," Ikenna said, helping the chief up.

"The way you ran was youth at its height," Tunde added.

On a normal day, he would have punished them for the mockery, but with the color of victory in his hands, he had no choice but to laugh.

Chapter 10

Pokzee went to the spot where his informant told him to wait with his complete army. There was something about the location that made him feel he should change his attitude toward this particular situation. Since the death of his wife and the reaction of these people that were now under him, he realized that his most trusted companion was himself. He had a Tikpapa and envoy just for the sake of protocol. The people he listened to were the elders, and they hardly ever made him do anything he did not want to. He looked at his army and shame gripped him at the thought of the kind of cheap victory they were all prepared for. He did not tell anyone what the informant had said. He just told them how they were entering into battle. If he had his way, the elders would never know about the situation, but as of now it was allowed.

Disgust erupted through him when he watched his Omees so relaxed about the battle they were about face. He looked above him to see the darkness laughing at him. Real men went into battle when the eye of the sun was wide open, when honor was not contaminated. His situation was getting unbearable as he squatted, awaiting his adversaries under the shade of deciduous trees.

The only reason he agreed to engage in such a degrading form of war was that it was in response to Oludu's sly concept of war. Pokzee knew there was something about the decision he made. He tried to find a reason why his information would deceive him, but nothing came to his head. This was his chance to prove to everyone that he was a master planner and not just a warrior who depended on brute force. He looked at the area they were going to stay in for about two to three days, depending on when Oludu and his men decided to pass through, and he knew this was going to be easier than opening a virgin. From the way things were, he would have preferred meeting him face to face, but there was also a problem with who he was going make chief of Ndemili. If only his son was of age, he wouldn't have to put in a stupid Omee who could change with the weather.

Pokzee's general divided the Ogwashi Omees in batches and allocated them to different points. The Omees all took food given to them by their wives and mothers, acknowledging the length of stay they had in the forests. The night crawled and the day feared to appear. Then one of the Omees fell into a very deep hole. From both the ground and the skies, all kinds of weapons flew, all kinds of traps consumed them— holes covered with rafia palms, firm branches held back with darts, trees held up by ropes.

The Ndemili Omees came from everywhere. Some were camouflaged like the bark of trees, some attacked from the top of trees. These Omees vigorously applied pressure on the Ogwashi Omees. Their men were confused when they kept seeing their comrades die but could not locate their adversaries. Pokzee was going crazy, he wanted to badly grab his enemies and crush them with his bare hands. The chief could not maintain stability amongst his men and they were dying with the more time they wasted. Their enemies were attacking them like ghosts.

When his Omees finally gained access to these men attacking them from strategic areas, the full Ndemili battalion attacked. Although at this time they were roughly the same in number, the Omees from Ogwashi were highly disorganized and the Omees from Ndemili exhibited an obvious contrast.

The attack on the Ogwashi battalions was merciless; men died like animals killed for a feast. Pokzee fought like a beast; the stroke of his sword was too much weight for any of his enemies to handle. He slaughtered his adversaries as they came his way. Now the light of day wanted to register its presence. The chief kept fighting without noticing anything in his environment; all he wanted was to kill every one of his enemies. At a point all his adversaries refused to confront him, he faced them with his sword and they all moved back without cowardice in their eyes and stood watching him.

"Face me, you bunch of liverless toads. Are you realizing what it takes to fight a real man? Come and design your blood on my sword."

Pokzee could not take it anymore and took his sword and hit an Omee's chest, screaming, "Fight me you coward!"

The Omee looked at the chief and said in a very calm voice, "I suggest you look around you."

Pokzee saw most of his men on the ground dead and the others on their knees pleading for mercy. He watched Chief Oludu come toward him with his assumed informant.

The informant noticed the man he betrayed ready to go into death and take him with him and he screamed to the Omees, 'Hold him down!"

The chief jumped with his sword to stab Oludu's general, but a dozen Omees held him down, pushing his big head to the shrubs. Oludu looked at Pokzee and seemed to be amazed that so many men were finding it hard to hold one man down. All through this extremely large man's struggle, his eyes were locked to Oludu's general.

"What burns your soul? Is it that you have lost the war, or that my general was never the spy you thought you owned?"

"Let them free me and you will find out."

"Free him." All the Omees were puzzled, even Pokzee, but they still did not completely loose their grip.

"My Liege, I do not think it is a safe decision under the circumstances," the general quickly said.

The chief ignored him and the man went to a safer distance. The Omees reluctantly freed Pokzee with his sword still in his hand. Pokzee got up, dusted himself off, then sat down with his elbows to the ground. When he was relaxed with his enemies standing around him he spoke.

"What burns my soul is of no relevance to you. I tasted the food of the gods and it has now consumed me. I have no hatred for your general, in fact I respect him now more than I ever believed I would. When he came to me, the lust for easy victory overcame me. I thought his goal was to become chief of your province, not knowing his eyes were on my province."

Oludu squatted to Pokzee's level and said, "I would let you go and from this day onward you would be an Ikaza."

Pokzee got up with revitalized energy that flowed in his voice.

"How dare you look at me up and down and think I would stoop so low to be an Ikaza. I am Chief of Ogwashi and I will die Chief of Ogwashi like these Omees lying here."

Oludu stood directly in his face.

"Pocket your pride and look around you," Oludu said, pointing at his Omees all ready for any wrong move Pokzee made. "You are a dead man already. Ikazas are men of respect."

"Correct yourself, Oludu, they were men who had pride." Pokzee's tone was still forceful. He started walking around the tiny circle the Omees did not occupy. "Did they ever tell you how chiefs used to go to war in the old days? When I say old days, I mean way back before the time of King Burobee."

Everyone paid attention to what the chief with a short time to live said.

"In fact, let me be a bit more specific. There was a chief who had a problem with another chief. Generally, they were to go to war with the consent of the King, but the problem was, one of the provinces was five times larger than the other. Now the chief knew that there was no honor in going against a province so small and his admiration for his adversary was optimum because the chief showed no fear in going against a province as large as his in those days, I might add."

The general fiercely interrupted.

"My Liege, can you see what he is trying to do? He is looking for a way to get into a physical battle. He thinks everything is by brute force because his brains hide behind his genitals."

"Shut up!" Oludu yelled at his general. "You may continue, Pokzee."

"So the chief who had the larger province said the two chiefs should battle individually to settle their disputes. Anyway, that was in the old days. I can never become an Ikaza, so I prefer to die right here and now."

297

Oludu knew this was one of the cheapest tricks in the war code. If he decided to kill Pokzee now, his Omees' respect for him would slide back and he could not let him go because the chief refused to be an Ikaza. It was a clear challenge of a masculine stand. Oludu knew that even if Pokzee eventually killed him in a man-to-man combat, Boodunko, his general, would not waste a second before he ordered the Omees to kill Pokzee.

"All right, Pokzee, if it is a challenge you want, then it's yours but I advise you to leave here an Ikaza."

The Omees started spreading and created a larger circle. An Omee threw a sword to Pokzee, who immediately started winding it in circles above his head.

Oludu faced all his men and men spoke out loud, "If the chief kills me in our confrontation, then he goes back to Ogwashi as their chief."

Boodunko walked to his chief and handed the man his sword.

"He lives as chief as long as you live," he whispered in Oludu's ear. "If I have to kill, I want you to know that it will be the first time I have ever disobeyed you."

"Let us begin," Oludu said.

Immediately, Pokzee attacked him with powerful thrusts of his sword, but his opponent deflected his attacks, as though the weight on Pokzee's sword was as light as a feather. Pokzee tried different kinds of techniques, but the chief maintained his composure. The spectators followed every powerful swing and movement during the metal collision.

The two chiefs clashed swords, then there was a halt as their swords jarred together and it seemed like a power struggle.

"Walk away an Ikaza."

This seemed to set Pokzee's blood on fire. He pushed Oludu with a super-human strength that sent Oludu flying back with his feet not touching the ground. Oludu hit a rock and immediately his men wanted to fire, but the general used his hands to tell them to halt. Everyone was surprised that Oludu had lasted this long with this man who was the size of a bear. Pokzee rushed Oludu as he was on the floor, but the chief returned to his feet still deflecting his attacks in the same relaxed manner. Pokzee fought again till the level where their swords met and this time he took out the knife at his side and stabbed Oludu in his shoulder. Blood gush all over his body.

Pokzee was impressed with his actions and, encouraged, he rushed at Oludu, but the chief seemed to disappear. Pokzee looked around, wondering where Oludu was and then he appeared in four places at the same time, twisting his sword without an expression on his face. Pokzee was confused, but determined. He started attacking all the images one by one. The spectators felt Pokzee had gone mad because they saw Oludu in one position, twisting his sword, while

Pokzee was making powerful attacks at the air. As Pokzee attacked the images, they seemed to multiply and, everywhere he looked, Oludu was there, twisting his sword. He did not want to take chances. He started swinging his sword in any direction. At a point he got tired and stopped.

Oludu gripped him from behind and put his sword to the chief's neck.

"I also heard the story about the chiefs way back then, but you forgot to mention that the chief with the smaller province killed his opponent in their confrontation."

As Oludu finished his speech, he slit the chief's neck, dropped him, and walked away. All the Omees were hailing their chief when Pokzee rose with his sliced neck, dying but not dead. He used his last ounce of strength and advanced toward Oludu with his bare hands.

Oludu did not notice the event behind him. Pokzee received more than a hundred stabs from the Ndemili Omees behind their chief.

Chapter 11

The Hurdene entered the bushes with her Ikuvamees. Her heart was pumping, not because she was in the bushes at this time of night, but because of the person she was going to visit. Whether it be man or beast, she had full confidence in her Ikuvamees. She knew there was no room for fear with the kind of determination she carried in her heart. The Hurdene got to her destination and then started contemplating whether to return. It was bad enough if anyone found out she was going to the home of Agreshi the witch, though she was positive no one had seen her and her Ikuvamees' loyalty was unshakeable. The Hurdene stood watching the house for a time she couldn't estimate before she gained the courage to enter alone.

*

A beautiful teenage girl in a small village got married to a farmer and they had a daughter. When the girl was six months old, her father died at sea while fishing. The widow raised her daughter on her own, tilling the infertile soils. When the girl was about five years old, the mother took her to the major town in a province to see her sister. The sister welcomed her warmly, but was not enthusiastic about seeing her niece. With time, the sister introduced the mother to a very wealthy trader who wanted to marry her as his second wife. The only problem was that such men did not marry mothers, so she pretended she did not have a child. In a few months, they were married.

The new bride took her daughter to her grandparents but they refused to take her because she was a girl. The brothers and sisters of her late husband all refused to take the child. The widow was frustrated and the sight of her child began to disgust her. She imagined everything she had to lose if her husband knew she had a daughter, so she made a hard decision.. She took her daughter deep into the jungle blindfolded. She was about to stab her child, when she looked back and realized she was lost. She laughed realizing that it was easier to abandon the child. Her daughter, on hearing her mother giggle, also laughed, hoping her mother was happy. The new bride looked around and decided not to kill the child, but instead she left her in middle of the jungle and went back to becoming the new bride.

After ten years, she had five sons and two daughters for the wealthy trader. On a quiet night, the wealthy trader died mysteriously. As the days followed, her children died one after the other consecutively. People brought many sorcerers to see the evil in the deaths, but they all said she had entered cursed waters and there was no way out.. When all her children had died, her sister, who was by her side throughout her tribulations, woke up one morning with the face of a woman four times her age. The problem reached the ears of King Burobee who sent the Awnu priest to consult the Oracle. The Headman to the Oracle reported that the curse on her was from negative forces that she had given an entrance to reality. The woman did not understand what this meant, but all she knew was that the worst was done— she had no family left and death would be better than the destiny of her sister's situation.

A teenage girl with eyes like fire came to the gates of the King's palace and ordered the Omees to open the door because she wanted to see the King. They all laughed at her. She faced the Omee in charge and told him to open the door or he wouldn't see the light of day. The man laughed louder and asked if she was going to make him blind. This she did by merely looking at him. Then she faced another Omee and told him to open the gate for her to pass, or her words would be the last thing he would ever hear. The Omee immediately opened the gate.

The young haggard girl with dirty dreadlocks and worn-out shreds of clothing covering her body passed the men who had nothing to say. She reached another barrier of Omees and one of them held her by the shoulder asking where she was going. The girl wiggled her way through without looking back at the Omee, who automatically became handicapped. The news about the girl in the palace spread faster than lightning; none of the Omees attempted to stop her again.

When she got to where the King was, she saw the Awnu priest standing in front of him ready for anything. The girl said she did not come for the King and even if she did, the Awnu priest knew she could not be touched. She told the King he had three days to banish the mourning widow from his kingdom. King Burobee refused to drive a woman under such pain out of the kingdom. She told him that he had three days to comply or else the curse would extend to him. Then she said when they banished the woman they should tell her that Agreshi placed the curse on her. The King, on heavy counseling from his high chiefs and elders, gave the order for them to banish the widow. When they told her that she was banished, she took it like nothing but a particle in contrast to monstrous punishment weighed on her, but when one of the Omees told her it was Agreshi who placed the curse on her, she killed herself. As time went by people went to meet her with different requests and she gave them all their desires, at a price. She always stated the terms before she provided what they wanted. She could give a person any material thing he or she desired: wealth, husbands, wives, love portions, children and a lot of other things in exchange for things like a short life span, sterility, a body part and a host of others things.

*

The Hurdene entered Agreshi's home looking for an excuse to turn around and return to her palace. She would have announced herself, but the hut was wide open. She saw her host burning something in a fire and at that point she knew she was in the wrong place.

As she attempted to leave, the witch spoke with her back to the Hurdene.

"State your request before you leave or else you might regret this day for the rest of your life."

The Hurdene was still contemplating whether to leave when the witch turned around. The Hurdene saw an aging woman who looked older than her mother. Agreshi got up and dragged a cut trunk and offered her guest a seat. The Hurdene tried as much as possible not to get close to her for fear of some evil contamination.

"You know we human beings are funny animals," the witch said in a squeaky voice. "I heard they burnt a girl, claiming she was a witch. They keep killing those people who accept the white man's god, using their horns and bellowing they are witches, yet no mob knocks on my door to tell me they want to burn me on the stake."

The Hurdene still refused to sit and looked for the slightest chance to leave this place.

"Believe I am creating new havoc."

The Hurdene could not take it any longer; she started to leave, but the witch spoke to her, still playing with the fire.

"You and I both know the son you gave birth to, does not belong to King Obi."

The Hurdene stopped and this time she went back and sat down on the seat.

"How dare you? My son is the child of the King."

"Yes he is and my hut contains all the oceans."

"What are you accusing me of?"

305

"It's amazing, before I mentioned your son, you were consumed with fear and now your tongue is as sharp as a blade."

"Why don't you tell me what you want to say?"

"No, you are missing the issue. Why don't you tell me what you came here to say? The question that has been punishing your soul all these years was never a question because you always knew the answer—the child is not King Obi's son."

The Hurdene was dumbfounded. No longer petrified, she wanted to grab the witch by her neck and strangle her.

"Don't worry, your secret will die with me. Now we have gotten over that, state your request."

"Since you seem to know everything, you might as well give me the solution."

"You must ask before we proceed."

"I want my son to be King."

"Is it really about your son becoming King, or is it about you ruling the kingdom? It's no secret that the Hurdene is the ruler before the child starts acting like a King."

"Now that you have uncovered the depths of my nakedness, I would like you to help me …I want you to help me…I beg you to help me." The Hurdene went down on her knees.

"Save your sympathetic gestures for a fool who has a weak heart. My rules are simple. For anything I do, there is a price. There are three chiefs who are your problem. So which one of them do you want me to get on your side?'

"Oludu."

Agreshi scratched on her dreadlocks.

"I will make things easier for you. Let me make the other two chiefs come to your side while you take Oludu."

"No, I have made my choice."

"See your mouth move. Have I told you my price?"

"I am listening."

"I want the life of your son when he gives birth to his heir."

"Impossible, I want my son to live as King."

"And so he shall until he gives birth to his son and then he will be mine."

"You are acting like I am a fool. Why do you think I came here?"

"You came here because you wanted to be King."

"Do I look like a man that I would be King?"

"Let me ask you a question. Is there any decision that an underage King can make without approval from his Hurdene?"

"None until he has seen sixteen feasts of Ezes," the Hurdene answered. "You can have his son but not him."

"That's too small a price."

"That would be the heir."

Agreshi thought for a while. Her crimson eyes fell on the fire and she said, "Oludu it will be, but your son is who we need."

"So let it be." She sighed, got up and walked away, not attempting to look back.

Agreshi then told the Hurdene, "If you can't convince the other two chiefs, and the high chiefs finally decide to choose the other child, I will come for you and your son."

"That does not really matter to me anymore. The people always kill the Hurdene and the person who does not become King, so I advise you to be faster than they are."

The Hurdene left, hoping never to return or to see the witch again.

*

Odagwe strolled into Abogima Province on foot with more than half of the Omees in his army on the day they were supposed to go to battle. He purposely entered the province on foot so everyone in the opposing province could see him walk in. As they marched, Odagwe could feel the sting of hatred that flowed through the eyes of the people and the feeling excited him. He walked in front of the battalions and was heading to the Haku that was formerly the home of Otuturex.

Some activists could not bear the thought of Odagwe taking control of their province, so they risked their lives attempting to kill the chief as he headed for the Haku. If only the men had known how useless their attempt was, they wouldn't have thought about it.

Odagwe entered the Haku with his general, Anossai, by his side. He looked around the Haku impressed with it, especially the colorful fur on the seats and animal skins hung on the wall.

"I have to admit, Otuturex had exquisite taste for a man so young. I hope his taste extended to his wives," Odagwe said to his general.

While the two men were laughing, Odagwe's messenger came in and bowed.

"Great Chief of every kingdom, the elders and envoy of Abogima are waiting to meet you."

"Let them wait. I want to drink wine with my general. By the way, bring that sweet wine I brought with us." The messenger ran to get what his master asked. Odagwe sat on the chief's seat and rubbed his buttocks on it.

"Come and try your seat."

Anossai was reluctant to obey the chief's command, but with a slight persuasion he sat on Otuturex's former seat. Odagwe addressed him like he was his friend.

"Relax and put your back to it. You are now Chief Anossai of Abogima."

The general flushed. It was hard for him to determine whether he was on the ground or in the air. The messenger came with the wine. Odagwe took it and served Anossai. The general took the calabash from Odagwe, looking at him as his equal and they both drank.

"You are a true friend," the general said. "You kept to your promise and I was thinking you would give your son the position."

"Apart from being a trustworthy friend, over a quarter of the Omees in the Ekpona Hills are more loyal to you than anyone else."

"That's not accurate, Odagwe...may I call you by name?"

"You may call me anything you want. Don't forget, as of now you are chief."

"They are loyal to me because of the times we have been together. Most of them know that I have been with you in combat since you were general at Ozuoba."

"Their loyalty to you is deep. By the way, did I ever tell you what my father used to do?"

"Not really, Odagwe, all I know is that he was an Ikaza." Odagwe put his head down and raised it.

Anossai realized he should not have reminded Odagwe of his father's position. *I should watch my mouth. He did not offer me the chieftaincy in front of witnesses. I am impressed with the chief. It seems I have traitors amongst my men. Odagwe found out of the assassination we planned on him. I know the man well, he would never have made me even near the chieftaincy. But why did he all of a sudden come out as the chief who keeps to his promises? It could just be* that he is afraid of my rapport with the Omees. He could be thinking that I will turn the men against him…That wouldn't have been a bad idea, but it would have taken too long. Now that I am Chief Anossai, I wonder if it is still necessary to go on with the assassination…Why not?

"Odagwe, did I say something wrong?"

"No, you did not. As I was saying, my father was a master in all forms of battle techniques, but what he was most popular for was his knowledge of the different kinds of poison and their cures."

"So?"

"Have you ever heard of pride burn?"

"No."

"Of course you haven't. It is a name my father gave to a poison that melts in a man's drink and when it enters the belly it starts burning you from the wine. It kills you in a day. It took my father years to find the antidote and even then, the antidote can only help its victim for thirty days...I think I am gliding in the wrong direction. What I am trying to tell you is that the wine you just drank contains pride burn."

"You are a liar. I did not see you put anything inside."

"To see me put something inside your wine is one thing, but the question is, did I or did I not." The general was looking at Odagwe with rage in his eyes. "Think about it, Anossai, if I had decided to kill you a long time ago, it would have divided the battalions, not to mention that you were chosen by the elders. All those years we were in Ozuoba, I knew it troubled you that I was chosen to be general instead of you. You were there from the beginning, raised to be Omee from a child and I came in after you through other means. Yes, the Omees under you respect you, but with poison no one will know how you died."

"Give me the antidote."

"I see you are beginning to feel the burn."

"Give me the antidote."

"This is what you will do for me. My son is going to take over here as chief and you will give him your full support."

The general was on the floor, holding onto his belly in pain, his voice was low.

"Antidote."

"Stop acting like a woman. I said it takes a day to kill you, so the pain you feel now is just the appetizer."

"Please."

"How many times do I have to say this to you? You are valuable to me alive, so don't worry, I won't let it kill you. Where was I? Okay, from now on, every thirty days I will give you your antidote. So if I were you, I would be praying for me to live forever." Odagwe squatted near the general, who was rolling around the floor grabbing his belly. "Have you started feeling like your belly wants to tear apart?"

Anossai slithered on the floor, begging without words.

Odagwe got up and went to get another calabash with wine.

"The antidote is in this calabash, but I should warn you, most herbalists you meet don't know the poison, talk less of the cure. If you take another substitute, it might affect this one from working."

The general drank the wine and quickly felt better.

"Get out of here and call the men waiting for me."

Anossai got up and was heading out of the chamber, when Odagwe added, "If you ever call me by my name again, I will make sure I put both your testicles in your hand."

Anossai nodded, knowing the assassination plans had to be forgotten; he was a prisoner for life.

Otuturex's envoy and the elders entered, all bowing to Odagwe the way they used to do to their chief. Odagwe was now sitting on the chief's seat and trying not to laugh because the faces of the men were filled with fear. Odagwe used his hand to tell them to rise.

"I have to admit, I was still expecting your people in battle."

"Chief Odagwe, we had no intention to go to war with you," the oldest elder said. "It was our late chief who made that decision and on behalf of our people. We appreciate your coming to take charge of this province."

"I would really like to thank your people for accepting me, but I am not going to rule here. My son Mukembe will be doing that job as chief."

"But Chief Odagwe, your son isn't yet twenty. He is still too young for a province this large," the youngest elder said.

"Are you trying to tell me when and who is ready to take over which and whatever I choose?"

"Great Chief Odagwe, I was only making a suggestion," the elder answered with consternation.

"And I gave a command." Odagwe called his Omees. "Take that old man and cut his body into small pieces so the wild animals won't waste time tearing it."

The youngest elder did not know what to say or do. It all seemed like Odagwe was playing a prank on him. When the Omees dragged him out of the chambers, he realized he was not going to see the next day.

"Does anyone have any suggestions? I am serious. Your suggestions are important to the betterment of the province."

They were as quiet as a dead night, looking at the chief as though he were crazy.

"My general, Anossai, will be acting as Mukembe's general. That's all I have to say to you men."

Odagwe lowered his head, stroking his beard, not noticing the men as they bowed and left. He stayed in this position thinking how cowardly the elders of this province were. It amazed him that at their old ages they still wanted to live. He wanted to die while he was Head-of-Government or else death would have been accepted earlier when he was chief.

Head-of-Government...Odagwe the Head-of-Government. Those stupid visionless Omees whom I told I would be the Head-of-Government, I wonder where they are. Probably bowing to a man above them or they are dead. I can still hear them laugh. Let them still come and laugh at the son of the Ikaza who would become Head-of-Government. My dreams are shaped for me to bite. What I have craved for from the day I was a man is now at my fingertips...the Head-of-Government.

The chief raised his head to see only the envoy still seated, comfortably for that matter.

"Did I not tell you that I am finished with you men?"

"Yes you did, but what I have to say to you is not the kind of talk that waits till the next day."

"Then say it. I have things to do."

The envoy looked at the Omees around them and said, "What I have to say is for your ears only."

Odagwe stayed a short while to let his power sink in before discharging the Omees in the chamber. He couldn't resist political gossip.

"Who are you?"

"I am Chief Otuturex's Envoy."

"Yes, I know you now. You are the son of Imukusade, the unshakeable warrior."

"No."

"Wait, do not tell me. From your looks and the way you talk, I am positive I have met your father. You are the son of Ojokei, the greatest man with the spear in all the kingdoms before his death."

"No." The envoy knew what the chief was trying to do and he quickly killed game. "I am the son of Tiwa the criminal."

"Really?" Odagwe pretended to be surprised while he was proud of his attempt to humiliate the envoy.

"Chief, I will get to the point. I found out that the King did not die of natural causes. He was killed before time by a man who knows poisons."

"But King Obi was the master of all kinds of poison. Did you not know he was raised by a man who cured different kinds of poisonous reactions?"

"Yes, I knew, but it depended on the man who gave it to him. An eagle child never wonders whether the food its mother brought is good or bad."

"So how can we find this man?"

"That is the difficult part. He could be anyone, probably the messenger in the palace, a friend of his, anyone who could give him wine to drink."

"Are you implying something?"

"I never said you poisoned him." The envoy grinned. The defensive role the great Odagwe was playing made him bolder. "All I am saying is that someone was involved in the poisoning of the King and that someone did not do it by himself. He had somebody else with a mutual interest with him."

"This is a logical deduction you have achieved, but you should be aware that such information could be dangerous for you to hold on to, especially if it is true."

"I am a man of principles. I have to let the world know if our King was murdered and apart from that, I have men I trust with my life scattered all over the kingdom who have this information and more. So the minute I die, they will spread it to the market women and everyone else, especially the high chiefs. I also told them to emphasize my major suspect and tell to the world what I heard from certain people before they died."

Odagwe got up from the seat and sat down near the envoy.

"I could kill you very easily."

"If you could, I would have been dead by now. I am a very understanding man when you get to know me." The Envoy got up. "I am aware that you knew the time he was going to die. It was disappointing that a man with a brain like yours would get involved with such a scheme and let that dunce of a general, Adu, know what happening."

"He was the closest person to Otuturex," Odagwe said, finally giving in.

"You could have come to me."

"Envoy, what do you want?"

"The same thing you want, Odagwe. It's an open verse that you want to be Head-of-Government and you planned everything from the beginning. You went to the meeting at the King's palace with intentions to go to war with Otuturex even before you saw him."

"That was not the question. What do you want?"

"As I said before, I am an understanding man. I want to be made the King's envoy whether you become Head-of-Government or not."

"If I become Head-of-Government then so shall it be, but if not, there is nothing I can do."

"Well you have to start thinking, because the only time you can evade the punishment for the murder is when you become a high chief. I guarantee you, if I don't make it as the King's envoy, the information will leak as a rumor and then the people will accept it as a fact."

Odagwe rose and walked toward the envoy with a devilish eye.

"I could still kill you now. First of all, I really don't believe your story about telling anybody what you just told me; and, secondly, if you have told anyone, then the story is out in the open."

The envoy smoothly swerved past the chief, talking as he walked away from the chambers.

"That should not be your problem. What you should be thinking of is how to convince the other chiefs to choose the boy you want as King."

Odagwe looked at the envoy as he left and hated himself for getting involved with Otuturex's general. He wanted to think of a way to deal with the envoy,

318

but none came to his head. He knew the man was smart, even before he got there. The envoy was even more of an asset to him than he could imagine and the man had a point. How was he going to convince the other chiefs to choose his choice as King?

*

Chief Oludu was asleep with his wife in bed when all of a sudden his eyes opened and he carefully shifted Ugonwa's hands off him so she would not wake. He got up and walked away from the bedroom into his private chambers as though he was being controlled. When he got there, he met a totally unkempt woman who used her clothing to show her nakedness and she was playing with the craft made by his mother who died the year before, but he did not seem surprised to see her.

She turned around and with her squeaky voice she spoke to the chief.

"What took you so long? I was planning on calling you from your bedroom."

"What do you want, Agreshi?" Oludu asked.

"What do I want, is that the way you treat your guest?"

She walked to the other end of the chamber, still playing with the other crafts, expecting Oludu to say something, but the chief just watched her.

"Stop looking at me that way. I have not killed anyone...yet," she said, grinning. "Did anyone ever tell you about your father? Not your grandfather, I mean your Omogor father."

"It seems you have nothing to say, Agreshi. I have things to do with my time, so you know how you came, so follow that way out."

"Oludu...Oludu...Oludu, how many times did I call your name?"

The chief did not reply, he just watched her seriously.

"Forget all this act of goodness you display, you and I are the same. We were raised by the same wickedness."

"You are the witch and I am not anything like you. Your heart is darkened by the wickedness you serve."

"And yours is supposed to be as clear as the heavens. Listen to me and listen to me well: I am a daughter of a god that gives you what you want at a price. If that's what makes me a witch, then let it be. I was running in the bushes, a lost child, and evil welcomed me with open arms and I am grateful to it. I see beyond what these beings desire."

"These beings...Then what are you supposed be?"

"I can be anything, but I am greater than what they can ever be. Look at their desires— power, wealth, lust and a lot of disgusting requests. They are ready to give their irreplaceable mortality, body and soul for such trivial things. I see these people and they irritate every inch of me. The big one is coming and I would be honored to be a part of their destruction. The forces

320

above me have sent me to call you from this illusion you live in called life."

"I knew you were a witch, but now I am sure you are a mad witch."

"You can call me anything you want, but we are the same. The evil that made me a witch shelters you and everyone knows it, especially your dead mother. Or is she your sister? That part confuses me."

"Get out of here." Oludu's hand clenched to a fist.

"I sincerely hope you do not think your mother-sister had you from one decent man somewhere or did not know how you existed. Your mother or sister had you by sleeping with all kinds of men, both short and tall, ugly and fine, rich and poor, dirty and clean, their sperms all mixed up in her womb. And did I mention that even all kinds of creatures dressed like men all dug into your mother?"

With a speed faster than any man could run, Oludu got to where the witch was and clawed his two hands to around her neck, saying, "I am not afraid of you."

Agreshi waved her hands around his face to cast a spell on him, but nothing happened. Then she dipped her two fingers into his eyes until he let go. As soon as he got his focus, he headed to finish her off, witch or no witch. Agreshi was on the floor, trying to regain her breath. Nobody had ever touched her without something dreadful happening to the person—to imagine the newness of strangulation. She saw the man coming toward her with death as his goal. Most of her life she sought death as the perfect refuge, but the way things were now, she was no longer in a hurry to get there, so she stopped playing games.

"If you kill me now, your wife will follow me."

"You have no power over her; she is Ogbanje."

Agreshi got up to strengthen her pride. She was happy there was nobody around to see a feared person like she, on the floor, nearly begging for her life.

"Yes, I can't kill her, but where her spirit plays requires her life on the earth. Any minute now her spirit will leave her body and be reincarnated, now that she has already given you a son."

"Your tongue speaks false words."

"I might be wicked in the way I carry out my actions, but I always let everyone know the truth about the actions they take."

"But her world is a different one from yours. How can you prevent this from happening?"

"Let's just say our worlds can collide. I can help you find her package and make her live a normal life as long as nature grants her."

"For this, what do you want?"

"I want you to join me in my world."

"Never."

"You do not realize it, but you know what it feels like to have the one person who feels your heart. It is not by having a thousand wives by your side, the emptiness still remains. People search their lifetime to have someone who can provide this fulfillment. Men

322

who have nothing go home with a smile if they have the right bride. You are complete and you do not even know it. Pure happiness is what you toy with and one day you will wake up to lose it forever."

"The day she dies, I will be at her side, even if it is in death, but I will never give you my soul."

"I did not ask for your soul."

"But you require my eternity, as they have yours. I will never join you."

Agreshi sighed and said, "I did not expect you to join me anyway, but I have another offer."

"What is it?"

"There is a certain contestant for the throne that I want to be King and I need you to make it happen."

"That decision has to be made by six chiefs and I am only one."

"Do you think I am stupid? There are only three chiefs who will make that decision, the other three are men who will follow."

"So how am I supposed to convince the other two chiefs?"

"You don't have to. All you have to do is stand firmly by the boy I want and the other chiefs will eventually follow because none of them are ready to die, now that they have grown more powerful."

"They might want to go to war instead before the eighty-second day."

"Take it from me, those men want peace. Why do you think none of them have called a private meeting on the choice of the successor till now?"

"Odagwe sent a message to me that he would like to meet with Ihua and me a day before we tell the high chiefs our decision at the conference room in Utagba."

"Hear his language: He would like to. That does not sound like a man ready for war."

"So when do you start with the ceremony?"

"I take it we have come to an agreement. But are you not going to ask which of the Hurdene's sons I want to succeed the King?"

Oludu looked at the witch's eyes and replied, "I know the contestant you want."

Agreshi realized that they had an agreement and that he knew who she had in mind.

"The ceremony starts now, but I should warn you, even if she gets to bring out the package, if her feelings for you are not as great as you have for her, she will still return to her world."

"I understand."

"I don't think you do. Even if she dies and goes back to their world, you still have to vote for my contestant, even if none of the other chiefs agree with you and you all die at the hands of the high chiefs."

"I said I understand."

Oludu led her to where his wife was and they saw her still asleep on the bed.

"So what happens now that she is still asleep?"

"She isn't."

"She isn't what?"

"Asleep," Agreshi said.

Immediately, Ugonwa's eyes opened and she dived at Agreshi with a knife in her hand. The witch stretched her palm to her, throwing white chalk on her face and the chief's wife stood lifeless, rocking to and fro.

Oludu looked dazed, watching his wife as though she was a pendulum.

"Oludu, have you ever been to a de-initiation of an Ogbanje?"

"I have only heard stories."

"Well, welcome to reality. I will say all I have to say once, so you better listen." Agreshi poured white chalk around the motionless girl as she spoke. "As I implied before, if she cares for you the most, her package that locks the key between you and the girl will be made up of something she cherishes that links the both of you together."

"One time I knew it was her father she cared for the most."

"You better hope her feelings deviated, because when she breaks out from the trance she is in, she will head for the place she hid it and I doubt if you and I can catch up to someone running back to Utagba." The witch stopped pouring the chalk and looked in the chief's direction. "You are supposed to be sure that she feels for you more than anyone. And I mean anyone, even her child."

"Only a fool knows what lies in the heart of a woman. All I know is that I feel for her the most."

"That is not good enough, but it is all we have right now."

The witch started saying incantations while she moved rhythmically around the swaying body. Then she started moving back while she spoke to Oludu again without looking at his direction.

"They always have a guardian on earth and a husband in their other world who protects them from any form of danger and sleeps with her in their world." The witch faced the chief with a grin. "Those nights she moaned in her dreams, someone else was doing all the work. At times her guardian gets jealous when she starts enjoying her life on earth and shortens her stay on the earth if he cannot get rid of what gives her the joy."

Suddenly Ugonwa jerked and her eyes closed.

"Any minute now she is going to run to where she hid her package and you have to be there when she reaches it or else her guardian will take her away."

"Supposing she hid it at another province?"

"As long as the person she cares about is living in this province, it will be somewhere close to where the person is."

Ugonwa's eyes opened and she ran. Oludu chased her. The Omees guarding the Haku saw their chief running after his wife and wanted to block her, but Oludu screamed, "Leave her!"

The Omees at the gates also wanted to stop her, but they heard the command of their chief running after her. Ugonwa ran like a cheetah, not looking back, and even showing a trace of getting tired. The chief and most of the Omees in the Haku chased her like a wave. The chief's wife ran into the bushes, still at the same pace. The men were only human and the number of Omees chasing her began to drop. They chased her, but they were beginning to lose sight of her because she was too fast.

Oludu was beginning to infer that she heading to another province. Whatever direction she was heading, it was in the opposite direction of Utagba. The chief at this time was the only man still chasing her.

This is not the way to Utagba. She cares for someone else the most. Why am I bothered? If it was her father, I would understand, or even her mother. Since I have been with her I have not even touched another, while her heart drips for another man. I thought it was real, but they are all the same...Why am I still chasing after her? It's a tragedy when the feelings you have for someone are not mutual. What am I thinking? She probably feels the most for her aunt. This is the direction to her place...yes what have I been thinking?

Oludu ran after her with all his energy, but he still could not catch up and he fell tired to the ground; he

327

was only human. As he lay on the ground, he cursed the time he spent with the witch. He was now positive that nothing good ever came out of the witch's negotiations. He started punching the ground and when he looked up, he saw the dust of his wife run past him in the direction they came from. He was extremely tired, but he still chased her again.

Her pace seemed to slow down as she neared her destination. Oludu looked straight ahead as he followed her. He was angry, yet pleased that her destination was back in his Haku. She ran all the way back to their bedroom and he followed her, panting like an animal. When she got back into the room, she stopped motionless again. Oludu wondered what next to do. He hoped the witch was still around.

She started swaying as though strings pulled her and then she walked in a dangling manner out of the room, out of the edifice, to a tree near the gates of the Haku and she started groping the ground with her hands. The Omees wanted to help her, but the chief warned them not to interfere. She stretched her hands into the hole she dug and pulled out a little package. Oludu squatted in front of her, then he opened her hands and wanted to take the package from her.

Her voice was as deep as Titan when she spoke.

"Who do you think you are?"

"Give me the package," Oludu said, breathing heavily.

"Do you really think she wants to be with you while she has me?" the deep voice replied. Oludu head butted his wife, twisted her hands and took the package.

She rose and with the same deep voice said, "Give it back to me."

Oludu got up and moved back. The witch never told him to expect this. All the Omees around were confused about what to do.

Then his wife used her two hands, grabbed him by the neck and raised him high enough for his feet not to touch the ground. The Omees wanted to fire on Ugonwa with their arrows, but Oludu, who was suspended in the air, used his hands to tell them not to. "Give me the package," the voice repeated.

The Omees had started attacking the chief's wife physically, so they would not leave any permanent injury, but she flung them away with one hand that was as powerful as that of fifty men. She suspended Oludu in the air until the chief dropped the package on the floor. She dropped him on the other side and bent down to pick up the little parcel. As she tried to hold it, it moved on its own back to the chief's hand.

The guardian in the chief's wife seemed angered by the event and she turned toward the chief with her eyes burning red. The chief suddenly had a frightful expression on his face. The wife rushed at her husband screaming.

Calmness came over him and he said, "Stop."

She stopped.

Agreshi stood behind the spectators, watching the event. She said loudly enough for only one person to hear, "What took him so long?"

Ugonwa stood still for a short time and then her body started jerking, as though something was trying to tear its way out of her. Again she suddenly stood still and everyone saw her standing calm, but Oludu saw something different. When she stood still, a perfectly handsome man came out of her. With a heavenly charm and with a sweet voice he said, "Come with me, my dearest."

Oludu looked at the beauty in the spirit and he did not have any words to say.

Ugonwa looked at him and asked, "Will you miss me when I am gone?"

Oludu still did not say a word to her. The spectators watching saw her lips moving, but could not hear her words. The chief seemed to be in a trance from their perspective, but they were patient.

"Look at the world I live in, it has no troubles or pain, just bliss in a manner that the earth can no longer provide. Everything I want is here."

The chief finally spoke.

"Everything." A tear fell from Oludu's eyes, but his face remained harden.

The guardian spoke to her again. "It is time we leave. We are running out of time, my angel. Collect the package from him and let us go home."

Oludu stretched out his hand, giving her the package.

She took it without saying a word to him and faced the spirit saying, "Your world is your own and mine is wherever he is."

As though she was hit by a mighty rock from behind, her body jerked enough for the spectators to see and she started falling, but before she landed on the ground, Oludu caught her. She looked at her husband and gave him the package. He opened it and saw a piece of his hair in it. She fell asleep immediately and he took her back to bed. The observers knew they had missed some parts of the story, but they had enough for gossip.

As Oludu watched his wife, without looking back he asked, "Is she really asleep now?'

Agreshi replied, "Yes she is."

Lying next to his wife and talking as though he were alone, he asked, "What makes you think you can trust me."

"I don't think, I know. And just in case of any breach, your wife is no longer an Ogbanje, so she is now susceptible."

"You are aware that if anything happens to her, I will be coming for you."

"I have to admit you are as powerful as I am, or even more powerful, but the difference between you and me is that I know how to use this power."

"'Really," Oludu said facing the witch, but she was gone and he was alone with his wife.

Chapter 12

Chief Odagwe stormed out of his bedroom and into the visitor's chambers in his Haku. As he walked to his destination, his anger proliferated, not because of the time he was awakened, but because of his visitor. He entered the chamber that served as a conference room and met his guest comfortably seated.

The Hurdene looked wickedly fine with her afro. She was present with six of her Ikuvamees and they all seemed ready for anything; despite their man-like appearances they gave an aura that put all the chief's Omees on guard. From the chief's perspective, the Ikuvamees had no chance at all if they decided to start anything here. First, his men in the room were three times their number and they were individually stronger, but there was still something about the women that made him uneasy.

"These seats are used when the master of the house gives anyone permission to use it and I am definitely not giving you permission to use it," Odagwe exclaimed.

Onyela got up from the seat. Her Ikuvamee went down on her hands and knees and the Hurdene sat on her back.

"I heard you were demanding to see me at this time of the night. Who do you think you are making demands of me? I could kill you now. How dare you demand to see me?"

"You do that and I will be eternally grateful to you. Then the high chiefs will be invited into our little web and they will make the decision in favor of the motherless contestant, after they have ordered your death. By the way, did I mention that both the Head-of-Government and the Ifa priest still despise your existence?" The Hurdene had a confident tone in her voice.

"They would not have to know how you died." Odagwe walked around Onyela.

"Seems you are enjoying your little walk around me. I suggest you look around you."

The Chief looked around to see the Hurdene's Ikuvamees in the Haku reaching for their swords.

"They are few compared to the number of men you have in this room, but I guarantee you will not be able to get a quiet death from me."

"They are only six women."

"And about two hundred scattered all over your province. The minute I die, you give the high chiefs the power to do to you whatever they wish. If you even attempt going to war with them, you become the enemy of the kingdom. As strong as your province has become merging with Abogima, you are still playing with the hands of a child where the fists of men feed."

"I am touched by your care. There is an old saying, 'You taste sweet wine a little and go, so you can remember the pleasure of the taste. But if you take it

334

too much, then you will get the real taste and realize it was actually bitter.'"

Odagwe stroked his beard as he walked around the Hurdene.

"You were always terrible at proverbs," she murmured.

"Let's not beat around the bush. I know why you came here and my answer is no," the chief blatantly said.

"Even your dreams cannot fathom why I am here."

"Onyela, I will not vote your son as King, even if I have to die the worst death."

"I would like to talk to you alone."

"What can you tell me alone that anybody here does not know you are going to say? Listen, woman, your wine now tastes sour, so please leave."

"This will be the last time I will ask to speak to you alone."

Odagwe knew this Hurdene since she had the mind of a girl and she always carried a cheerful face even in times of her sorrow. But now the wickedness of her expression made him realize that he did not know who she was. She still looked the way she had when he met her. The only difference was that the child in her had been killed or there never was a child. It was a thought that he recognized for the first time, the native child always knew her way home. The power in her speech had a dangerous foundation and the chief stood trying to understand the situation.

The Hurdene got up from her Ikuvamee and started walking away; her soldiers followed.

Then Odagwe ordered everyone to leave them alone. The Hurdene stopped and told her Ikuvamees to also leave.

When the two of them were alone, Odagwe started feeling uneasy.

"It is pointless, Onyela. I will never vote in your son."

Onyela started walking around the seats, rubbing her hands on them.

"I see that your pain is rooted to the past."

"Is that what you came here to say?" The chief was still standing and watching her.

"There is a saying that the cause of the pain is the only one that can make you forget."

"Listen, I have better things to do with my time, so you can forget about trying to seduce me."

"When and if I want to seduce you, that would not be a problem. You still drool at my presence."

"You are a dreamer."

"Why don't you ask me what is really on your mind?"

"Next you will tell me you read minds. Listen, woman, I have things to do."

"If you wanted to leave, you would left a long time ago. I suggest you listen to what I have to say."

"Then say it."

"It is a very large word to play with. Which of the its do you want to hear about: why I left you for the King or why you are going to vote my son as a King?"

"As I said earlier, you have lost touch with reality."

"I also have things to do. I heard you and the other chiefs have agreed to meet a day before your decision is expected. I thought you were all ready to argue till you die."

"You have nothing to tell me. I suggest you start your journey back."

The chief walked past the Hurdene and was headed out.

"It's terrible, now you have to let another woman's son become King while your son is closer to it."

The chief stopped and walked back to the Hurdene.

"You will do anything to get what you want," he snarled.

"Think about it, Odagwe, I got pregnant immediately after I married the man. He is not capable of producing sons and you have nine."

"You lie, witch," he said, grabbing her shoulder.

"Rephrase that. A lying witch who is the mother of your son."

Odagwe dropped her on the floor.

"Your sweet rose has thorns all over it. Nobody played love more than you when your husband lived and now I will not dance to the beat of your drum. Your son's father is dead and I will not let you see me. Never!" Odagwe started walking away then he came back to face the Hurdene who was on the floor with an innocent look on her face. "Even if he was my son, do you think your husband would not have known, or even Queen Ifrareta?"

"He never knew I slept with you. All I told Ifrareta was that we were courting and even when he slept with me, I made him believe I was a virgin."

The seriousness in Odagwe's face faded away and he smiled as he replied to her.

"No matter how wide your hands are or how deep a bowl you can find, you will never be able to capture the rain...only the waters. I already told him years ago that I slept with you and even tried to spice it up by lying to him that I raped you. So take yourself out of my Haku or I will personally throw you out."

The Hurdene got up from the floor, her face transformed from the innocent child to a deadly woman. She started leaving and without looking back she said, "When next you see the boy, look at his eyes and tell me he is not your son."

The chief sat down on the floor for a while. Onyela was not the person he thought she was. His mind started working. The way she even got married to the King was impressive to him. Hundreds of women were raised to be brides of the King and very few were chosen. Most of these women were raised pure from aristocratic families, but how a girl from an unknown background got access to the King confused him.

338

The way he got in contact with her was more comprehensible. She used to serve under his first wife when she was a little girl. Weruche's marriage was logical to him. She had a son for the man. That was enough to marry any woman, not to mention her beauty. His second wife was the perfect bride for a King—young, from a notable family, and unadulterated by society. Ifrareta was acceptable in every way. She was his first wife, but all that made the Onyela story a little complicated. How did Ifrareta get in contact with such a girl? He knew she was easily loveable, but he was positive that the Hurdene went out of her way to create a coincidence with Ifrareta.

While I was courting that witch she was busy planning how to marry the King? How she got in contact with Queen Ifrareta is the part I do not understand. So Obi did not tell her that he knew, I slept with her. All that time she was playing virgin in bed, the man would have been looking at her as a fool. She is a calculating witch. So she thinks I am a fool who would let her bastard son become my King. Amazing is it not? I had to always watch every step I took, expecting that stupid King to attack me. Now I live. I could have sworn my plan would not work. I am getting ahead of myself—her plans not mine.

The chief grinned as he walked to his destination.

Obi must have known that he died from the asite poison. The symptoms are very obvious. It takes half a day to kill the victim and yet it has no antidote. Our father spent all his life trying to find its antidote. I should hear myself, our father. Stupid boy, why did he not follow me when I begged him to? We would have been invincible. No…he decided to spend his life being the son of an Ikaza and then he became King. Why do I hate him so much, yet somewhere inside I still love him? When she asked me for the poison, I did not expect her to use it. I thought she was just trying to show how powerful she could be. Somehow I knew she would do it. Head-of-Government is not the kind of position you come across everyday. Ten generations from now the children of my children will still remember their ancestor who was an Head-of-Government.

The chief got to his bedroom and saw Weruche still asleep on his bed.

If I was the one to have dropped the poison…I would never have been able to do it…to my brother.

Odagwe carefully sneaked back into the bed so Weruche would not wake up, and he slept with his mind still working.

*

Chief Ihua was in a room in the Haku with only four of the elders and nobody said a word to each other. Ihua looked at the old men around him and realized that the youngest elder was only a year older than he was. He knew he was getting old and the vitality he used to possess had taken another turn. It was time he retired and he had no intention of remaining in this phase. He thought of farming, but he was already too rich to suffer. He thought of trading, but he never was a traveling man, so he decided to just stay in his houses and continue getting young girls pregnant.

The Okpala among the elders spoke first.

"Ihua the Immortal, we have come here today over a number of issues. The first is who are you going to make chief of Alloida."

Ihua was looking in a different direction from where the elders were.

"Why don't you ask me the question that is lurking in your minds, am I going to put any of my sons as chief of Alloida? The answer is no. If I make any of them chief, one of those two madmen, either Ikenna or Tunde, would have to be his general. I give them a year or two at most—an accident will happen and my son will be dead with one of them talking his place. I doubt if they believe I will ever retire. They think I want to stay here forever. If I put both men as chiefs of Alloida and Ahoda, they would not hesitate to go to war with each other. With them as chiefs, my two sons, Akpononu and Nwojo, will be their generals. If both chiefs intend to kill themselves, then let it be. I have to walk away from this circle before it kills me. Tunde will be the next chief of Alloida and the ceremony will begin tomorrow. In three days, he will follow me to Utagba, so we can vote in the new King. His general will be Akpononu."

341

The elders seemed pleased with his decision.

One elder then asked, "How about Ikenna?"

"Ikenna will remain my general until we have a new King. Then I will retire and he will take my place. Nwojo will be his general."

"But if the two of them are made chiefs in separate territories, they will not hesitate to go to war against each other," the same elder asked.

"I handpicked these men personally. Take it from me, war is no longer on their minds."

If you believe that, then you will believe I own the heavens. If I made one of them chief and not the other, I am positive that I would be dead before the sun shines again. So they should understand that a man has to do what a man has to do. I am so glad that I won't be here when they are killing themselves. It's time I enjoyed my wealth and I am not interested in any elder position.

The Okpala asked another question.

"So who are you choosing as King?"

Ihua sighed. These men are beginning to get on my nerves. They just want me to say Weruche's son to get them convinced. I have no choice but to choose her child. She is from Ahoda and a daughter of our province. My choice of her son is firm, but I am not ready to die because of this choice. Life is sweet and I am just beginning to enjoy it.

"Odagwe arranged a meeting for Oludu and I to attend a day before the six chiefs give their unanimous decision to the high chiefs. That is in about five days. Then, and only then, will I announce my decision. I would like to be alone now."

As the elders left, Ihua thought, That was easy.

Chapter 13

The three chiefs were present in the palace on the day they had agreed to meet, which was the eighty-first day since the King died. They all came with their sidekicks, who were now all chiefs still temporarily under their masters—Tunde of Alloida, Boodunko of Ogwashi and Mukembe of Abogima.

Odagwe was the first chief to arrive with his son, Mukembe. The other chiefs assumed he came a day before to humbly beg them to vote his choice. They were all received by Queen Ifrareta, whose pregnancy was ripe for delivery, but she insisted on them being shown into the rooms where they would sleep, have a bath and then she gave them food to eat, before she allowed them go to their meeting.

The chiefs were tense and they did not know exactly what was on the other men's minds. They knew that if one chief decided not to conform to their general decision, then they all would die. The three men were not ready for that. These kinds of meetings between chiefs were to try to convince the other party to accept your candidate.

At times a chief might be adamant and refuse to accept any other person's candidate, eventually leading to their death at the hands of the high chiefs. That would leave the high chiefs to choose the most suitable candidate as King. At times, if a particular chief strongly held to his candidate, the remaining chiefs eventually changed their choice to have an unanimous decision.

The three chiefs—Odagwe, Oludu and Ihua—entered the same day to prevent surprise attacks. Their meeting took place in the palace, where it was forbidden for any man to kill another except by consent of the King. As the chiefs were meeting, the whole palace was aware of what they were discussing. Time started taking short paces.

Then the three chiefs abruptly came out with expressionless faces. No one could deduce what had happened in the meeting and they had no way of finding out. The first thing the chiefs did when they left the conference room was to send for their sidekicks.

*

The eighty-second day arrived and the six chiefs were all seated around the conference room awaiting the high chiefs. Queen Ifrareta came earlier to make sure they were well taken care of. She was still the number one woman until the new King got married and she didn't hesitate to show it, whether she was pregnant or not. Going back to her palace, she felt dizzy, the baby inside her starting to kick and pushing its way out. Her maids and Ikuvamees surrounded her, knowing there was no way they could move her as the baby was about to come.

The high chiefs all came together in the same entourage. They were laughing and very cheerful when they arrived. After they stepped into the conference room, their expressions went dim. On entry, all six chiefs got up to greet them. After they all took their assigned seats, the Head-of-Government asked the messenger to call in the two Hurdenes and their sons.

The women around the queen had a hot bowl of water with a cloth in it and they used their wrappers to make a fence around the pregnant queen. They were on the road connecting the palace with the queen's palace. There weren't any spectators around the area, but the women still held the fence high. Ifrareta did not even need to be told to push; she already had five daughters. As she pushed, she felt a sharp pain in her abdomen that stretched down her thighs; the child was too big. The women dabbed her head with warm water. The queen kept pushing and the head of the child finally found its way out into the world, but the child's body was still in the belly.

The two Hurdenes were present with their sons and five Omees surrounded all four of them. The Head-of-Government got up, slowly looked around the room and then began.

"This is the second time we meet like this and I am aware that we have three new chiefs. Congratulations, but you still have to undergo a confirmation ceremony that will require the blessing of the King. Before we start what we came here for, I would like to announce that the Ifa priest and I are retiring as high chiefs and we will no longer disassemble your modern society with our ancient ideologies."

Odagwe said with careful sarcasm, "But why would great men like yourselves retire at your prime?"

"Our retirement is when the King has been crowned, so if you have not reached a unanimous decision," he said, ignoring Odagwe, "we will still have to kill you before we retire. But you are all mature men and I am sure you have reached a decision."

Both Hurdenes' heartbeats were like wild horses and neither was sure of the fate of her son.

"I will name the province and I want your decision. You are all aware that at this point there can be no more negotiations, so whatever decision any chief makes is permanent. Do you all understand?"

All the chiefs answered in agreement.

As Queen Ifrareta pushed, the upper body of the child had found its way out. Soggy blood was all over the child's head, not a sound came out from its lips. Everyone urged Queen Ifrareta to push faster because something had to be wrong for the child not to cry. The queen pushed harder and harder and the child kept slipping out without an expression. The women could not take the child's silence any longer, so they added a little pressure to pull the child out. When the child was out of the mother, they cut the cord, expecting the child to at least cry, but it still refused to make a sound. Then the women turned the child and tapped it. They still did not hear a sound. Slight taps became heavy slaps on the child's bottom, but he refused to make a sound. They looked at the baby's eyes, which were open. His heart was beating, but the child was not crying while the mother had fainted.

The Head-of-Government started.

"Ahoda."

The Chief answered briefly, "I am in favor of Hurdene Onyela's son."

"Alloida."

Chief Tunde got up and said, "I am in favor of Hurdene Onyela's son

"Ndemili."

Chief Oludu rose with these words on his mind, Agreshi my debt is paid. Take your candidate and do what you wish. I have completed my end of the bargain.

Oludu said, "I am in favor of Hurdene Onyela's son."

"Ogwashi."

Chief Boodunko rose, answering before getting on his feet, "I am for Hurdene Onyela's son."

"Ekpona Hills."

Chief Odagwe rose sluggishly, taking time to decipher the power of the thoughts in his head. How can you hold a scorpion in your fist without it stinging you? I was lucky I came the day before, to see the eyes of the child that prostitute called my son.

Odagwe said, "I vote in favor of...Hurdene Onyela's son." Weruche, you are a scorpion and you sting because it is your nature. I saw the eyes of Onyela's son and they were mine. He is my boy and my son will be King. That is greater than any Head-of-Government position I need.

"Abogima."

Chief Mukembe got up and answered rather enthusiastically with his squeaky voice, "I vote in favor of the Hurdene Onyela's son."

The Head-of-Government ordered the Omees outside the conference room to imprison Weruche and her son until their execution, the next day.

When the Omees grabbed her, she realized her son was not going to be King and the both of them would soon die. She tore off their grip and pounced on Odagwe like a cat, using her bare hands as her weapons. As she clawed the chief's neck, the Omees pulled her away. She struggled with the viciousness of a lunatic.

The Omees found it hard holding onto her while she kicked, punched, slapped, scratched and shouted. All the men in the room were positive she was deranged. The only person who understood her instant madness was Onyela, because she knew she would have been doing the same thing if she were in her position.

As they led her away she kept screaming, "Odagwe, tell them how we poisoned the King together. The bottom of the fowl must show!"

Odagwe shouted back at her, "You are a mad woman, a deranged excuse for a human being."

They tugged her from the conference room, but her screams were still audible.

"You did not seem to bother about how deranged I was when I slept in your bed."

Odagwe faced the men in the room. "The woman is definitely mad. She is looking for someone to share her predicament."

The men in the room nodded in agreement, but all of them believed every single word the supposed mad woman said.

When Queen Ifrareta gained consciousness, she saw herself in her palace. Lots of women were all lined up outside to congratulate her. The first thing she asked for was her child. The maid rocked the child, playing with the baby as she took it to the mother.

The queen screamed at her to bring the child. When the queen got the child, she looked at his lower body and then asked the maid if they had started the meeting. The maid replied they had finished and told her who the new King was. Queen Ifrareta raised her son, with her weakened hand, admiring what came from her belly. The maid told her that the child refused to cry. She ignored the maid. You my son. The flesh and blood of Obi will be King, even if I have to die making you it.

*

Weruche and her son died the next day. Onyela's son was crowned King and his name became Iwureshi. Gbangba retired as Head-of-Government and the Ifa priest followed him later. His Head-of-Government was Oludu, who initially refused the position, but was later forced to take it. Odagwe claimed not to be offended by the position being forced on someone else when he was available, making his hatred for the Hurdene multiplied. Ihua retired and moved away to another kingdom. Otuturex's envoy became the King's envoy, through Odagwe's constant recommendation to the Oludu. Odagwe died two years later from the same poison that killed the King.

Chapter 14

King Obi woke up, touching both his palms and his thighs to feel rugged rashes around those areas. He noticed that those areas had turned green. The King smiled and got up from the bed quietly, not wanting to wake Queen Onyela, but a certain weakness gripped him.

He walked sluggishly toward the conference room, trying to calculate the time between the initiation ceremony of the new Okpalaukwu, who replaced the last one who died of old age, and now. He found it difficult to see, but he tried not to let the Omees and servants notice. He didn't need to see his reflection to know his eyes had turned bloody red. He was positive he was suffering from the effect of asite poison, but the effect of the poison was not his problem. How long he had to live was what bothered him. His Omees came toward him, trying to support him, which made him aware he was not doing a good job hiding his predicament. Even so, he did not want any help.

When he got to the conference room, he told his messengers to call the missionary Michael, Gbanga, and the Ifa priest. Sitting alone, he tried to figure out when he must have taken the poison. He knew it could not be from the food he ate because his meals were always prepared by his wives and they had to eat with him. He thought about who gave him what he drank the day before, but all his four wives presented the drink given to him during the initiation ceremony. They did not drink from it.

It was clear he was poisoned by one of his wives, but he did not want to believe it. He tried to analyze why they would do it and his suspects shortened to two. The Hurdene title came into his mind. He was aware that asite poison was not the kind you easily got access to. There were over a thousand kinds of poisons. Why did the person have to use the poison that his father, Ifeanyi, could not find a cure for? It was as clear as an open book to him—Odagwe was involved, but he chose not to wonder which of his two wives conspired against him. He longed to stroll all around the conference room with his hands at his back, but when he tried to get up his legs were completely dead; he could no longer feel them.

The missionary came in first, as he was a guest in the palace. The man bowed to the King. Obi wanted to use his hands to tell him to rise, but he realized he had no control of his hands, so he told him to have a seat.

"Michael, tell me why do you feel we live?" the King asked.

"To grow in the ways of God."

"I like that. A world belonging to the gods that men play in."

"I believe in only one God and I dance only to his tune."

"We believe in a lot of gods and for a funny reason—they are always at war with each other."

"Are you all right, Your Majesty? Your voice sounds croaky."

"I will be up and jumping soon. So what do you believe about death?"

"Eternity."

"We believe in reincarnation. If you lived a worthy life on earth, you come back a greater man. But if your life was spent poorly, you come back a lesser man, animal, or even a plant."

The King at this time could no longer see, although his eyes were still open, he could only hear.

"It is general opinion that a good man is not afraid to die. Supposing, I mean hypothetically, if I was about to die and I want to meet with your God you've been talking about all these years, what do I do?"

"Take him as your only God and believe in his son."

"That's easy. My gods are a little bit impotent." He attempted to laugh, but he felt too much pain. "So I take it that when I die, I will see your God…But if he has a son, then he should have a wife."

"No Sire, he doesn't have a wife. Actually he—"

At that time the Ifa priest and Gbangba busted in. The Ifa priest rushed to his King and the Head-of-Government gave the missionary a polite nod for Michael to leave the room.

Michael then said to the King, who was drifting further from reality, "Goodbye, Your Majesty."

The King did not hear him with the Ifa priest's examination on him, but he meant the words deeply. He was not a specialist, but he could see the man was fighting to live. He wanted to go to his friend and hug him, but any attempt and the Ifa priest would have killed him instantly; you never touch a King unless he touches you.

The Ifa priest was giving the King a thorough check up. Gbangba was getting impatient so he asked, "Is he going to be okay?"

In an unconvincing tone the Ifa priest turned to the Head-of-Government and said, "He is going to be okay."

In a slow, broken voice the King said, "If you believe that, then you will believe the sun touches my head. You are talking with a dead man."

Gbangba did not realize he was in tears. Watching his friend helpless on the seat, skin discolored, burnt his soul. Even before he asked the Ifa priest, he knew his friend was flowing on death's path. He was no longer seeing a King, but instead the boy he wrestled. He remembered the day as though it was part of him.

The Head-of-Government did not have anything to say to his friend, he just looked as he tried to pretend he was painless. In his heart he cursed life for making him meet his only friend, just to watch him die and vengeance burnt inside him. Someone or people were going to be punished for the atrocity that was before his eyes. He didn't care how long, but the owners of the crime would pay for it. The day before, they were laughing like children. Now he knew he too was old.

"I feel like a roasted cock," the King said.

"Nonsense, you are okay. You will be up and running in no time. Right, Gbangba?" The Ifa priest addressed the Head-of-Government, who was not ready to hear or say anything to anyone.

"I was poisoned. Or do you want to tell me nature wants my life?" Obi asked with a grin on his dying face.

"You were poisoned, my Liege, and it's a miracle you are still alive," the Ifa priest said.

"Can you hear it?" Obi raised his head to the molded roof. "Death is calling."

"There is something I have wanted to tell you for years," the Ifa priest said.

"Talk quickly. As you can see, I am a dying man."

"About your two sons, I found out late that they belonged to another, but by that time you had grown deeply in love with both of them. I intended confronting you with my observation when a true heir was born, but considering the circumstances, I have to address the issue now."

"It doesn't make any difference now," the dying King said.

"I am sorry, my Liege, but it makes all the difference now. Death is their destiny along with their philandering mothers. There is no place for an unclean blood on the throne of this kingdom."

"I don't want any of them touched."

"I am sorry, Your Majesty, but that is one order I cannot carry out," the Ifa priest replied.

"Ifa priest, do you think me a fool? Weruche told me her husband was impotent. She thought I was a fool. Onyela told me she had never been touched by a man. She rubbed alum on her vagina to tighten her walls. She thought I was a fool. Do you take me as a fool, Ifa priest?"

"No, Your Majesty," the Ifa priest said, his eyes locked on the dying man's feet.

"The Oracle gave my grandfather, King Burobee, a proverb that seemed very complex, yet elementary. The answer stared at us like the heavens. That was why it required my father, King Nwosa, killing his only son, me. I believe you men know what the message from the Oracle was. I am too weak to recite it again…But it meant that the generations of all the kings that have stepped forth into this great kingdom will end with me. That was why my life was required to change the prophecy. So no matter what happens, my heir can never rule."

"If that's the way it has to be, so be it, but as long as I am high chief, those two frauds and their mothers will die," the Ifa priest said with his head still low.

"Listen to me. I prefer that one of those two frauds—let me emphasize frauds—who could bring joy to my heart, be my heir rather than anyone else."

"With all due respect, my Liege, I cannot concur." The Ifa priest kept firm to his decision. The Head-of-Government stood speechless.

The King tried to move as he was talking to the Ifa priest, but every part of him was no longer moving except his mouth and he fought for every breath.

"Ifa priest, when I first laid eyes on those boys, they disgusted me. I didn't see my eyes in any of them, but I grew to feel for them like children, then eventually like sons. I trained them like Omees, taught them how to walk, talk and think like a King. I am asking both of you…those are the wrong words…I am begging both of you, as your King, but more especially as my friends, to let them be treated as my heirs when I die."

The Head-of-Government replied first. "Your wish is my command."

The Ifa priest reluctantly followed. "As you desire, Your Majesty."

"Thank you," the King said then sighed. "Can you hear her voice?"

"What voice?" the Ifa priest asked.

"That sweet voice. She is coming back to me."

The two men looked around, but saw nobody.

"I can see her. Are you men too blind to see beauty?"

Both comrades just stood watching him.

"You are not going to run away from me this time, Amina."

The two men were unable to hear what he was saying.

Obi saw his first wife in front of him, smiling, and he heard her calling him. He chased her and this time he caught her. He said, "Forever."

EPILOGUE

Gbanga stood outside the church, looking at the wooden house with shaded leaves and he began to lose himself in the wonderment of the essence around him.

"You can walk in if you want to; nobody is in."

Gbanga turned to Michael.

"So fragile your building is, yet so strong."

"The congregation put their hearts into attaining perfection."

"I see."

"So what happens now you're no longer high chief?'

"Return to my shell and wait."

"Wait for what?"

"Life's most predictable destiny...Disaster."

"What makes you so sure?" Michael asked Gbanga, who had his eyes hooked to the church.

"There are questions that already have answers. When asked, one then has the power to look at the other as a fool."

Michael said nothing; he just stood watching him.

"Do you know why I put so much energy into trying to hate you?"

"Why?"

"Because you speak from the heart. You think the best in everything, which was what Obi feared about you. The only difference between Obi and me is, I know you are but one. I know there are lots of others like you, but not you."

"What I offer is a belief, a pure free belief."

"But what comes with that belief? Our culture is based on our belief, a belief we have studied for centuries, a belief that has built the peace of mind we gather till now. What you offer might be free and pure as you say, but it comes with its own culture. The more you initiate people into this, the more people will lose what they have. And even if they do accept your dogma, they will be decades behind you. And when they finally get to where they are supposed to be, another level will be attained, making them slaves to the past."

"But the generations after them would catch up."

"Catch up to what, your way of life?" Gbanga sighed. "Kings fight wars with their sons by their side, killing men looking into their eyes, showing their soldiers and their enemies why they rule. Your people kill without even facing their enemies. Everyone has enough food to eat, and palm wine to drink. The harder you work, the bigger your land. We tell tales to the young ones by moonlight, tales they themselves will tell to their children. We dance to celebrate the seasons of harvest. Your wife looks upon it as barbaric, but it's our joy."

"My wife?"

"Her expression tells everything. The sickness from our land, we know the cure, but that foreign to us, that which comes from lands lighter than our skin, we can't understand, and your people laugh at our ignorance."

"But the things you do, in kingdoms other than this…they kill children because they are twins, female circumcision—even in this kingdom, polygamy"

"And who made you a god to judge?"

"I'm not a judge."

"You do not judge, but others do. The death of twins is a practice confined to a tribe, which believes that is the way to purify their land. A practice cursed by most kingdoms, but like most of you preaching your beliefs, you look for the most negative thing in our land and shout it out continually amongst the people in your land, announcing why you think your people are better. Tell me now that your land has no secrets. Tell me now that your land bears no wickedness. Tell me now that your land is not ready to crush everything that stands in its way just to grow bigger."

"But we are ready to accept what we believe is wrong and make it better."

"The death of twins is one of a tribe. You condemn the act. Condemn the tribe, but not the kingdom."

"But is the tribe not part of the kingdom?"

"Understand why they do the things they do and then tell them why they are wrong."

"But they are your people."

"No they are not, Michael. They are of another kingdom. The advantage you missionaries have is, everything you say is accepted as selfless and it gives room for understanding. If I walked to that kingdom saying that, they'd think it a catalyst for war."

"And the female circumcision?"

"Are you not circumcised?"

"Yes but..."

"Why?"

"It's the norm."

"That is the point, my friend. Over here it's also the same for females. I see the way your wife walks when you walk, talks when you talk and picks the meat in the pot before you. That is your way in your culture. We let the woman be the woman. She is there to serve her man and her man is there to protect her and provide all her wants. You let a woman grow a penis like a man. She cannot be a woman anymore. She desires the things a man desires."

"Does she not live, eat and breathe like a man? Why should she be treated as inferior?"

"My dear man, you need to understand life. Only a fool believes a woman is inferior to him. A woman is more cunning than a fox. They know the things to do or say to get what they want. Why do you think they hate themselves? Because they see through each other. Ask yourself this: Why is it that royal women remain uncircumcised, yet they force every other woman to be circumcised?"

"I don't know."

"I will tell you why, because sex is power. A woman of royalty married to an inferior man can do what she likes and he can do nothing about it. But that power she possesses, she would rather lose her left eye than let every woman have it, unless everyone else is doing it. Obi as King." He chuckled. "Who do you think planned everything? Obi—you believe that, you believe stars grow in my yard. Ifrareta ruled this kingdom during every breath he took on that throne. The only power a man can have over a woman, beyond strength, is sex. Once that is lost, the only thing stopping them from ruling the world is themselves."

"That's why you engage in polygamy."

"Polygamy is our way. Unlike your kingdom, we don't divorce, so even when a woman begins to shrivel away, her breasts falling down like over-ripe paw-paw, we keep her in the authority of the position she held: the first wife. Put only one woman in the house and she would twirl you with her wrapper and you won't even know it."

"I don't think that's the right way."

"You people come here claiming disgust for our ways, yet your men come in here sharing diseases we have no cure for, blind our women with things they haven't seen. And as you preach, we have all the diseases. Tell me if I lie. Do your people not preach us as sexual beasts who sleep with everything, including animals, because we are like beast?"

"Some say."

"Have you seen this, or heard it from any kingdom with men the color of my skin?"

"No. How do you know these things?"

"To be Head-of-Government you have to know things. Women they slept with heard their words when drunk, heard the excuses and the riposted versions of their wives' defense of their infidelity."

"But sex is…more open here."

"And in your kingdom, it's more hypocritical. When next you see a woman, an African woman, if she is married, she is married. Not even the flashiest beads or stones can caress her out of her fidelity. That is what matters. Tell a man his wife is in bed with the King and he would laugh at you. That was how it is…" He stopped to think. "How it was, before you people came."

"What would you do if you ruled?"

"Kill every one of you, those who come in peace and those with wicked hearts."

"Why would you want to kill me?"

"Because your intentions are good, but even you don't understand, that for men to feel good about themselves they have to make others feel worse. Obi was a great King; the reason the oracle wanted him dead was because of you, because you would open us to your world, to your religion. Your religion would only set us back to a place where we would have to start—"

He stopped as Michael's wife called out for him from the hut next to the church.

"Would you like to—"

"No. But I would like you to know, Michael, if I saw the hearts of a hundred men like yours, then I might consider changing my stance. For now, be glad I am no longer in power."

"No disrespect, but I am glad you are no longer in power."

"For now," Gbanga added with a smile and walked into the veriscent shades of Africa.

About The Book

I walked into an open bar in the University of Port-Harcourt, and I met a man. He told me a story about his perspective of the Benin culture. He was apt in reaching his cliffhangers, with an empty beer bottle. He kept using the Godfather line, I need to wet my beak, so I kept the beer flowing. Years later his stories remained and I began querying my father about our culture and his very rich back-story and that is how the book began. I began by writing the book and it eventually began writing me. This is the first book I ever wrote and the third I ever published. It has many characters that I still adore until this day.

CPSIA information can be obtained
at www.ICGtesting.com
Printed in the USA
BVHW031037031220
594748BV00050B/161